MERCY
and
GRACE

OTHER TITLES BY ANOOP JUDGE

The Rummy Club
The Awakening of Meena Rawat
No Ordinary Thursday

MERCY
and
GRACE

a novel

ANOOP JUDGE

LAKE UNION
PUBLISHING

Published by Lake Union Publishing, Seattle

www.apub.com

Amazon, the Amazon logo, and Lake Union Publishing are trademarks of Amazon.com, Inc., or its affiliates.

ISBN-13: 9781662509216 (paperback)
ISBN-13: 9781662509209 (digital)

Cover design by Kimberly Glyder
Cover image: ©cat_arch_angel / Getty

Printed in the United States of America

For Amaraj and Ghena:
my heart, my soul, my lifelines.

AUTHOR'S NOTE

Scholars in India and around the world agree that the demolition of the Babri Masjid on December 6, 1992, and the deadly riots in the weeks that followed changed India. More than thirty years later, most moderates will agree with this. With the rise of Hindu nationalism, the alienation of Muslims, and the erosion of the rule of law, Indian society has become more deeply divided and polarized than ever.

PART I

PART I

CHAPTER 1

NOW

"Please," Gia Kumari beseeched the Mother Superior. She struggled to stop the tears squeezing out of the bottom of her eyes, because the nuns of Mercy & Grace Orphanage would always say that tears should only be cried for Jesus Christ and the sacrifice that he made for everyone's sins. Today it was hard, though, and the tears felt like they were running ragged red lines through the whites of her eyes, desperate to escape in their panic, which was the same panic that the rest of Gia felt. The sheer, utter terror of being forced to leave the only place she had ever known.

"I am sorry, Gia," the tiny Mother Superior Elena—not more than five feet with a pronounced dowager's stoop—replied from behind round wire-rimmed glasses, a heavy crucifix around her thin, wattled neck. Osteoporosis had its iron claws into her, but she seemed unperturbed by her awkward posture as she sat behind her wooden desk, a desk that had already been old and marked with ink and graffiti and scoured with scratches when it had been donated to the orphanage. Like the Mother Superior and Gia both, the desk had become a relic of the institution, as familiar as the whitewashed walls and the rotting, unlockable multiple-sash window affair of the girls' dormitory, facing the fumes rising from the adjacent Lux soap factory as if it was a panoramic view.

When Gia had arrived in the orphanage—before she was old enough to remember it—Mother Superior Elena had been Sister Elena and had been at least a head and a half taller. Seeing her become the Mother Superior had been a decades-long process of watching the nun shrink and wrinkle and fold back into herself, disappearing into her white habit—there was, apparently, only one size available—and sitting smaller and smaller in the ratty chair behind the desk. It was as if one day she would shrink to nothing and become another dust mote dancing within the myriad specks in the shaft of sunlight that shone through the office window between the hours of two and three o'clock in the autumn and spring months.

Yes, Gia had been at Mercy & Grace Orphanage a very, very long time—all her life, in fact—and now they wanted to throw her out. A wooden clock on the wall behind the desk ticked away, the sound of it like a crow pecking the remains of a dead tree stump.

"You are twenty-one years old, Gia," Mother Superior Elena said in response to Gia's best doleful look, the nun's tone stiffening a little. It was a fact that orphans, much like puppies and kittens, learned from a young age to make their eyes wide and glistening and in need of anything you might be willing to offer them. Nuns, for the most part, quickly became immune to it.

"But I am the most helpful of anyone here, am I not?" Gia argued. "I take charge of distributing duties, and I am a mentor for every new orphan that comes into the orphanage. And I have even begun teaching math classes."

"All of which is commendable, Gia," the Mother Superior said with the air of someone who was not bothering to disguise the sizeable *but* that was coming, "*but* these things have only meant that we could justify not moving you on before now. Most orphans move out at sixteen," she went on. "Eighteen in a few cases. At some point—"

"I could be a nun!" Gia tried desperately. And it *was* a desperate effort, one which the Mother Superior was never going to fall for. She

4

knew as well as Gia did that, of all the things that Gia had found at Mercy & Grace, God was not one of them.

"End of the month, that's the best I can give you." The Mother Superior said the words with such an expression of sympathy and regret that—although doing nothing to tamp down Gia's rising panic—she found it impossible to unleash the anger that wanted to explode out of her. Nuns had their wiles too; *Uffffff,* Mother Superior Elena.

"So, start making plans now, Gia," she went on. "You're a well-educated woman, thanks to your stay here. You could make a man a good wife." Gia reflexively screwed up her face at that, and the Mother Superior huffed. "Or get a job. Event management is what you got your diploma in, isn't it? You love weddings, don't you?"

"Who is going to employ an orphan?" Gia grumbled. "It looks bad. We're like a walking tragedy. Who wants that organizing their wedding day?"

"Either way," the Mother Superior cut in with a hint of finality in her voice, "we have so little resources these days, Gia, and even less space since the west wing collapsed last year. We've had to begin turning little ones away, so you're going to have to make room."

Gia put on the bravest face she could as she backed out of the office and onto the uneven surface of the terra-cotta-tiled corridor. The half-ruined right heel of her chappal caught in the depression made by a missing tile and bent the open-toed shoe so that the tear that snaked along its length opened just a little farther. That was the final straw, and Gia's tears began to flow.

She pressed her hands hard against the upper part of her cheeks, and she ran. Not to the dormitory that she shared with nineteen other girls but out the door and into the yard, where several boys were playing among the puddles of the monsoon rains. There had been a brief respite in the rain since the previous evening, but now the winds were rising again, blowing the thick green branches of the peepul tree that grew untamed, dominating the yard, and the roots of which, Gia suspected, had probably contributed to the collapse of the orphanage's west wing.

She clambered up onto an old, rusty metal drum with the name DALDA VANASPATI OIL still legible in faint letters, which was set against the half-plastered, half-bare exterior wall, and pulled out the mobile phone from her pocket. Standing on top of the drum, she could see over the wall and out to the houses and businesses of the rest of the town. But Gia was not looking out. She was, instead, looking at her mobile phone, moving it around until she got the desired bar of signal.

The phone screen was cracked in such a manner that sometimes dull rainbow colors played across the text on the screen as she turned it over in her hand. The mobile smartphone was the only thing of value that Gia owned, bought secondhand from an unscrupulous and lecherous old man with a brilliant gold tooth in his mouth, the owner of Pramod Phone Store in Kirti Nagar, New Delhi. She bought credit when she could and always did her best to make it last, but the number she was about to call would burn up the rest of the credit she had in just a few minutes. Yet Gia *needed* to speak to him.

Every time she spoke to her uncle, she thought of the day nearly three years ago when the Mother Superior had called her into the office and changed her life forever. Already at that point she had been one of the "senior" orphans, a responsible link between Mercy & Grace's many little urchins and the nuns who ran the orphanage. Yet the look on the old nun's face had given her pause as Gia entered. So grave, so serious—even by the joyless standards of a nun.

"You have family," she had told the eighteen-year-old Gia without preamble. "An uncle in America has been in contact." Gia's chest had almost burst open right there and then with the excitement of it. The story of an orphan was one of abandonment and hopelessness; almost every child she had grown up with was a nobody, a blank slate defined by a lack of parents or family willing to take care of them. Now she had an uncle, and in America of all places!

"He is not in a position to take you on," the senior nun had continued as flatly as she had while informing Gia of her new relative. If Gia had not known Mother Superior Elena for all her young life—although

6

not always as the Mother Superior—she would have thought her heartless, yet Gia understood that this was how she often gave difficult news. It was about getting it over and done with as quickly as possible, like ripping off a Band-Aid. "But he would like to arrange to speak to you soon."

"What is his name," Gia had asked, "my uncle?"

At that moment, the Mother Superior Elena's eyes had betrayed her for just a fraction of a second. Here was whatever it was that the orphanage's senior nun did not like. "Mohammed. Mohammed Khan."

"Is he . . . ?"

"Muslim," the Catholic nun answered, her jaw tight. The problem would not be that he was not Catholic—very few of the orphans in Mercy & Grace came from a Catholic background, many being Hindu, some Sikh, and some Muslim. All were the same in the orphanage, even the backward caste kids were not thought so different. "We will let him explain."

And he had, after a fashion, telling Gia that her father—his brother—had been a young Muslim man who had died before he and her mother could be married. Gia's mother had been a Hindu and, although Gia understood that this specific religious difference would have made things difficult for them, and it explained the reason for the nun's reticence, it had done little to alter Gia's own view of herself. Orphan, religious mongrel . . . what was the difference?

She hadn't thought it mattered to her uncle, either, but nearly three years later, they still hadn't met in person. "Uncle?" Gia now said on top of the barrel in the yard, pushing the phone hard against her ear as a gust of wind drowned out the first words on the other end. In fact, the gust of wind was so hard that she teetered on the rusting oil drum—even close against the wall as she was—and almost toppled over.

"Gia?" came the deep, vigorous voice of a middle-aged man on the other end. Although there was still a South Asian lilt to the way he spoke, decades living in another country had made his voice a very different one to any other that she knew. Hearing it tended to bring a level of comfort to her. "Do you know what time it is?" he went on, in a sort of half hiss, half whisper.

In her haste, Gia had not thought even one little bit about the time of day. It was, she guessed, about three o'clock in the afternoon where she was in India. Which meant . . .

"It's half past two in the morning here, and you just woke your aunt up."

"I'm sorry, Uncle," Gia spluttered. She did not want to make him angry; she had never made her uncle angry, and it would make what was already a terrible day even worse. "I . . ."

Gia's Uncle Mohammed, who lived all the way over on the West Coast of America, must have caught on to her tone straight away. "What is it?" he asked hurriedly, all thoughts of whispering or awoken aunties seemingly brushed aside.

"They are making me leave the orphanage, Uncle," Gia sniveled, the tears threatening to come straight back again. "I don't know what I will do, where I will go."

"I thought you were teaching there," he said. "That you were too valuable for them to be getting rid of you."

Yes, Gia had told him that rather boastfully only the last time that they had spoken just a few weeks back. She didn't need reminding of it now. "I am scared that I will end up living on the street, Uncle, since I have no connections to get a decent-paying job. Or, even worse, that I will have to marry someone."

"Marriage isn't so bad, you know—"

"Uncle!" Gia admonished the man on the other end of the line. Guilt streamed through her as she imagined him wincing at that. She had never met him in person, although there was a picture of a middle-aged man with receding hair and a black beard that covered his cheeks that she always kept tucked safely among her things. He was with a dumpy woman in a brown sari—Aunty Farha, his wife—and two boys who both looked to be in their teens. A smiling family photo that gave Gia pleasure and pain in equal measure, like chewing on a too-spicy chili pepper. Gia had only ever spoken to her uncle, so the others in the picture were like characters in a static TV show, people she imagined and assigned made-up characteristics to based on one toothy smile on one family day out.

"I know, Gia, not helpful," he said in a soothing, apologetic voice. "I—"

"You wish you could afford to bring me over, to let me stay with you," Gia cut in, not unkindly. She had broached the subject before, multiple times, but although fortunate enough to live in America, Uncle Mohammed was not, apparently, a wealthy man, something which he sometimes whispered was not a popular fact with her Aunty Farha. His lack of wealth seemed strange because, as far as Gia was concerned, her uncle was perhaps the most well spoken and cleverest man she had known or heard of. These things usually went hand in hand with wealth, or so she thought. Unless you were an orphan or a Dalit, that was. He had let it slip that he had a degree and was once a lecturer but that he had never been able to do these things in America, instead working production-line jobs and, eventually, driving a taxicab.

On the other end of the line, Gia's uncle hadn't spoken again, and she was suddenly worried that she had hurt or offended him with her words. A monthly chat with her exotic uncle, the only family member she had ever spoken to, had been the best thing in Gia's life these last few years. Well, that and Instagram. Just a bit after she had become aware of Mohammed's existence, he'd given her a gift of a little money, which she'd used toward buying the phone.

"Look," he said, the word coming out in a long sigh. "Let me see what I can do. If we can get you here, maybe we can find a way to apply for you to stay."

Gia's heart leaped and did somersaults inside her. Hope was a powerful, sometimes almost overwhelming, thing. "Thank you, Uncle. Thank you so much," Gia called out in an almost shrill tone, drawing attention from the boys playing in the middle of the yard. The wind blew another strong gust, causing the fingers of Gia's free hand to have to scrabble at the loose masonry on top of the wall to stop her from being toppled. The sky had turned a dark gray, like a koel's egg, suggesting that the monsoon rains were early this year.

"I can't make promises, Gia," her uncle quickly put in, "but I won't see you put out on the street. Or . . . married, I guess."

Gia got off the call before her dwindling credit had the chance to cut her off altogether. She knew she could rely on family to help her out. It wasn't just that she feared being on the street, forced to do anything that she might have to for the money to eat, or married to someone she did not like—although she was scared of both of those things—but Gia also felt sometimes that something awaited her over in America. Opportunity and perhaps the chance to find out a little bit more about who she was. Maybe she could cajole her uncle into telling her who her mother had been. Any time she questioned him about it, he changed the subject, saying it was too painful to talk of the past.

She imagined it at night when she lay alone in her bed, alone with her longing, the need to find out everything about her parents like an ache in her bones. "We love you so much, Gia," she heard them say in her imagination. She wondered how it would be to be a real family, just the three of them. Many nights she fell asleep with this fantasy inflating her like a balloon and lifting her into the sky.

A crack of thunder sounded nearby, and she knew that she should jump down from the oil barrel, but she had a little credit left, so she held up the phone, pointing the camera at the raggedy-looking boys playing in the yard, each of them trying to shove the others in a puddle. What with everything, she had not yet posted on Instagram today.

Sister Agatha appeared at the door from the main corridor and called for the boys to come in before the rain fell and soaked them through in seconds. That was when Gia took the picture, making it look like the nun was shouting at the boys and their game.

"Gia," she growled, "I'm not about to be on Instant-Gram, am I?"

"No, Sister," Gia answered with an angelic smile and a suppressed chuckle. "I won't post you to Instant-Gram," she went on *kind of* truthfully, then tapped the button and added to the collection of stories she had on Instagram that were marked with #AngryNun. The last time she had checked, it was trending, and she'd garnered 1.2K views. #NotBadForAnOrphanKid.

CHAPTER 2

THEN: 1992

The shamiana was close to the weed-encrusted green water of the mighty Ghaghara River, partially screened from the distant road and the rest of the small gathering by fronds of tall grass, as if the tent was hiding. Its canvas was a deep, almost scarlet red, the lining gold, and it shuddered in a breeze that had been slowly building all morning, coming in across the river from the east, where distant clouds sat menacingly on the horizon. Those clouds just had to stay where they were for another hour, and that would be enough, the wedding would be done.

Sometimes, with this wedding, it felt like that. Like it just needed to be done. Which wasn't fair at all, especially as Saumya had seen the Bollywood film *Deewana* when it came out in the cinema just a couple of months ago, and was caught up with idealized conceptions of intense, obsessive love. She wanted it to be perfect.

"Did you hear that?" Saumya asked her little sister inside the tent; she was looking back over her shoulder. "That was thunder."

"I dn ear en-thn," Bindu answered around the pin that she held between her teeth. She pulled the pin out of her mouth and, one eye squinting, aimed it toward the cloth of the sari that Saumya wore. "Now hold still, *Didi*," she grumbled, referring to Saumya by the respectful Hindi term for her older sister, "or the next pin will be going into that perfect skin of yours."

Saumya was standing on a tiny stool, the three legs of which, despite the woman's slightness, were pushing great grooves into the carpet that covered the floor of the tent. The ground this close to the river was still soft after several months of the monsoon.

"I knew the rains were not yet finished when we set this date," Saumya moaned. "It's going to be a washout, I know it."

Bindu smiled up at her older sister, who had always been the most eligible of the two of them, with her perfectly symmetrical face and her skin that was just a shade paler than her sibling's. "You are just having a bride's nerves," she replied dismissively and turned her attention back to the dress she was pinning, which—and this was no accident, anyone who knew Saumya would have understood this—was the same deep shade of red as the tent and similarly embroidered with gold. "Anyway, the sooner you are married, the less chance there is for a fuss, you know this." She made a small, distasteful noise, a clucking of the tongue. "But I would have liked to have longer to get this dress right. You are too small for everything. Bah, it makes me hate you."

Saumya did her best to look aghast, although the beginnings of a laugh twinkled around her eyes and tugged at the corners of her mouth. "You can't say that you hate me on my wedding day."

Bindu's own grin faded as she finished what she was doing and stepped back. "I am used to being envious of you, my beautiful *Didi*. But in this . . ." Bindu's expression was hard to read, although Saumya fancied that she felt her sister's affection shining through the more complex emotions like a sun slowly brightening a cloud.

"Why can't you just marry a suitable Hindu man?" Bindu said in a gruff, throaty voice, launching into an impression of their older brother, Jeet, who in recent years had become the de facto head of the family. Their father had been diagnosed with a degenerative illness that had eventually stopped him from working. Once a strict patriarchal figure, he had shrunk, physically and morally, only for his eldest son to replace him—stricter, angrier, and seemingly without the undercurrent of love that always underpinned their father's sternness. "Why does it have to

13

be a damn Muslim?" Bindu added belligerently, still mimicking their older brother.

Saumya put a hand to her lips, but a short burst of childishly guilty laughter spluttered out from between her fingers.

Bindu sighed as the laughing petered out. "You can't help who you love, eh?"

Saumya huffed dismissively and stepped down from the small stool with not enough care, causing her younger sister to raise an eyebrow for fear that all her hard work would be undone. The pinned wedding sari stood up to its first test well, though. Saumya crossed to a dressing table set with makeup and prepared to finish what she had started before her sister had come to perform the last-minute adjustments to her bridal attire.

A low rumble of distant thunder drifted into the tent, unmistakable this time, and as it rolled into the distance it revealed another sound, like raised voices. Bindu quickly crossed the shamiana and pulled back one of the tent flaps. "Oh, fucking Jeet!"

Any other time, Saumya might have been mildly amused by her sister's use of a cuss word, as Bindu was usually so well spoken and mild mannered. But not today, when all Saumya needed was for things to go smoothly for an hour or two. "What?" Saumya started to get up and cross over to see what was going on. She, and likely everyone else, had noticed that Jeet had been drinking whiskey all morning—his way of getting through the day that his sister married that "beef-eater from the wrong religion," as Jeet would have put it.

She had been born into a Hindu family and raised in the faith, but the emerging Hindu Nationalist movement in her country scared her. The latest controversy revolved around a sixteenth-century mosque, Babri Masjid, in her hometown of Ayodhya. The mosque had been built when the Mughals—Muslim emperors—had ruled India. The Mughals had built hundreds of mosques and forts during their reign, including the historic Taj Mahal. According to legend, the emperor Bābur had built the mosque in the exact spot where an ancient temple dedicated to Lord Ram—the hero of the holy epic the *Ramayana*—had stood, and hard-line Hindus had been calling for its demolition for years so that they could restore it to its former glory. The facts of this story were disputed; many moderate Hindus believed that rumors of the historic temple were spread by British colonizers who intended to divide and conquer the people of Ayodhya.

By 1991, though, the mosque in Ayodhya had become the biggest political issue in the country. Saumya had seen the recent footage on TV, until she'd begged Bindu to turn it off. A mob of Hindu fundamentalists marching toward the mosque—angry red tilaks pulsing on their foreheads, chanting *Jai Shri Ram*, with iron rods and flaming torches in their hands—had left her heart pounding with an all-consuming fear.

Now, as she strode toward Bindu, her stomach scrunched and crumpled like a sheet of tinfoil.

"It's alright," Bindu said, waving her back, "I'll go and deal with it. Send him home if I have to." Saumya cast her a doubtful look, as Jeet was not one to suffer a woman telling him what to do and where to go at the best of times. "Maybe Father will help to calm him down," Bindu added, catching her expression. "You just be quick finishing up, eh?"

Bindu disappeared through the clear sheet-plastic flaps, giving Saumya a brief glimpse of the setting for the wedding as she went. A tin-roofed tea stall too small to enter stood solitary in a wasteland of gray grass with a row of crumbling shops nearby—a broken neon sign blinking Popul r El ctric Store, wedged between Gokul Sweets and Yasmeen Ladies Tailor. A short way beyond them stood acres of flats with yellow-stippled walls, the dull sheen of the Ghaghara, illuminated in mercurial strips where the sun broke through the clouds. And then, down a poorly asphalted road, teeming with people on bicycles and scooters avoiding *gobar* patties left by wandering buffaloes, stood a pillared temple with peeling plaster, a leathery-looking banyan tree beside it. Across the river, in the distance, she could see the ruins of a hunting lodge that dated to the Mughal emperor Jehangir and its *chattri*-topped minarets with a group of women rushing by in black burkas.

The location was as discreet as it could be, away from their home-town that lay just a little east of the city of Ayodhya. There were several— at least several—locations in her city that Saumya would have picked over this field of dun-colored grasses and scrubby trees, where the holy river sat stagnant like liquid jade, but they were making the best of it. Marrying for love was what mattered to her, and it was a luxury still not always afforded.

The flap fell, cutting off her view of the awkwardly milling guests, consisting mostly of close family from both sides who didn't seem to know quite what to make of each other. If the rain came, their wed-ding finery would get soaked, that would be that, and Jeet was now in the hands of the rest of her family, so Saumya pushed the worries that were building inside her aside and turned to finish her makeup. Only thoughts of Hassan, her husband-to-be, drifted across her mind to occasionally break her concentration. Let them be married, then all would be okay. It had to be, *right?* Instead, she felt her insides tighten and crackle.

Saumya could not have said how many minutes she had been sit-ting like that when Bindu came back into the tent.

"Don't you hear them, *Didi?*" Bindu demanded, the two sisters' eyes meeting in the reflection of the mirror as Saumya sat ramrod straight with her back to the entrance.

"Is it time?" Saumya asked. The simple act of applying her makeup, occasionally punctuated by memories of stolen moments and of gentle touches, had brought her into an almost trancelike state.

"What?" Bindu looked back at her, incredulity creasing her forehead.

Oh no, Jeet had hit one of Hassan's family or something, and the whole thing was about to descend into a farce. Saumya had already seen this in her mind several times as a sort of waking nightmare. "Jeet?" she asked, but still Bindu's face did not change in the way she thought that it might.

And then Saumya did hear it, realized that she had been hearing it for some time yet hadn't registered it for what it was: angry shouts, a loud thwack like a chair being bashed against something hard, a strangled female cry that melted into a long, drawn-out wail. That was her mother's voice.

Saumya froze and listened harder, raised eyebrows twisting together in a deep frown, her breathing getting faster and faster.

"They came," Bindu said, her words coming in short gasps, "from the city. They have Hassan."

Saumya rushed past her sister, slipping from the grasp that tried to stop her. Outside, the storm clouds had overtaken them to the north; the brooding gray darkness that had been some way across the Ghaghara had now slipped around to the side, like it was trying to surround them. Saumya searched beneath it, past the rows of chairs that had been set out—several of which were now knocked over and all now devoid of guests—to where a small crowd was moving toward the river a few hundred yards upstream. They were dragging a single figure, and Saumya knew straight away who it was.

"What are they doing to him?" she shrieked and instinctively started toward them, but one of her sister's hands clamped tight around her upper arm, fingers digging in painfully as she struggled.

"They . . ." Bindu didn't manage to get it out at the first attempt, then blurted the words in a rush on the second one. "They said they were going to make sure he is fit to marry a Hindu woman. Get him ready for his wedding night."

"What?" Saumya's legs faltered beneath her, and she bent forward like someone had just punched her in the stomach. Bindu half caught her, gently but firmly attempting to push her upright again.

"You need to get away. The mob is looking for you too."

CHAPTER 3

NOW

Take the red-eye flight from Delhi to San Francisco.

"You will need to stow your table and fasten your belt for landing," said a polite but insistent voice that seemed, to Gia, at once right next to her and also very far away. A few moments later, just a little more firmly, the voice said, "Miss?"

Gia came fully back to consciousness. She had been dreaming, and her mind swam as if she had awoken out of some deep trauma. It was hard to focus, even to lift her head for a moment. Fragments of the fading dream held her; she had imagined a still male form, shrouded in darkness, looking tenderly toward her. "Father?" she had whispered, her fear replaced by yearning that was as old and illogical as anything she could remember. She knew so little about her Muslim father, and her Hindu mother. Who was this man who had defied all odds to marry her mother? Surely they came from very different backgrounds, and yet they had fallen in love. She never knew anything for sure because no one would speak to her of them.

A shiver went through her, and she felt at once sweaty and extremely cold. This was her first flight to anywhere, and it had been long and exhausting. Takeoff had been terrifying, as the big airliner climbed into the brilliant-blue sky so different from the orange, dusty one she had left behind, and the Air India flight attendant, whose green sari matched the color of green Gia was feeling, asked her if she was doing okay. The flight attendant brought her a cup of Ayurvedic detox tea to calm her nerves. The rest of the flight had been surprisingly boring, save for the in-flight movies.

"When you came on board," the flight attendant told her, "you were so wide eyed and excited that I thought we would have to peel you from the top of the cabin." She shook her head ruefully. "Then you slept for most of the flight."

Gia sat up straight, felt her hair plastered unflatteringly against the right side of her head, and was fairly sure that she could sense the tautness of some dried, crusted drool at the corner of her mouth. "Did I miss it?" she asked the flight attendant. "I wanted to see it from the air."

"You're fine," the attendant answered kindly, then wagged a finger at Gia's midriff. "Just get your belt on. The cloud cover's high today, so we'll drop through it with plenty of time for you to get a good look. Put your seat back into the upright position, too, please."

Gia nodded and pressed the button that would bring her seat upright again—she had played with it so much when she first came on board that she soon heard annoyed huffing from the seat behind—and then retrieved the belt from somewhere below her posterior. Gia had been so tired when she finally boarded this flight back in Delhi, a flight over to the West Coast of America. It had been the culmination of nearly two weeks of frantic activity by someone uniquely ill positioned to suddenly move to the United States the way she was doing.

The clasp made a satisfying click, and Gia rubbed a hand through her hair before leaning her cheek against the cool glass of the airplane window. Her hand reached habitually into the hand-embroidered, mirror-work sling bag that she used in place of a handbag and found the letter that had been with her like a talisman for these last two weeks. She never left more than a few hours between reads, just in case she had read it incorrectly or had somehow interpreted the perfectly clear words in a way other than that in which they were meant. Just in case she had imagined the whole thing and was living in some dream where the miraculous had really happened and she had been saved from a life of desperate poverty outside the orphanage.

Dear Miss Kumari,
Please allow me to introduce myself. My name is Sonia Shah, and I am the owner of Golden State Weddings & Events in San Francisco in the United States of America. As a part of our Global Equality Initiative program, we obtained your curriculum vitae from Mercy & Grace Orphanage, which we understand has been your home for many years.

Given your qualifications, your specific interest in event management, and the attitude demonstrated both in your CV and by testimony of the nuns at your orphanage, we believe that you would be an excellent fit for a designer position that has opened up at our company.

As she did every time, Gia read the last sentence twice, still marveling at the fact that her Uncle Mohammed had somehow pulled the biggest of strings to arrange this for her. He always professed such humbleness, yet it seemed that he must have some big influence and connections.

So many questions had swirled around in her head like boiling milk when she received the letter. She had not been able to afford the credit to call him since receiving the letter with the enclosed airline ticket, and her time had been consumed with arranging a passport and all the other little items of business that would allow her to take up the position as soon as this Sonia Shah wanted her to.

It was all so perfect; not only to be saved from destitution but to have gone from that terrifying prospect to her wildest dreams—to America, a dream job, and to living just across a short stretch of water from her uncle . . . it was almost too good to be true. Gia's fingers caressed the letter as she placed it back into her *banjara* bag. She turned to the window again as the airplane dropped through the clouds, revealing only the tossing sea below them.

Gia pressed her face right up to the window to look past the plane's wing and was struck by the ruggedness of the landscape below her. It looked dead, as if they were flying over the moon. Then, they flew over one last set of mountains and all of a sudden everything was green, and there were about ten million little houses, laid out so neatly in orderly rows. So alien, even from thousands of feet in the air—and Gia found her stomach clenching as she viewed this city of uniformity and equal angles, without the fanciful lines and ornamentation forms she'd been used to from Delhi, that awaited her.

When you exit immigration and claim your bags, we will have someone waiting for you.

"It will be a culture shock when you arrive in America," Sister Agatha had told Gia as they stood in the airport check-in terminal in Delhi. The sister had gently put a hand to Gia's cheek and turned her face so that their eyes met. Gia was already experiencing "culture shock," as the sister called it, while still in the airport in her own country. The seething mass of people of all colors, creeds, shapes, and sizes, with their trolleys and luggage, elbowing fellow travelers out of the way. Then there were the tensile barriers, which made nonsensical mazes to contain the throng surging toward the check-in desks. The closest thing Gia had known was enrollment day at Polytechnic Academy for Event Management, and that was only a fraction of . . . *this.*

"But remember, Gia," the sister had gone on, "you are an orphan of Mercy & Grace, so you will not be overwhelmed by it, and you will not succumb to it."

"Succumb?"

"Everything will be 'more' in America, child. It will be bigger, brighter, shinier. But all these things sit on the surface of everything important that you already know. The values we have . . . *tried* to bring you up with. Do not let it confuse you; do not get lost."

Gia had nodded while not having the slightest idea what Sister Agatha was talking about.

"It is like a wedding ceremony," the sister said, obviously trying to put it in terms that she thought Gia would understand. "You can buy all the jasmine and marigold flowers and have the prettiest sari and the most ornate *mandap*, but underneath it, the ceremony is always the same, and it means the same to everyone involved, however much money is spent on it."

Gia nodded again, thinking that, as far as she was concerned, there were weddings and then there were *weddings*. Her Instagram highlights were full of celebrity weddings—Shahid Kapoor and Mira Rajput, Rani Mukherjee and Aditya Chopra—which she had devoured for hours, poring over every venue detail. Now, as she pulled her battered suitcase behind her through the arrivals lounge of San Francisco Airport, its broken wheel under it like a sick bird's claw, Sister Agatha's words were echoing through her mind, although probably still not with quite the effect that the nun had intended.

Gia was aware that she must look like some provincial idiot as she turned small circles and stared at the digital displays on the arrival and departure boards, across at the athletic apparel and candy stores, and even at the potted palms near the entrance. Her breath caught in her throat, her chest ached, to think a country could be so alight, so clean and dazzling. It was hard to stop turning, and even harder to stop snapping posts for her Instagram story. #AMERICA.

"Miss Kumari?"

Gia spun around to be faced by a bald man with skin so white that Gia could see the little pink pinpricks in his nose and the blue and purple capillaries in his cheeks. He was wearing a black suit and cap, with a glowing white shirt underneath. He regarded her seriously as he held up a small whiteboard with her name written on it in black marker.

"Yes."

"Welcome to America," the man said in a deep voice, and Gia fell immediately in love with the accent, which slid over the words like ghee melting over *paranthas*. "My name is Roger, and I'm going to drive you to your apartment. Did you have a good flight?"

"I . . . slept."

"That's good," Roger answered in a slightly robotic tone, like perhaps the answer would have been the same if Gia had said, "Well, we nearly crashed twice." He looked down at her ancient cloth suitcase, which had been among the smallest on the luggage carousel. Waiting for it to come out had been equal parts nerve-racking and thrilling. "That's . . . all your luggage?"

Gia nodded dumbly.

"Let me take that for you," Roger offered. Feeling like things were becoming more surreal by the moment, she let him take it.

When they came out of the airport, the air felt colder, and everything was brighter. There were not the masses of people darting into traffic as there had been in Delhi, squeezing past cars, bulls, lumbering trucks painted with gaudy gods, nor the blare of a hundred horns or the shrill whistles of loitering policemen. There was not a single person haggling with a cab driver or eating roasted corn from a cone, crumpling the newspaper print and throwing it on the ground for birds to peck at or stray dogs to lick. There were no idle groups of men smoking *beedis* and watching passing women.

A car waited for them. Black, stretched and sleek. Gia did not know much about cars, but she could appreciate the inside of the rear section, which had a cream-colored leather covering on the seats, with a lacquered, reddish wood on the inside of the doors and on the outside of the small cooler that was open in front of her.

"Help yourself to a drink," Roger called from the front seat. "You want the screen up or down?"

"Um . . . down, please," Gia replied, randomly picking an option as she didn't have the slightest clue what he was talking about. She picked up a can of Coca-Cola from the cooler and opened it with a satisfying hiss, sticking the thing straight in her mouth as it threatened to bubble over and make the upholstery sticky. The ice-cold sweetness flooded through her, a taste that she had enjoyed precisely twice before in her whole life, both times when some wealthy patron or other had treated them to a free lunch at McDonald's in honor of their kid's birthday. And here they were, handing it out for free in the back of a chauffeured ride to the apartment that had been provided for her.

Gia loved America already, even while fear gripped her that something *had* to be wrong with this picture. She was to be an employee at an event company, yet she was almost feeling like royalty. Did they think she was someone that she was not, someone who deserved all *this*?

"First time in America?" Roger asked with the air of someone picking the question from a selection of possible ride-conversation openers.

First time anywhere, Gia almost replied.

Take your time to settle into your apartment. There is a gift waiting for you on the table in the living area.

The apartment had an electronic entry system, which seemed very futuristic to Gia. There had been very few doors in her world that even locked. The code had been in the final set of email instructions sent to Gia before she had left India. She had been trembling with anticipation, her heart soaring with happiness before she even crossed the threshold. The ride from the airport through the changing landscape had kept her engrossed—rolling hills dotted with eucalyptus trees and then the loneliness of the streets and the sidewalks and the houses. *Does anyone even live here?* she had wondered, her face pressed up against the window as she greedily guzzled her Coke and then eyed the other drinks in the cooler. Sister Agatha's imagined face and wagging finger had stopped her from snatching up another. Instead, she busied her hands with taking pictures on her old, beat-up Nokia phone.

Just walking through the apartment complex and finding her own door had felt overwhelming. It was on a narrow tree-lined street where the midrise condominiums had large north-facing windows, and the sidewalks were clear of litter. Across the street was the back of a concrete parking garage. She felt swallowed by the glass and steel facade of the entrance as she walked past the elderly gray-uniformed concierge who waggled his sun-bleached brows at her. She took the elevator up and walked along the carpeted hallway to . . . she took a moment here . . . a place . . . that would be . . . her own. Excitement rose in her like the hot dry wind that blew over Delhi from the desert of Rajasthan in the summer months.

Inside was another level of awesome—a uniquely American word that Gia had already decided she was going to use liberally now that she was going to live here. She ran around, turning on all the lights and turning on and off the faucets in the bathroom and the little kitchenette. All hers, *all hers*. Roger had explained that, according to Sonia, this would only be for the next few months, until the company found something more suitable—*something smaller for her* had been his words—but she intended to enjoy every thrilling moment she was in it. The cozy-looking couch upholstered in pale blue with throw pillows patterned in green leaves, the flat-screen TV on the wall, the bed with luxuriously pure-white linens. She lay down on the bed for a moment, her fist clenching the soft folds of the silk sheet under her as she remembered the large, unheated dormitory she had slept in with nineteen other girls—on a single cot with a rusted metal frame and coils that creaked and squeaked whenever she moved. How she huddled under a holey wool quilt with a wary eye cocked on a mousehole in a corner of the stone floor.

And then there was the package on the table in the living area. The gift. She had never had a gift so beautifully wrapped, and it seemed a shame to undo the bow and ruin it. Yet somehow, she managed.

"Oh my, my," she said out loud, the tears that had been threatening to some degree since the moment she arrived at the airport finally beginning to spill forth. *For work*, was all the card said, then it simply had Sonia's name beneath it. And lying there on the opened candy-pink wrapping paper, still in its box, was a brand-new iPhone.

CHAPTER 4

NOW

Gia was almost late for her first day of work. It had been a combination of things.

First, there was the problem of assembling an outfit, and she'd gone with a blue-and-white polka-dot blouse with a long A-line denim skirt that the nuns had given her as a parting gift. It had a chocolate stain on it because she had already worn it on the plane, but she'd sponged it with a Tide pen she'd found in the laundry closet, and was delighted to see it looked as good as new.

Having arrived on a Thursday, she had been given three full days to settle in and work on her "jet lag"—a term that had sounded entirely made up to Gia before she slept until about two o'clock in the afternoon and woke up feeling worse than when she had gone to bed. She'd first tried to contact her Uncle Mohammed, and had left him two voice mails, which he hadn't yet returned. She wanted to meet up with him as soon as it was possible. That was because she wanted to see him, of course—she so dearly wanted to finally meet him in the flesh, to hug him, to meet her cousins, to thank him for what he had done for her— but also because she hoped to, over time, tease more of her past from him, to understand at least a little more of where she was from, which had always been something Uncle Mohammed had seemed reticent to discuss when they spoke. Gia had sensed he was worried about being overheard, as if the answers Gia sought, about her mother and father and why she had ended up in an orphanage, were things he could not say in front of others.

With nothing else to do, and not wanting to call Uncle Mohammed a third time, Gia had lazed about the apartment for another day on Saturday, getting up at odd hours and eating all the goodies from her welcome basket—two packets of Ruffles potato chips, something called Funyuns that were shaped like rings and reminded her of the pinwheels the vendors sold outside India Gate park, an assortment of nuts, even pistachios (which she'd never eaten before), and tons of chocolates in every flavor imaginable. She'd watched lots of cable TV and taken three baths before deciding, on Sunday, that perhaps she should explore her neighborhood a little, and—countless hours and several hundred pictures on her iPhone later—she had arrived back home in darkness.

Gia had awoken on Monday morning with almost all the clothes that she owned—a sum total of two outfits, some cotton underwear, and one brassiere—in dirty piles around the apartment, along with a general sense of time wasted and preparations not made. Oh, and rising panic. That too.

Then there was the train.

Gia had been informed in her last instruction email that the best way for her to get to work was on the BART train system, and she had seen on Google Maps that the nearest station was just up the street. It turned out to be a much longer way along the street than expected, as they had some very long streets in America. And—who could have guessed?—it was a really bad idea to stop and take pictures of interesting things for Instagram along the way. #coolgraffiti. #manwalkingcat. #OhDearGodIsThatTheTime?

It was not the first time that Instagram had led her astray.

Gia burst into the station and found that getting a ticket was not something that could happen in the forty-five seconds she still had to get the train. Panic had gripped her then. Images of the as-yet unmet Sonia Shah's deep disappointment with her lateness and the subsequent

immediate return of the disgraced employee to India and a life of squa-
lor—but, worst of all, one that she had brought upon herself . . . Until
she had realized that the next train would be along in another five
minutes. Panic over. She had already been planning to beg her uncle
for work at the cab company; *anything rather than be sent straight back.*

All the same, Gia still felt like an unprepared and sweaty mess as
she approached the office building where Golden State Weddings &
Events was based. In this part of the city, almost all the buildings were
so big, and she, a small-town girl, had found getting to the right address
hard when each of these steel-and-glass monoliths seemed to take up as
much space as a whole shantytown that recently had sprung up on the
outskirts of Noida. Staring straight up at it, she could not believe that
she would be working somewhere inside. It made her feel so important,
like she must really be someone to be standing where she was, and just
a little of the nerves melted away.

Instinctively, Gia's hand came up to take a picture for a post, but the
time on the home screen said that she was due in the office in another
four minutes, and it seemed that getting anywhere in this place always
seemed to take longer than she was expecting. Best to get moving.

At the top of the steps a revolving door was partitioned into three
segments, and the whole thing traveled agonizingly slowly in a coun-
terclockwise direction. Gia stepped into it, and, a few seconds later,
a tall man with a smooth face accented by a high forehead beneath
tousled black curly hair made an athletic leap from the foyer and into
the other side, turning sideways to make it through the closing gap.
He was dressed in a charcoal-gray suit, the jacket undone and flapping
about, revealing a crisp white shirt that clung to him and was almost
see-through in places. The tie he wore was loosened a little, the top
button of the shirt undone, like he was closer to the end of the day than
the beginning of it, even though it was not yet nine.

His skin was of a lighter tone than Gia's, almost olive, and he looked
young to her—no older maybe than she was—yet carried an older man's
confident air, especially in the way he smiled at her through the glass. He

had a knobby nose, although it suited him—perhaps the result of breaking it while competing on the wrestling team or gymnastics at school. He rolled his deep-set eyes and made a show of plodding slowly behind the glacially slow progress of the glass partition, looking at his watch and tapping it, before throwing Gia a final grin and leaving the revolving door to head down the steps and away. Distracted as she watched him go, Gia completely missed her chance to exit and found herself doing a second circuit through the revolving door, watched by the woman sitting behind the reception desk inside.

Finally exiting the revolving doorway, Gia stood all but speechless in the foyer as she tried to absorb the splendor of the most opulent expanse this side of a luxury five-star hotel in south Delhi, where there had once been a high-society wedding that had gone viral on Insta. It really was an unnecessary amount of space for the lone woman who occupied it, over to Gia's right. She finally dared to take a delicate step toward the desk. The floors and walls were covered in Italian marble in a chocolate-and-cream harlequin pattern that sparkled under the glass-bubble chandelier. As she looked up at it, Gia found herself holding her breath for fear of shattering the glass. The soft amber-colored light dispersed by the voluptuous bubbles made the stainless-steel doors to the elevator appear almost golden. Aside from the dark-haired receptionist and her large walnut desk, the only other features in the space were a potted palm tree in the far-right corner and a creamy-white leather sectional along the left-hand wall, which sat on a fluffy rug a shade darker than it.

The receptionist glanced up at Gia as she approached but then straight back down again. She had shiny black hair tied back in a bun so tight it looked as if the skin was going to split along the lines of her wide cheekbones. Her skin was pale, almost like talcum powder; her jaw, her cheekbone, a subtly dimpled chin—all of them poking through her smooth complexion like rocks through snow. *Hai bhagwan*, the woman was so imposing, so . . . coldly glamorous. And this was just the receptionist.

Moments passed to the echoing clickety-clack of the receptionist's keyboard keys, and Gia wondered if she was being purposely ignored, whether she was expected to speak or clear her throat, or something. Perhaps it was some sort of test, she wondered a little crazily. Finally, the receptionist took her hands away from the keyboard and looked up with a delicate intake of breath. The smile was at once dazzling and professional, the eyes bright but guarded. The woman was both a human welcome sign and a barrier to entry. "Can I help you?"

"Gia-Kumari-employee," Gia blurted out, hearing her Indian accent ringing like an alarm bell in every syllable. "Er . . . Sonia Shah," she added hopefully, dropping the name of the business's owner like it might have magical properties. "Golden-State-Weddings."

"Fifth floor," the receptionist told Gia before looking back at her screen. And that, apparently, was the end of their interaction.

"Thank-thank you."

The elevator made a self-important ding as it arrived, and Gia stepped into a space with mirrors on both sides—her reflection coming at her in a pincer movement. *Oh dear*, she did not look at all how she would have hoped. Her long, usually silky hair—that Gia often felt was her best feature—was disordered and frizzy at the ends. She tried running her fingers through it, briefly revealing the mole behind her right ear, but rather than falling elegantly back to her shoulders, it kind of held the shape that her fingers had pulled it into. In a panic, Gia pressed the flat of each palm against her head, trying desperately to press the hair back down. It did not work.

As the elevator slid upward, Gia looked at the young woman that stood across from her in the spotless mirror. For the first time she realized that she *was* a woman, that person looking back at her. The thing with growing up in an orphanage was that, although she'd grown up fast and lost her innocence at an incredibly young age, in many ways she had stayed a child. Going shopping in a mall, watching a movie in a theater with girlfriends, letting her rosebud lips graze a boy's for the first time—these freedoms that other young adults took for granted were foreign to her.

The next thing Gia thought was how plain that girl looked. Just an ordinary-looking South Asian girl with eyebrows that always grew back too thick, a nose that was too flat and pudgy, and ears that seemed a little too big in proportion to the size of her head. At least her skin—the color of milky coffee—had finally shed those adolescent pimples.

Then there was one more thought that came merely a moment before the elevator pompously dinged her arrival at the fifth floor: She did not know the face staring back at her. The thoughts and feelings, the hopes, dreams, and expectations that made up Gia Kumari were not reflected in that face. The two did not align, and that person in the mirror might as well be a stranger to her. Yet she was not sure if *that* Gia Kumari, the one who had never inhaled the scent of a man, who had never experienced the kind of love they depicted in the classic Hollywood movies she'd watched, was the young woman who belonged in a Noida slum or in a San Francisco apartment.

Ufff, she wasn't even Gia Kumari, not really, "Kumari" being a name given to orphans who knew no family name or could not take on the one that they might have had. She might, indeed, have had another family name—perhaps Khan, like Uncle Mohammed, or Ali, like the famous boxer.

She stepped out of the lift to face three plaques on the wall in front of her. Crozier & Co. Attorneys at Law was on the top, with an arrow pointing to the right. Gia's mind flitted to the confident, nattily dressed South Asian man in the revolving door at the front of the building, wondering if that was where he worked. He looked capable enough, she fancied, to be something like a lawyer. The next plaque down belonged to WhiteBrite Dental, which again was to the right, while Golden State Weddings & Events, last on the list, was to the left.

Gia pressed a buzzer to be let into the office, heard the officious voice of an older woman say, "Come in, Gia," over the top of a crackling bed of microphone static, which flicked straight off again. *Is that her?*

she wondered, this woman who had hired her, who was the key not only to a better life but to a career doing what she loved? Sonia Shah.

The office's lobby was decorated in a sunflower-yellow shade and accents of vanilla, with six burnt-orange upholstered chairs. Crimson-red and flamingo-pink silk maharaja turbans with richly jeweled plumes spilled out over a hat rack. The left wall was dotted with multicolored *gota* dreamcatchers and tiny burnished-gold temple bells. To the right was a wall of pictures. Happy couples in wedding *lehngas* and sherwanis smiled back at her. Thank-you notes and newspaper cuttings of local socialites attending weddings organized by Sonia Shah and her team were scattered throughout the photos.

There was nobody at the reception desk, so Gia stepped on through to an open-plan office space painted in magnolia and punctuated by rectangular roof supports, with navy-blue square tiles of carpet under-foot. Clear acrylic chairs surrounded a long, medieval-looking table that held an assorted variety of decorating odds and ends—there was a clump of tangled artificial mango-yellow-and-orange marigold garlands on one, another desk bore an elephant-god-Ganesha-imprinted paper backdrop in gold and burgundy flattened out, probably to be used imminently for wedding decor.

What the room did not have at that moment was any staff in it. There was a door against the back wall and another toward the far end of the right wall, then over to the left there was what might be an office with a half window set in a narrow door. The door and the windows had horizontal blinds that were pulled almost entirely shut, and the space beyond looked dark and empty—at least until Gia saw a hand slightly part two of the slats and a pair of eyes appear briefly, before they quickly vanished again.

Before Gia could wonder any more about that, the door against the far wall opened, and two people came out, arguing. "Ugh, honestly," said a young Indian woman with dark-black hair that curled thickly all over her forehead. She wore a thin, mustard-colored wool sweater and dangling gold earrings that swung when she tossed her head. "Your room stinks like bad flatulence," she complained to the other one, a short man who was muscular and stocky, with bleached-blond hair that stood upward in a lazy Mohican. "I can't stand to be in there a moment longer."

"It's not me!" the man protested, holding up a Tupperware box in one hand while carrying a fork in the other. "It's the boiled eggs."

The woman stopped, turned around, and held up a hand to stop him. "Well, don't keep following me around with them then!" she exclaimed. "Really, what sort of a weirdo eats a whole box of boiled eggs for breakfast?"

The man glared sullenly at her and muttered, "It's for protein," then seemed about to turn around again when he spotted Gia. His face instantly transformed, exploding at once into an expression of utter joy, like the argument was instantly forgotten. "The new girl!" he shouted, pointing at Gia. She noticed now, as his navy-blue blazer drew back from his broad chest, that his T-shirt bore the words *Keep Calm and Eat Healthy*.

The woman turned, her face lighting up, too, and she bounded over to Gia like a child riding an imaginary horse. As she got closer, Gia saw that she had a tiny birthmark at the top of her neck, just below her chin. It was strawberry-shaped and could almost have been intentionally placed there, tattooed perhaps. Somehow it suited her precisely.

"Gia!" the woman cried as she reached her, then she threw her arms around Gia and enveloped her in a tight, long-lasting hug. Gia went stiff—unused as she was to casual human contact—and just waved her hands about, which were pinned to her side. "I've been so excited," the woman said by way of explanation when she finally stepped back. "My name's Dolly, Dolly Khatri." A hand was thrust forward, and Gia gingerly shook it, thinking that hugs usually followed handshakes, not the other way around.

"I love-love your sweater," Gia said, transfixed by its vibrant color and the light fibers, which bounced around a little like the woman's curly hair did.

"Thank you," Dolly said, seeming to blush. Gia thought that she loved this woman a little already, even if it was all somewhat overwhelming. Something tight in her chest was loosening a little, and she wanted to cry joyous tears, although she held them back.

"I'm a set designer and decorator," Dolly went on, "but I'm also a mean seamstress and a whiz with costume advice. Basic all-around company asset"—she flopped the fingers of a loose-wristed hand against her chest—"if I do say so myself. And this"—she turned to indicate the man who was now shoveling boiled egg into his mouth—"is Chad. Weird human being, great videographer."

The door to the corner office opened noisily with a clatter of dangling blinds, and a hard-eyed, grim-faced woman strode out. Surely this was not Sonia Shah, whose picture on the "About" page of the company website was a professional and glamorous headshot with diamond solitaires dangling from her ears and a knowing smile playing about her lips. Well, there was at least a passing resemblance, Gia supposed.

On this woman, the salt-and-pepper pixie-cut style made her look serious and efficient, and it contained far more "salt" than it had in that photo. Her silver gray looked almost platinum, a wintry background to those small eyes. She wore a simple white dress with black trim, and a long silk scarf that hung gently around her shoulders, like she was ready to breeze among the guests at a wedding ceremony whenever called upon to do so. The pink-and-purple paisley patterns on the scarf made the design look like it was moving when she grabbed the fabric in her hand and pulled it lower against her wrists, while masterfully balancing the oversize mug she gripped as if in a talon. The mug read YOUR HAPPILY EVER AFTER, yet this woman's peremptory look made her seem a little more like the wicked stepmother of that particular fairy tale, and not the fairy godmother.

Another woman followed Sonia out, and this one could not have appeared more different, although she was also South Asian and probably of about the same age. If Sonia was smart but austere and formal, the other woman was also smart, but stylish and flamboyant too.

An expensive-looking purse swung from an extended wrist, and the woman wore huge sunglasses, her face shining with the effects of a lot of immaculately applied makeup. She had an abundance of hair that was intricately piled up on top of her head, somehow defying physics by remaining where it was.

"Thank you, Sonia," she sang, "you've been so helpful. It's so good to get an idea."

Sonia briefly caught Gia's eye before stopping and turning back to the other woman. "No problem at all, Mimi," she answered, a little warmth sitting on top of the officious-sounding voice. "So good to see you, and I'm happy to help."

"Do make sure you say hi to Ranveer for Pat," Mimi added. "He made me promise."

"I will."

"Pat still calls him 'the best salesman in recruitment,' I swear it. Cannot say your husband's name without getting that in there."

Sonia slowly stepped toward the main office door, leading the way. "I will not say that part," Sonia joked, "his head does not need to be any bigger."

Mimi laughed—very hard, Gia thought. "Oh!" The woman had suddenly stopped, very close to the door. Gia thought she noticed Sonia's brow twitch, but, if the other woman saw, she did not appear to show it. "I hear you're doing the Jimmy Singh wedding."

"Yes."

"In New York it would have been such an event," Mimi simpered. "Millions spent on his last wedding, I heard. Incredible location."

"Not so much this time," Sonia admitted, "but it should be lovely nonetheless."

Gia flicked her eyes over to Dolly and Chad, who both stood by the nearest desk trying to look busy, while clearly listening in, she felt. Gia took their cue and did the same, although she got the sense that this Mimi lady—some sort of client, she guessed, though she obviously knew Sonia quite well—did not even notice any of the employees were there.

"Imagine," Mimi went on, hushed and yet not hushed, "having to come all the way down here to find a farm girl after that scandal with the ex-wife who would not be quiet."

"Oh," Sonia said—a noncommittal reply to Gia's ears.

"I heard there is some secret there," Mimi added. "Who knows what?" Then she shrugged and seemed to move immediately on from the conversation. "Anyway, my hair appointment is at ten."

A moment later, she was gone, and Sonia turned and came over to where Gia, Dolly, and Chad were standing.

"New girl," Chad said, pointing to Gia.

Sonia gave Gia a closemouthed smile. "Welcome, Gia."

"Is that Pat Malik's wife?" Dolly asked before Gia could make any sort of reply.

Sonia glanced over her shoulder briefly. "Mimi, yes."

"I didn't know you knew them," Dolly said, sounding almost upset. "He's worth more money than everyone I will ever know will ever earn. He even has one of those Learjets." Dolly sounded like she would like a Learjet.

"Ranveer did a lot of hiring for Pat when I first met him."

"Pat . . ." Dolly repeated wistfully. "Are we doing an event for them?"

"I doubt it," Sonia replied. "Wanted an idea of prices."

"Does that matter if he is so rich?" Gia asked, never one to keep a question to herself. Questions, Mother Superior said, were the key to learning; although Sister Agatha hadn't always agreed.

Chad scoffed. "The richer you are, the more value you want for your money."

"That can sometimes be true," Sonia agreed, "but I got the sense that half the reason for Mimi's visit was that last bit of investigative gossip; gossip is her favorite pastime." She chewed her lip thoughtfully, then looked up at her new employee. "Gia," she said, "would you like a fun job for your first day?"

CHAPTER 5

"Better to be safe than sorry," Sonia had said to Gia, before asking her to check out Jimmy Singh's social media for anything suspect about his previous marriage and the way it had ended. "No big deal, but we need to cover all bases, and make sure there's nothing scandalous about his past that would make Tasha or her family reject him at the *mandap*. In this business, we don't like surprises—we like to plan for every eventuality. In fact, it's the job of the 'planner' to be ahead of the game; I would even say it is implied in our job title, wouldn't you?

"Dolly will want some help with the wedding decor, as well, but fit it in around that where you can."

Gia did not even know who Jimmy Singh was, so she started her research there. "Diamond merchants," she said out loud, causing Dolly to look over from a nearby table.

"Yup. Beautiful, expensive stones." Dolly told her with great authority. "Mimi has a point." She kept saying Mimi's name like they were now best friends, even though they had not spoken a word when the woman had been in the office. "I mean, Jimmy Singh and a girl from Yuba City, of all places?"

"Yu-ba City?" Gia tried quietly, repeating the unfamiliar name to herself. "What is wrong with this place?"

"You're kidding me, right?" Dolly put in, clearly forgetting that Gia had been in America only a few days. "It's, like . . . Hicksville, California."

"Yoo-bah," Gia silently mouthed to herself again, still not sure what Dolly meant.

Sonia caught Dolly's eye as she crossed the office and pulled a face. "That's a little . . . It's quite pretty out in Yuba City, after all."

"Yeah." Dolly rolled her eyes. "All those walnut and raisin farms."

Sonia paused to take a long swig of her coffee, her eyes glinting before she went on, "The bride—um, Tasha—she's got a finance certificate online with Berkeley." Sonia took a sip of her coffee again, reminding Gia of her PE teacher, who used to drink his tea from the saucer, and blew—*phoo phoo*—over it, to cool it fast. "She's not just a dumb country girl, you know. I'm sure she would do well without Jimmy Singh."

Gia glanced over at Dolly, who looked unimpressed by this online certificate. "New York . . . Diamonds . . . So-o-o much money," Dolly said, her teeth slightly gritted, her neck extending slightly to show her distinctive birthmark.

Sonia gave an exasperated sigh and carried on her way, then seemed to remember that she had her coffee cup in one of her hands; she held it out to Gia. "Put that back on my desk, would you? I will need a fresh cup in a moment."

"I could—" Gia began, wanting to be helpful.

"No," Sonia interrupted in a clipped tone, "thank you, Gia. No one touches the coffee machine but me."

Gia flushed purple; she had not expected to find that a sensitive subject. With rapid strides Gia walked into Sonia's office, which should have felt like sacred ground but was a disappointingly slovenly, disorganized mess, and Gia could not believe that she had recently entertained a potential client in it. It reminded her of a private investigator's office from a black-and-white movie that she had once watched projected onto the water-stained walls of the orphanage. The detective had been a disgraced alcoholic ex–police officer with a big belly and mud-splattered boots.

The office was dim, the horizontal slatted blinds that faced the main area still pulled halfway shut, while a thick, roll-down blind blocked the only external window. Most of the light came from the doorway that she was standing in and a desk lamp placed over to one side with a fluted marble base that looked like it might have belonged in the black-and-white movie. Gia looked around for a main light switch but, after several moments, decided that she would have to do without it.

An espresso machine, which must have weighed easily three hundred pounds and that had a billion different flavors of coffee capsules stacked on top, stood on a table against the back wall. An antique-looking mahogany desk was placed against the near wall below the glass interior window, which was partnered with a mahogany chair, the padded seat covered in well-worn green leather and held in place with brass studs. Although it had a keyboard, a mouse, and a monitor on it, much of the remaining surface was overflowing with writing pads covered with notes, pencils, pens, bridal magazines, and periodicals, some left open with pages crinkled.

Gia wandered back into the main office and toward a table in the center of the room where someone had laid out pictures from a Pinterest board titled "Tasha weds Jimmy" next to large-scale printouts of a floor plan. Dolly was crouching at the table, leafing through the pictures. "Ugh," she grumbled as Gia drew nearer, "I've got to go shopping for more coral and cream chiffon fabric. We don't have enough for the drapes that the bride wants us to hang around the *mandap* like arched doorways, and I've got a million things to do here."

"If you're doing that now," Sonia said from across the office, "why don't you take Gia with you to Preet Fabrics?" Dolly seemed to brighten a little at that.

"Should I not be researching Jimmy Singh?" Gia asked.

"When you get back," Sonia snapped impatiently. Gia saw a frown flicker across her face as she gave Gia a long, lingering look up and down. "And while you're there, pick up an Indian outfit to wear to the wedding."

Dolly clapped her hands together excitedly. "Oh, clothes shopping for Gia! Happy days!"

Gia didn't quite know what to say. Sonia Shah was an enigma—stern, yet suddenly so generous. "Thank you," Gia managed. Then she remembered to add, "And thank-thank you for the iPhone and for the lovely accommodation."

"The mobile phone is necessary for work," Sonia answered, "and you will be making a contribution out of your own wages for everything else."

Okay, so not *that* generous.

CHAPTER 6

"I don't hate it really, you know," Dolly said, punctuating the sentence with sucking noises, which she made around the candy lollipop she had bought at a little store just around the corner from Preet Fabrics. The two-story clothing store sat in one of the many commercial plots with a maze of overhead utility lines following the sides of the state highway—surrounded by wide orchards of peaches and walnuts.

"Fabric shopping," Dolly elaborated as they walked down the store's long central aisle. "I might have made it sound like a drag before"—she reached out a hand, the four tips of her fingers lightly touching the bottom of a thick roll of golden organza fabric, woven with silver sequins—"but really, this place is, like, where I find a lot of my inspiration."

It was overwhelming, Gia thought, that was for sure. The space was huge with high ceilings, and naturally lit by many tall windows with low sills that ran most of the way along one side. Although there were fabrics of all sorts and colors—variously rolled up on shelves, in stacks, dispensers, leaning against the wall, or folded or draped as part of a display—the store leaned toward a distinctively South Asian aesthetic. Indeed, it looked to Gia like there were the base materials for a whole lifetime's worth of saris in this one place—a different one for every day that she lived, perhaps.

Without thinking about it, Gia stuck her own lollipop back in her mouth and lifted her iPhone to take a picture. Well, several pictures. This would make a great theme for a series of Instagram posts. #sariseduction.

"That is one of the best features of the place," Dolly said, pointing toward the large window that dominated one side of the loftlike space. "Because, to truly understand color, you need to realize that it looks different depending upon the lighting." She indicated the overhead fluorescent light that painted everything in a sickly milky-white hue. "The color of natural light is different to the color of a striplight, or other types of artificial light. Even natural light is different depending upon whether it's a sunny or a cloudy day, if the sun's high or low in the sky. All these different types of light bring out colors in different ways."

Dolly found the fabric that she needed and then guided Gia over to a far corner of the store housing ready-made clothing, with an especially large collection of saris and traditional men's outfits. "Right," she said, "now for the fun part." She rubbed her hands together and gave Gia an up-and-down look. Although there was no judgment, Dolly's appraising gaze still made Gia feel a bit naked. "Let's get you something appropriate for the wedding, shall we? If it actually goes ahead, then you might even get to wear it," she added with a humorless laugh. "I'm hoping this gossip that Mimi was talking about turns out to be nothing significant." She shifted her feet impatiently, like a horse kicking at dirt.

"Anything you like the look of?" Dolly asked her after they had been browsing the section of ready-mades for a minute.

Gia shrugged, not because she did not know or had not yet seen anything that she liked, but rather because she was overwhelmed. So many of the outfits were beautiful beyond anything she had ever imagined owning herself. She could not believe that she was really here, in this moment, and wanted to pinch herself.

Dolly appeared to take her noncommittal answer as a prompt to begin pulling examples off the rack. "You saw the cloth that we've got for the drapes, right?" she said to Gia. "So, what do you think of this? How will it look on you?"

It was a bright-red sari like the Holi colors of the festival, with an ombre at the bottom, fading from crimson to dusty-rose pink on the hem and at the end of the blouse sleeves. Gia felt like this was somehow a test, the way that Dolly was asking, even though Dolly's eyes did not betray any such thing.

"Something a little lighter?" The cloth looked too richly colored for her, like something that royalty might wear.

"I think you're right," Dolly said, holding the sari at arm's length again, screwing up her face around her cute button nose. "You don't want to show up the bride. Jimmy Singh might end up running off with you instead."

Gia blushed and chuckled at the compliment.

Dolly held the dress against herself. "Hmm," she mused with a mischievous grin, "I could certainly do with all that Singh money." She shook her head, almost as if she were shaking those treacherous thoughts out of it. "No, I've already got something to wear."

"The best part of this job," Dolly said a few moments later as she selected a *salwar-kameez* several shades lighter than the previous sari, "is that you get to live other people's dreams with them, but without the aftermath of actually being married to someone. But heck, if I *am* going to get married, it's going to have to be someone rich like Jimmy Singh. I could even handle a little scandal, you know. He wouldn't have to be, like, totally faithful, not if I had a credit card."

"Is he very, very rich?" Gia asked, trying to divert Dolly from more casual talk about sex as she could feel herself flushing. *Hai bhagwan*, men's private parts she knew a little about but had never seen nor touched them. Nor did she know anything about these people whose sex lives Dolly was speaking so casually about, even though she was shopping for an outfit to wear to their wedding. From the way Dolly was speaking, Gia supposed they might indeed be royalty.

"You've never heard of Singh Imports?"

Gia shook her head, supposing that she had never heard of most companies, but one called Singh Imports could have been just about anything, including the man who sold fake Gucci clutches outside Hanuman Temple in New Delhi.

"Jimmy Singh's father is one of the biggest diamond vendors in New York," Dolly said, sounding like she was salivating as she said it. She held up the outfit. "Try it. There's a fitting room behind that rack there."

Gia went into the changing booth, which was just a hanging rail with a strip of one of the shop's heavier fabrics—it was either velvet or chenille—run through with curtain loops. She felt a little exposed as she got changed, although it was not a feeling that she was unused to. She found herself looking down at her own body. She still had the long, awkward limbs of an adolescent, even though she was now twenty-one years old and here in a business establishment in America, with a serious job and having a (kind of) serious conversation with Dolly, who seemed every inch the responsible adult, despite the girlish outbursts that seemed to occasionally punctuate the things she said. Dolly was so comfortable in her own skin, it made Gia wish that she could spend every moment with this cool "American Indian," if only for the hope that some of that confidence might rub off.

Dolly gleefully pressed her hands together when Gia emerged, rocking back and forth on the balls of her feet. "Yes. Yes, yes. Let me just . . ." She moved forward and took the *pallu*, which Gia had draped in the traditional style, and began fussing with it. "This is not how we . . . Just . . . pull that gorgeous hair of yours up, would you?"

Gia did so, and, a moment later, Dolly stopped fussing and began, "That's much—"

"What?" Gia asked after a few quiet moments, still holding one side of her hair up and out of the way. "What is it?"

"That mole," Dolly asked, sounding puzzled.

"I've always had it," Gia answered. She could sort of picture it, although it was behind her ear, so she never saw it unless with clever placement of a mobile phone or mirror. She did not like it, but her long hair almost always covered it, usually even when she wore it up. Dolly's sudden fascination with it was unnerving, making Gia self-conscious. "What-what about it?"

"Nothing," Dolly said quickly. "Just . . . familiar."

Gia stepped back, letting her hair fall and regarding Dolly, who now wasn't meeting her eye. "How can that be?" Gia asked.

Dolly finally looked back at her, the smile slowly returning to her eyes, and she shrugged. "Oh, you know. A mole is a mole." She pressed a finger to the birthmark below her chin. "Like just that, eh?"

"Thank you, Mr. Shah," Dolly said to the man who let her and Gia back into the Golden State Weddings & Events office. He appeared to be about sixty, or well on his way to it, and in what Gia would have called a sweatshirt, striped in black and red, along with light-gray joggers that did not go with the shirt in the slightest. Add in the flip-flops, and he was definitely dressed for lounging around the house. The man's hair was almost white and in the kind of thick buzzcut that suggested a pair of home clippers and an aversion to barbers. A matching moustache looked a little better cared for.

Although Gia had not seen this man before, the surname was a big clue as to who he might be.

"Ranveer, please, Dolly. How many times must I ask you?" the man replied, crossing his arms and looking questioningly at Dolly. Gia was taken aback when Dolly returned his glance and replied in a similar, affected tone.

"At least once more, Mr. Shah," she said, "as always."

Both of them broke into giggles, and Gia hurried on past them, panicked by the surreal air that was suddenly filling the space.

"Ah, *Pirates of the Caribbean*," he said seemingly to no one in particular, shaking his head. "A classic."

"This is Gia," Dolly put in quickly, as Ranveer helped Dolly with her bags. The shopping had not ended at Preet Fabrics, after all. Dolly had brought along a company credit card and had talked Gia into acquiring two new dresses at a store called Macy's, telling her airily that her current wardrobe needed an update, and that it would come out of her paycheck. Gia was getting the feeling that Dolly had the potential to be a terribly bad influence; indeed, she had been fretting all the way back that she would somehow get in trouble for spending half of her first day not actually at work.

"Ah, the legendary Gia," he replied dramatically, giving Gia an appraising look. His accent was strongly Indian, even though his English was impeccable. "All the way from beautiful India. Oh, how I still miss her, and the things I relished—masala chai with sizzling samosas and a bit of *imli* chutney, in the city of my birth." His eyes became dreamy.

"This is Sonia's husband, Ranveer," Dolly put in. Gia, too, had noticed that he hadn't introduced himself, even though she had already taken an educated guess. A part of her mind had screamed that it could not possibly be *Sonia Shah*'s husband. He was dressed like a—how did they say . . . couch potato—and had the air of someone's errant grandfather, perhaps undergoing the first unfortunate stages of dementia, not the sleek silver fox that Gia might have imagined.

"Go on then, Gia," Ranveer said, "test my film knowledge." He said the words as if they were perfectly normal words for a person to say moments after they had met someone for the first time. "Throw me a movie quote."

Mr. Shah's—*Ranveer's*—unexpected challenge filled Gia's stomach with trepidation, with the acute possibility of embarrassment or humiliation. She thought back to the movies that a pastor from the local church used to show from the picture projector against the moldering walls of the Mercy & Grace refectory. Those films represented most of Gia's lifetime movie experience so far, and she remembered them more clearly than anything else she had seen. When she remembered one and spoke, it was with the awkwardness of feeling the English words heavy on her tongue, enunciated by someone of the wrong age, the wrong gender, and who was most definitely not an actress.

"Of all the gin joints in all the towns in all the world—"

"She walks into mine," came a familiar, sharp voice, and Sonia appeared behind Ranveer, her large coffee mug in her hand. She gave her husband the tiniest flicker of a smile as he turned around. "Leave the poor girl be, she has work to do." Sonia's eyes moved over, settling on her with subtle strength. "Don't you, Gia?"

Moments later, Ranveer had left, and the office was settling down again, Dolly having disappeared to her room in the far corner, Sonia back to her own office, and Chad nowhere in sight. Gia sat alone at a desk, investigating. It was not too hard to find the name of Jimmy Singh's ex-wife: Suzy Kerala. Gia was, however, as good as any millennial at exploring the rabbit hole of information that could be found on social media sites, so she set about uncovering everything she could about the woman.

Beautiful, successful. Probably marrying upward with the Singh family, yes, but who wouldn't be? She was definitely not a country bumpkin, Gia could tell that. But then she found something particularly tantalizing. Suzy Kerala's phone number.

Gia glanced over at Sonia's office. She should ask permission before she went any further. Then again, if she could come back with an answer about why and how Jimmy Singh's previous marriage had failed, without any help, how impressed would Sonia be?

CHAPTER 7

"Mrs. . . . Miss K-Kerala?" Gia stuttered in reply to the curt voice on the other end of the line, her strong accent creeping further into her voice in the moment of panic. She was sitting in the company restroom, a small, cornflower-blue sticky note held between two fingers.

"Look, don't you get tired of trying to con hardworking people?" the voice on the other end of the line snapped. It was a haughty but well-spoken voice, although there was some subtle undercurrent that Gia could detect as being of South Asian origin.

"What?" Gia was confused and getting the sense that the telephone was about to be slammed down on her.

A minute ago, needing somewhere quiet and discreet to make the call, she had told Dolly that she needed to go to the bathroom, which left Dolly looking a little nonplussed. "You don't have to tell me," Dolly had replied, her mouth twisting with amusement. "And we call it the 'restroom,' by the way." Even as she had dialed the number, Gia had wondered if she was doing the right thing, that perhaps she should ask for permission, yet Gia had never liked asking for permission when she thought that there was a strong chance of a no. She would get to the bottom of things, have a wildly successful first day; it would be fine and would cement her future at Golden State Weddings & Events straight away.

"I know everyone has to earn money to live," the woman who she had not yet established as Suzy Kerala said, "but I don't have a problem with my broadband, and you are not getting access to my computer. Stop stealing from people!"

"I . . . please, Miss, can we discuss about . . ." *Your Indianisms are not helping you, Gia.* She sat up straighter and breathed in deeply, channeling the image of their yoga *Masterji* at the orphanage as he sat cross-legged on a padded mat every Sunday morning. Dressed in only a loincloth, his face and body streaked with ash, the traditional red thread of a Brahman running over his shoulder and diagonally across his chest, he would roll a rosary of sandalwood beads through his fingers as he droned on. *Inhale, exhale. Inhale, exhale.*

"I am Gia, calling from Golden State Weddings & Events in San Francisco." *Shouldn't have said that. Should not have said that.*

Her words seemed to have brought about a pause in the woman's rant, however, and Gia heard a chair scrape on the other end and a door close. "You're doing Jimmy's wedding," she said eventually, all the righteousness having emptied from her voice.

"Yes," Gia went on cautiously. "Jimmy and Tasha."

"And I guess Tasha's having second thoughts."

"Uh . . ." Gia had not been expecting that.

"Did she squeal on me?" Suzy Kerala snapped, a slight edge of hysteria quickly finding its way into her voice. "I told her not to bring me into it. I only wanted to warn her that it would be an unconsummated marriage for her, woman to woman, because nobody warned me. However, I still have to live in the same city as these people, and you do not want to upset the Singhs."

Gia's mind raced. She had instantly stumbled into something more than she had expected and did not want to say something to stop the flow of information coming. Yet, as the silence on the line lengthened, she felt she had to say *something*. "Did you bring yourself into it?"

"Hey!" Suzy Kerala complained. "That man broke my heart. I . . . loved him."

"I am sorry," Gia put in quickly, not entirely sure whether she was apologizing or empathizing.

"And you want to know what the ironic thing is?" Suzy went on, the fire back in her voice. "I'm used goods now. Ha, used! I could have had almost any man I wanted. And I did; I had Jimmy Singh. *Jimmy-bloody-Singh!* But who wants a twenty-nine-year-old who's already divorced, eh?" Suzy went on, a South Asian inflection creeping in there. "And, who would believe that the prom queen's husband never touched her?"

Never touched her? "Why?" The word escaped Gia's lips before she could consider whether it was a sensible word to utter.

Suzy sniffed. "I wish I knew. I went through all the usual things. His preferences, those problems that men don't like to talk about. I steamed open letters from his doctors like some movie psycho. But I never found a reason and . . ." Gia heard Suzy release a long breath as if she had more to say. "I want kids, I want them so much. Time is getting on." She let out a sharp, bitter laugh. "And the irony is, when a baby doesn't happen, I'm the one everyone is looking at."

"Did you try speaking to his parents?" Gia asked. A part of her could not believe they were having this conversation, that this stranger was unburdening herself to her. Yet, perhaps it was because she *was* a stranger that Suzy Kerala was sharing so much. Catharsis.

Suzy's voice dropped to a whisper. "He was never in work when I called the office, and when I complained about his constant absence to his parents . . . Let's just say that they're not natural liars." She snorted in disgust.

Gia had never been in love, but felt she understood this woman, her anger that this Jimmy Singh might now go and give his affections to someone else when she had never been provided with answers. All the same, warning off the bride-to-be was a dangerous game to be playing.

A few moments later, Gia dropped her mobile phone away from her ear and let out a long, deep breath, running her palms across her face. She did not have an answer—in fact, she had even more questions—but surely this was enough to take back to Sonia. All her new boss had asked for was a little bit of poking around on social media or the internet. Also, it seemed that the bride-to-be, Tasha, knew of the issues in Jimmy

Singh's previous relationship, and that was surely something that Sonia would want to know.

But Gia wanted to come back with an answer, something more definite that would prove how invaluable she was. Gia *needed* this job to work out; she knew that, even after only a few days in America. This was her place.

Think, Gia, think. She sat there for another minute on the lid of the closed toilet seat, pulling up anything she could find on Jimmy Singh. Who was he with, what places did he go? She couldn't sit in the bath-*rest*room for the remainder of the day, or questions would soon start getting asked.

He was never in work when I called the office. Suzy Kerala's words suddenly popped into Gia's head, as if placed there by some divine intervention. She looked up Singh Imports, found the number of the head office in New York. It was a long shot, but, then again, Suzy Kerala had kind of worked out. *But maybe this time don't tell them where you're calling from . . .*

"Singh Imports, can I help you?"

"Hello, I am calling from Mr. Singh's office. He has been trying to reach his son urgently about some personal arrangements, but he is not answering his mobile phone. Is he there, please?" Gia was concentrating hard, trying to use her best voice, trying not to laugh at the irony that this stall was kind of like her new "office."

The voice on the other end of the line seemed to pause ever so slightly before answering. "He is not in the office at the moment, can I take a message?"

"Mr. Singh says it is urgent. He asked me if you still have that landline number, the one he could sometimes reach Jimmy on during the day? He is desperate to reach his son; it cannot wait."

"I . . ."

"I don't know if you have ever experienced Mr. Singh when he is impatient . . ."

That did the trick. "I think I have it here somewhere."

51

"Thank you, you are such a help and will be saving my ears from another bashing."

The voice on the other end of the line gave a small laugh, and, a few moments later, Gia brought her mobile phone down from her ear and saw how her hand was shaking. Her heart was thumping painfully, and she felt a little sick, but there was a number on the little notepad in front of her, and it just might be the one she needed.

Several deep breaths later, she began to dial again. One last call, she had come this far . . .

"Hello, can I help ya?" It was a woman's voice, thick with that kind of New York accent that Gia had only heard in movies before this moment. Again, Gia was momentarily back in the orphanage when, on one of the special occasions like Christmas and Diwali and Holi, Father Brian would bring over his projector and DVD player—always with an American movie that spun lazy afternoon offerings of love and betrayal, murder and long-lost sons—and use the decaying walls as a screen. It happened rarely, and the pastor's taste had never been more up to date than the classic films of the fifties and sixties, but Gia had loved those nights and, in her head, each time had lived with dreams of America for months after. And here she was. For her, the voice on the other end of the line seemed straight out of *West Side Story*.

"I'm looking for Jimmy," Gia replied as confidently as she could.

"You are, are ya?" Gia had expected caginess if her theory was correct, but the woman on the other end of the phone sounded mildly annoyed. "How many people is he giving this number out to now? I don't mind, but he's the one who always worries."

"I—" Gia stopped herself from admitting that she had phoned his office. She didn't want to get the woman who had helped her in trouble. Attempting to sound stern—angry, even—she demanded, "Look, is he there, Miss, um . . . ?"

"Symonds," the woman answered with a growl. "Angela. You just missed him." When the woman spoke again, a note of suspicion was present. "Who's calling?"

"You know he is due to be married soon?" Gia asked, surprising herself with her plain language. It was a gamble, an attempt to smoke out the theory that had been forming in her own mind about Jimmy Singh, yet some of the fire in her own voice was real. She waited for a blast back from the feisty-sounding woman on the other end of the line; instead, silence dragged on for several seconds.

"Are ya . . . her?" Angela Symonds's words came softly over the distance between them. It was the sound of someone who had been waiting for a long time for the axe to fall.

"No," Gia answered. Then, after a moment's thought, which maybe should have been much longer than a moment, "He doesn't know it, but his last wife has called and . . . warned the bride-to-be off." Gia winced, unsure what she might be unleashing on Suzy Kerala, or even if she was completely correct in the way things were happening. She suddenly felt so very much at sea for her first day in a job—a job that she never expected to include what she was doing now.

"Are ya a friend of his fiancée, this . . . Tasha?" the woman asked, pronouncing the name with evident hesitation. "What are ya going to do?"

"Let's just say I am an interested party," Gia answered, sure that she had gotten the line out of one of those old movies. "And . . . I don't know," she added honestly. It would not be up to her, although she thought this might change things. "Why are you with a man who will not marry you?" Gia went on to fill a growing silence, sure that she was right in her assumptions and wanting to understand it herself. "A man who is-is marrying someone else?"

There was a long silence, and Gia began to think that the woman she had called on a whim was not going to unburden her heart to a stranger. But then, she spoke.

"He *can't* marry me," Angela Symonds replied with a whine. "I'm too white and too common for the heir to the Singh fortune. Just some broad from Queens, ya know?" Gia did not know, but she got the general idea. People judged places, families, *caste*, all before they made any attempt to judge the person.

"But . . ."

"But why won't he just marry me anyway and damn his parents?" It wasn't the "but" that Gia had been thinking of, yet it was a pertinent point. "All I really want is him, and I don't care about no diamond business."

But maybe Jimmy does. "What about the woman he's going to marry?"

"Maybe she'll like the money more than me," Angela Symonds replied acidly. "But I can tell you this, after so many years, I know him better than any other woman ever will." There was a defiance there, although Gia did not feel that any of it was aimed at her. At some point, Angela Symonds had claimed ownership in her mind, possession of Jimmy Singh. Maybe that was more important than ever when the person you loved could not even acknowledge you. She felt sorry for this woman on the other end of the line and thousands of miles away from her, but it did not feel right to tell her so.

"I'm sorry," Gia said, not quite knowing why she was apologizing, then she hung up, blocking the number on her mobile phone before she got up and left the stall. Jimmy Singh—and all the Singhs for that matter—had a lot to answer for.

"That was a long bathroom break," Sonia observed as Gia walked back into the main office. Her boss was standing by Dolly's desk, her large coffee cup in her hand, and both Dolly and Chad were there, too, Chad eating a tub of boiled potatoes. All three faces were fixed on Gia—staring with an intensity like a devotee before an idol of Lord Shiva. Gia willed herself to appear composed, although inside she was a churning mess.

"I was . . . investigating."

"In the bathroom?" Sonia scoffed. It was hard with this woman to tell how good humored—or not—she was being.

"Jimmy has a Caucasian girlfriend," Gia told them, her phone still dangling from her hand. She felt tired, drained, weighed down by the dirty secret she had uncovered. "The parents know but won't let him marry her and I think will—what do you say?—cut-cut him off if he doesn't marry the right sort of girl. They've been together for years, and, from what I can tell, he won't be giving her up if he marries this Tasha from Yu-ba City."

Sonia's jaw fell open, which was oddly satisfying. Dolly's jaw had, too, although Chad just continued shoveling food into his mouth. "I said do a little light investigating. How . . . ?" Sonia shook her head as if banishing the thought. "Never mind, I'm not sure I want to know. You, Gia, are as tenacious and resourceful as I hoped you would be."

Sonia did not smile along with the compliment, instead pausing to sip thoughtfully from her **YOUR HAPPILY EVER AFTER** mug, pursing her lips with relish as if noting the rich, strong taste of the coffee with pleasure. Gia, however, was suddenly filled with pride, almost bursting with it.

"What is wrong with people, eh?" Dolly put in. "All the money, and they can't find a way to be happy in their lives, like they have to make things complicated and stressful."

Sonia started back toward her office. "Anyway, back to work, everyone. The rehearsal has been put forward to tomorrow, so we want to put on as good a show as possible."

"Are we not telling Tasha that he has a long-time girlfriend squirreled away?" Gia asked, a little surprised. "This could affect things. He never consummated his previous marriage—and probably won't consummate this one, either."

Sonia stopped, surprise stretching her features too. "Hell, no, we *are not* telling Tasha. This will absolutely affect things."

"But—"

"But our job is to put on a wedding, Gia," Sonia interrupted, "we are not here to fix their relationships for them, or counsel them, or save them from themselves. We give them a wedding, and they figure things out from there."

"Then why did you ask me to look into it at all?"

"As I said," Sonia said patiently, "we don't like surprises. Information is like insurance in our business. We need to have it, but we don't want to have to use it."

"But shouldn't she know?" Gia pushed, thinking of Suzy Kerala and, in a way, Angela Symonds. "I would want to know."

Sonia crossed back over to Gia. She was shorter than her newest employee but still easily trapped her gaze with eyes of dark steel—Gia felt overcome, as if seized by some occult and irresistible force. "We do not tell Tasha, Gia, do you hear me?" Sonia tapped the side of her mug hard with her fingertips, nailing her point in place with an insistent tink-tink.

Gia's mouth worked as if to protest again. This was not fitting the romantic view she had of the wedding business. No words, however, came out under Sonia's rock-solid gaze.

"What good would come of telling this to Tasha," Sonia went on, "except that she might call the whole thing off? And who among the families do you suggest we go to with this?"

Gia swallowed involuntarily; she could still feel her jaw working—like she was a puppet made of wood—but Sonia suddenly relaxed. "That was exceptional work. Now why don't you join Dolly at her desk for the rest of the day?"

CHAPTER 8

THEN

Saumya could hear the chaos of the main road, not only the hum—and occasional roar—of vehicle engines, but also the hoots of irritated horns, the screech of tires, the barking of a pack of stray dogs. It was Friday afternoon, and the sound of the Imam announcing the call to *junna* prayers at the three-domed mosque at the end of the bazaar was loud. Saumya heard it echoing off the corrugated-sheet-metal walls of the shed in which she sheltered. It had been three days since she had seen an angry mob drag her fiancé away on the banks of the Ghaghara, and much of that time, the incessant swishing of water—that magnetic sound of the monsoon—had been part of the background tableau as well.

She had always been able to block out this kind of noise before, slowly becoming used to it until she did not even realize it was there, but not this time. Now Saumya started at every shout and flattened herself against the wall when the excited chatter of those passing by veered close to the two-room abode, because any of them could be the sound of the mob that was coming to get her. But every time she worried about herself, she was beset by a wave of guilt that she still did not know what had become of the man she had been about to marry.

She had lost her virginity to him in a hut not unlike this one. Hassan had done his best, though, surprising her with flowers and candles and a meal that they had shared. Never pressuring her, although, that night, they had both known why they were there together . . .

Saumya was brought from her painful reverie when the listing door with its failing hinges opened, making a loud scrape as its bottom corner cut an ever-deepening gash into the dirt. Saumya let out an involuntary squeal at the harsh noise and the shadow in the doorway, even though the face she had been expecting was the one that appeared through it.

"Bindu." She said her sister's name only to hear her own voice, hoarse from its long silence and sounding like someone else's entirely.

"Those damn mobs are out there again," Bindu complained. "I've heard reports of stoning, stabbings, and police shootings." Bindu gave her head a disgusted shake and muttered, "Why are these men not back home with their families, eh? Leave the politics of the Babri Mosque to politicians, huh."

Hopelessness swelled within Saumya as she sat with her knees drawn up on an old velvet mustard cushion that Bindu had brought with her on a previous visit. She wanted to wail and keen and beat her fists on the rotting-wood-plank floor. She had told Hassan when they met in college and romantic sparks flared between them: Don't pursue her, she'd said. Her family would never allow it. A Hindu and Muslim could never be together, everybody knew that timeless truth. He had pushed and pushed, telling her this was the new digital India, shiny like a new rupee coin. That they would be like a modern Sunil Dutt and Nargis: Hindu and Muslim, man and woman, husband and wife. She had given in, charmed by his boyish smile, his charisma, and the sense that he was somewhat of a rebel. But look at what happened finally. The old India had triumphed—cleaved not only by the political and geographical upheaval of Partition but also by the timeless flood of hatred that divided its citizens.

Saumya had not thought much about the controversy surrounding the location of the Babri Masjid in the past. But what she saw on the news, the way those *kar sevaks*—red paste smeared on their foreheads, eyes ablaze with religious fervor—climbed on top of the dome and started hacking at the mosque with hammers and spears, then set fire to nearby Muslim homes, chilled the blood in her veins to ice.

But, to Saumya it was about politics. It had been happening from the time of the British. If you wanted to create a rift between Hindus and Muslims, you cut a pig and threw it into a mosque. Very soon there would be a retaliatory attack, and news would arrive that Muslims had slaughtered a cow in a Hindu temple. Trying to deduce which community began a riot was a classic chicken-and-egg problem. Back when India wasn't even a country yet, people in power were frying juicy politics meat in the oil of religion, and the *netas*, desperate for votes, only continued what they learned from their masters. Religion was the biggest business in the world. They used the fear of God to get votes, to rule over people.

Bindu handed her a plate of the food she'd brought with her and continued, "Bloody bigoted men with nothing better to do, that's what they are. I was terrified one would recognize me and follow me here."

Saumya let out a slow breath, although it came out more like a wheeze that morphed into a brittle cough. The shed, which a friend of Bindu's sometimes used as storage for their export business when they were carrying an excess of stock—although never during the rains—was damp. The bare shabbily aligned walls made the place more like a meat locker than anything else. "Any news of him?" Somehow, it was too hard to say his name.

Bindu's face twisted in sympathy at her sister's plight, and she squatted down in front of her. "No, and I don't think I will get any. Hassan's whole family has vanished, and it would be almost impossible for me to reach out to them, anyway, even if they were still in town. They—our brothers and their friends—watch me, you know. Every time I come here, I fear that I am leading them straight to you. We cannot do this much longer, Saumya."

Saumya, who had been staring at a roti held loosely in her fingers and thinking that she had felt hungrier a few moments ago, looked up sharply. "What do you mean?"

"I mean we have to think ahead. You cannot stay in this"—she waved a hand at the decrepit surroundings—"place forever, *Didi*, and things are not going to magically calm down here in Ayodhya. It is too small a town, and they know who you are and where you live."

Saumya let her expression harden, even though she felt like a shell, and Bindu's words were threatening to crack the brittle exterior and expose the emptiness inside. "I cannot go until I have found what has happened to my husb—" She stopped herself from saying the word.

"He's dead, Saumya," Bindu snapped. She almost never used her sister's actual name. "They dragged him off along the river, and no one has seen him since. What do you think happened?"

Saumya recoiled, the food falling from her nerveless fingers as she shrank back against the cold wall, unbidden images of her would-be husband's body floating face-first down the river crashing into her mind.

The momentary anger melted from Bindu's chiseled features. "I'm sorry," she went on softly, "but you are my first concern, and if you stay here too long, they will find you and . . ."

Although Bindu didn't finish the thought, Saumya knew that the choice she had made, the man she had fallen in love with, had made her less than nothing in the eyes of the Hindu fanatics of Ayodhya. Everyone knew that men became savages with the women they regarded as less than nothing. Unconsciously, she brought her hand down and laid it gently on her belly. The same reason that had made her want to stay until she knew for sure what had happened to Hassan now made her realize that Bindu was right.

Saumya nodded. Staying in Ayodhya was simply too dangerous right now. She gathered close the memories of how Hassan had written great, throbbing poems for her so melodious that tears streamed from her eyes. How he bought her hot chili *pakoras* from the street vendor and how together they washed it down with the rich, piquant cola of Thums Up like a postmeal tonic. She ran them through her mind like a reel. Her nose ran a wet trail to her lips, her eyes reddened. She would leave. Who knew when it would be safe for her to return?

CHAPTER 9

NOW

"Here's to Gia, our private investigator," Dolly said, raising her glass and nodding at Gia to do the same. They were in Pepe's, the first restaurant that Gia had been to since arriving in San Francisco. She *had* ordered a takeout from an Indian restaurant, which had been a strange experience. The food in the outrageously priced takeout had been good—richly flavored, dripping with oil—yet not the snapshot of home that she had hoped it would be. Rather, it only very distantly reminded her of India and of the orphanage.

Guilt had come with memory, as she sat there eating more food than she would sometimes have come across in a whole week. Her appetite had waned, replaced by a dull sickness and a surprising longing for somewhere she had never expected to miss.

Supposedly in celebration of Gia's "fabulous detective skills," Chad had offered to buy dinner after work for all three of them, although Gia got the sense that Chad and Dolly did this a lot, and perhaps did not need much excuse to dine out after work. They had not been able to go for the meal until late, because of the frenzied preparations for the wedding rehearsal the following day. Gia had tried to be as helpful as she could be, although that had mostly ended up with her carrying bins overflowing with decorations, errand running, and being a human clothespin.

Pepe's was an Italian restaurant with a small, intimate feel and a sense—or so Dolly had sold it to Gia, who had already been persuaded at the words *free dinner*—of being on the Mediterranean coast. She had to take Dolly's word on that, but the place surely was a sight. Mosaic panels alternating with planters of ivy and geranium lined the walls on either side, while the tables were covered in cheery white-and-red checked cloths. A dome-shaped porcelain lamp was suspended above each one, held aloft by a chain massive enough to hold up the Golden Gate Bridge (which Gia had yet to visit but recognized from the "Welcome to San Francisco" glossy on the plane). Click, click went Gia's phone as she snapped picture after picture of the restaurant and their meal for her Instagram story. #FoodPorn.

Dolly called the bubbly honey-colored drink in the tall flute that she had shoved into Gia's hand "prosecco," while Chad raised his own much larger glass full of a thick, slime-colored concoction. ("My third smoothie of the day," he said—*more like a green sludge,* thought Gia). The ladies clinked their two more delicate glasses enthusiastically, causing a little of Gia's drink to splash out onto the table.

"I liked the way you stood up to the boss-lady there, as well," Chad said, taking a long sip of his drink that left a foamy residue on his upper lip. "You've got some balls there, young lady."

Dolly huffed her displeasure in Chad's direction.

Gia took a sip of the alcoholic drink, the bubbles tickling her nostrils. It was deliciously sweet, even as she tasted the alcohol. "I still don't understand how we are going ahead with the rehearsal," she said.

"All joking aside, I would leave that one alone, if I were you," Chad advised a little more seriously. "Sonia Shah isn't as scary as she seems—not until she actually *is*. She has her limit, then . . ." He made a silent *pow* with his mouth, while clenching and springing open both hands. "I would not cross my boss for anything."

"You look like you're doing jazz hands," Dolly teased, then turned a little more seriously toward Gia. "He's not wrong, though."

"I didn't mean that," Gia protested, trying to think of a way to explain what she was getting at. "Just . . . why is it that Tasha is still going ahead, with warnings like that from his ex?"

"Money!" Chad coughed into his hand. "It's a strong motivator in any wedding match."

Dolly took a long swig of her prosecco. "You could show me all that Singh money if you wanted to, I wouldn't say no."

Chad chuckled and, without warning, screamed out, *"Show me the money-y-y!"* While some of the patrons in Pepe's turned and looked at Chad—and others did their best to look anywhere *but* at Chad—the staff either just frowned or raised their eyebrows.

"Show me the money-y-y!" Dolly screamed in response, bringing a slightly more irritated look from the owner, who was over behind the bar, although still no one questioned their behavior, and Gia, sensing the tightness of a shocked expression pulled across her own features, was starting to feel like she had just entered some parallel universe.

"You better show me a tip," the waitress who had seated them said as she passed their table on the way to take an order, "troublemakers."

"Have you never seen *Jerry Maguire?*" Dolly asked, finally picking up on Gia's stunned look.

Gia shook her head. "I know it is a Tom Cruise film. I remember seeing his movie *Top Gun*, which they screened at the orphanage one time. It might be the only movie I have seen that was made after the nineteen sixties."

"Jerry Maguire is a Tom Cruise classic," Chad put in enthusiastically. "Dolly's favorite."

"All that Singh money," Dolly repeated with a sigh as the waitress returned to take their meal orders.

Gia ordered tagliatelle with pesto, two things she had never had before. The creamy sauce with the thin, long-strand pasta was delicious, and she carefully mimicked how Dolly and Chad used their forks and knives, trying to curb her bites and extend her enjoyment of the food, instead of shoveling it into her mouth with slurps and smacks, fingers hungrily working, as she would have done not long ago with the usual rice and dal meal they ate at Mercy & Grace. Tonight, she did not miss the orphanage or feel guilty that she was eating so well, she only felt guilty about what seemed an extortionate price, even though she had gone for one of the cheaper things on the menu. Although originally tempted to join them by the promise of a free meal, Gia found herself offering to pay her share, especially as Chad had hardly eaten anything himself. But Chad's offended look was the first truly stern expression she had seen him adopt, so she didn't push the point any further. Even Dolly looked nonplussed by her offer, and Gia got the sense that she had perhaps made a social faux pas.

Gia wet her lips with a satisfied sigh—eating dinner with Dolly and Chad was the first time she had felt like she belonged anywhere. Apart from the orphanage, of course, but no one ever *really* wanted to belong there.

The prosecco was making her want to pee buckets so Gia excused herself to go to the toilet—or, rather, "restroom," a name she still found quite odd. After flushing, she opened the stall door and staggered over to the sink to wash her hands. On the next sink over, an older woman pressed her thin, wrinkled lips together and swiped a bright-coral color on them. Gia moved over to the automatic blower to dry her hands. She searched in vain for a button to push, her hands dripping.

"It's automatic. Just put your hands between the two arrows and it will start," said Coral Lipstick Lady.

"Wow," said Gia as the dryer began to blow, and feeling her hands somewhat dry, she removed them and patted them on her skirt.

"Yes, it's so much fun. Look, I can make it turn on and off all by myself!" said Coral Lipstick as she delightedly moved her hands back and forth in front of the blower, causing it to start and stop.

"Yes, Miss, you sure can," said Gia with a shy smile, wondering if Coral Lipstick had had too much to drink.

"And it wouldn't be the first time, I can promise you that. I happen to be quite good at turning things on." She had a big smile on her face, stretching past the shaky lipstick lines she had drawn. "I've been married three times, dear, but the one time I went out with a French man . . ." She rolled her eyes with great exaggeration and fanned herself with her fingers. "Oh my, he simply followed me when I'd gone to the lavatory, and before I knew it we were kissing frantically, like teenagers. I couldn't believe it. He smelled like cigarettes and gin and had the most amazing tongue! At one point, I heard a banging on the door, but he insisted that we ignore it. He kept saying in a low, deep voice, '*Vous* must let me make love to *vous*. We'd make zee most beautiful fireworks.'"

Gia was blushing by now to her roots and wondering if the over-sharing of candid confidences was normal in America. If so, she liked it!

Coral Lipstick giggled nervously, then her voice trailed off as she put her hand to her yawning mouth. "Oh dear. Those martinis sure are strong. I better go before I fall down. Time to get Edward and go home."

Gia hurried out after her, wanting to tell her coworkers about this weird encounter she'd had in the toilet, and hear their thoughts on it. But the bill had just arrived, and Dolly and Chad were arguing about how much tip to leave.

After settling the bill, Chad got to his feet while Gia and Dolly were still finishing the last of their second glass of prosecco each, citing the need to fit in a workout since they were leaving for Yuba City the next afternoon. By the end of the first glass of the alcoholic drink, Gia had begun to feel a nice, warm fuzziness—and that was no doubt why she was laughing more and loosening up, basking in the invisible glow of the camaraderie with her workmates, the comfort of feeling like she fit in. The second glass, however, was beginning to get the better of her, and those Indianisms that she usually worked so hard to keep under control were beginning to creep back more and more into her speech.

"I think we're going to have great fun together, Gia," Dolly said, crossing one arm over her chest, resting her chin in her opposite hand. "You're like my sister from another mister. I have three brothers, you know. Three brothers and no sisters." She turned to face Gia directly and grinned—a slightly lopsided grin that showed just the slightest hint of intoxication. "Where were you when I was growing up, Gia?"

You don't want to know, Gia thought but she smiled back, showing the small gap between her front teeth. She was genuinely flattered by Dolly's enthusiasm. "I cannot believe that I am here," Gia admitted, thinking of how recently she had been facing a much worse life. She would have probably ended up trying to make her way in the metropolis of Delhi, and, however much she liked to think that she would never compromise, would have almost certainly taken any retail sales job at any seedy shop with a lecherous employer to put food in her mouth and a roof over her head, rather than sleep homeless in the filth-ravaged, poverty-stricken slums of that huge city. "I . . ." She didn't want to say it, like she might be breaking some magical spell to do so, like she might end up putting everything back to the way it was, waking up tomorrow back in her bed in Mercy & Grace, the thin, coarse blanket over her, rather than the thick, fresh-smelling duvet at her apartment.

Gia went to take a sip of drink instead but found that the once-sweet smell seemed to have soured slightly. She put the glass down; perhaps she had drunk enough prosecco.

"What?" Dolly pushed, her face that of someone who had just sensed something juicy beneath Gia's hesitation.

"I am just wondering, why me?"

Dolly scoffed, rolled her eyes, then sat back and drained the last of her prosecco. "Sonia knows what she's doing; and she evidently saw something in you, even from the other side of the world."

"And what if she is wrong?"

"You were resourceful enough to get to the bottom of the Jimmy Singh mystery in one afternoon. I think you're going to be just fine."

Dolly held her gaze, and—perhaps it was the alcohol—Gia did not look away. The next words bubbled up to her lips before she could stop them. "I cannot go back. I need to belong here now."

Dolly's face fell a little at that. "Was it bad, where you were?" Before Gia could reply, Dolly shook her head, as if shaking her previous words away. "Stupid question, sorry."

"It will be worse if I must go back. After being here."

Dolly leaned forward across the table and took Gia's two hands in hers. The other woman's hands were a little clammy and had an unexpected roughness to them, which was reassuring. Gia had tensed but found herself relaxing as their eyes met again.

"Never going to happen," Dolly said, and, although the woman's eyes were a little dilated and her grin reflected her own intoxication at the hands of prosecco, Gia wanted so much to believe her.

It was dark when they left Pepe's, the taller towers glittering as they reflected the street lamps and the lights from the windows of the lower buildings, the largest of them patterned by little dots of light, like a giant punch card of the sort used in early computers. For Dolly, the bus was the quickest way home, so they went their separate ways just after going back past the office.

"Be safe," Dolly told her as they parted, but downtown was not busy, and Gia was already beginning to feel safe on the streets of San Francisco. She was not worried, even at night. As the warm, fuzzy glow from the prosecco and the happy, full feeling of the meal returned pleasantly to her, Gia began to congratulate herself about how quickly she was starting to feel at home in this place that was so different to anything she had known before.

They did not have to be at work until ten o'clock the following day—due to the late finish and the likelihood of a long day with the rehearsal tomorrow—so she had plans to meet her uncle for breakfast in the morning, which she was looking forward to very much. He had finally called her back, apologized profusely for not responding earlier because he had been slammed over the weekend with some big tech conference in San Francisco. He said he'd been up two nights, picking up and dropping off customers, and had missed her calls when they came in. "Never mind," she'd said benevolently, just happy to have arranged a date to meet him. To finally see him, to embrace him, to get that little extra sense of who she was by actually meeting a blood relative for the first time. She had planned to quiz him about the job, how on earth he had managed to arrange it, yet she was coming to realize—thanks largely to Dolly—that it did not really matter. She was here, and she just needed to make the best of it. Stop worrying about what was or what might be.

These were Gia's thoughts as she suddenly stopped at the subway entrance that would take her home. *Make the best of it, Gia.* Going home right now would not be making the best of it. She loved her apartment, the incredible place that was all hers, yet—and maybe this was the prosecco talking—she had not come to America, to San Francisco, just to sit at home. She wanted to explore, to see a little more of it at night, when it was all lit up and inviting.

Looking over, Gia saw that a tram was stopped in the middle of Market Street. Now *that* would be a good way to see a little of the city, rather than the boring old BART service that had shown her nothing of the city during her journey to work.

Before the impulse could fade, Gia turned and crossed the street, almost stepping out in front of a cyclist with a food-delivery box on the back of his bike. The cyclist wasn't offended, merely tilting the bike one way and then the other to slip around her, silently disappearing off into the night, as she was about to do.

CHAPTER 10

"Two twen'y-five," the operator barked at Gia after she had stood at the entrance to the car for several seconds looking expectantly at him. He flicked his eyes down toward a machine that said *Cash Only* on it. Gia felt about for some money, but the smallest she could produce was a five-dollar bill. Which, in and of itself, seemed embarrassing. "No change," he added in the same almost monosyllabic way. Gia gulped as she fed more than twice the cost of the fare into the machine, this whole escapade suddenly feeling extravagant and wrong now that she was wasting so much money to do it.

Another part of her knew that she earned several times that amount each hour at work, that the meal at Pepe's had cost many tens of dollars between them, that everything here in America worked on an entirely different level to what she was used to, yet the panic attack that the whole thing set off inside her still felt right. Reasonable. She did not know when, or even if, the cost of things here would stop shocking her.

Sitting down in a window seat, Gia slowly stopped hyperventilating, and the fuzzy, fun feeling of the recently consumed alcohol crept back in again. She was on a "proper" San Francisco tram—green and cream colored with a red band around the middle, as she had noted when crossing the street. She had also noticed the letter *K* on the front, so figured that at some point she would want to get another *K* going in the opposite direction. As it started moving, the fact that this was the entirety of her plan seemed very exciting and spontaneous.

Gia's face stayed glued to the window, her nose pressed against its coolness as she took in all the different buildings, the people, the vehicles and signs and bicycles . . . and the flurry of all of it. She ached to belong here.

Soon the towering buildings became smaller, and the street's central island became occasionally populated by a strip of two or three palm trees lined up in a row. Somehow, they seemed out of place here, like a fish in a tank. Then the buildings were rarely above four stories high, and all the glitter and glamour of the front store windows of the downtown shopping area was gone.

Yet still there was life here, the sidewalks thronged, although the people were different. There were fewer suits and shopping bags, and a lot more laughter. A rainbow-colored flag flapped from a flagpole and, instinctively, Gia brought up her phone and snapped it. The flag looked hopeful in the half light cast upward from the streetlights below it, and Gia's finger lingered over the screen, as she never posted without a hashtag. There was always something to say about every photo she took.

#LoveSanFrancisco. She smiled at that, even more at the forty-seven likes it had already earned only a minute later. Glancing around further, she could see that this area was full of bars and restaurants, some of them spilling out onto the roadway in half-boarded, covered seating areas that were painted in various colors—although, again, rainbow stripes seemed to be a popular theme. Next to one of them, a young Caucasian woman no older than she was reached up and tenderly took the face of a tall, light-brown-skinned man's face in her hands, as both pairs of eyes looked deeply into the other.

Just then, the tram came to a stop, and someone familiar stood up from his seat. She hadn't noticed him when she got on. Her day had been full of so many new faces and a lot of new information, so it took her a moment to remember where she had seen him. *Revolving Door Guy,* she thought, remembering the well-dressed man she had seen coming out of the office building that morning. A lawyer, perhaps, she had thought at the time, or someone who had just been to see one. He had the same suit on, now slightly rumpled, but he still looked elegant.

He got off the tram. Gia did too. She had probably traveled far enough away from the place she would have to return to. Besides, this area looked colorful, and the mystery man was getting off here. She resolved to do some exploring by foot.

Gia looked around for Revolving Door Guy once she was off the tram, but he had already melted away into the busy throng. *Oh well.* It really did feel like she had arrived in party central, and there was such an energy to the place. Quickly picking a direction, Gia came onto what she was discovering was one of many San Francisco streets that descended before rising again into the distance. A banner hanging above the street said **WELCOME TO THE CASTRO**.

More rainbow banners hung from streetlights, and she came upon a movie theater with the same name as the district on her left. Why hadn't she thought to go and see a movie in a real movie theater over the weekend after arriving? She felt a strong desire to slip inside the vintage building. Gia would watch anything, anything at all, just to see a movie that hadn't been made some time before she was born. But tucking herself away in the darkness of a movie theater was not why she had got onto the tram. She wanted to explore.

Gia stopped next to an ornate wrought-iron lamppost capped with a white globe. It glowed like a full moon in the increasingly frosty night air. Perhaps it wasn't *that* cold, but she was used to Delhi heat. Then she spotted Revolving Door Guy again, now standing not far away from her in the middle of the sidewalk outside of the cinema. He was talking to two men—one tall and South Asian in appearance, the other shorter and Caucasian. Both had the same bleached-blond hair, and both were, in different ways, fashionably dressed.

They were all laughing, and the tall South Asian guy was gesticulating quite a lot. Gia found herself entranced by the three of them. All three looked so comfortable, as if they belonged. Watching them suddenly felt voyeuristic and she started moving again, wanting to walk past them, wondering whether she might stop somewhere and buy a drink—a soft drink, no more prosecco—or whether she would look lonely and pathetic if she were sitting all on her own at a table in this place where, as far as she had been able to see, *nobody* was alone.

"I know you," a voice called out close by. "You're Revolving Door Girl."

The words made Gia freeze. She turned slowly to see Revolving Door Guy standing less than half the pavement width away from her. His two friends appeared to have vanished in the last few moments.

"You're Revolving Door Guy . . . ?" she tried.

"Oh, I love your accent," he said, his eyes lighting up like she had just sung some sweet melody to him.

"Thank you?"

"Hey"—his eyes narrowed, and his face tilted to the side; Gia thought she saw mischief in there—"are you following me?"

"Since-since this morning?"

A hand came up to rub his chin. "Unlikely, I guess." The thoughtful look effortlessly melted into a winning smile again. "Wishful thinking."

"I'm . . . um, exploring," Gia said, then wondered why she had. It sounded even more stupid than it had in her head.

"I'm Adi," he said, holding out his hand a little daintily.

"Gia," she answered, taking hold of the offered hand, which was unexpectedly rough and textured on the palm.

"You want to get coffee?"

And that was kind of that.

"I love it here in Castro," Adi said about ten minutes later as they sat outside of a coffee shop just another minute or so walk from the cinema. "Everyone is themselves here."

They each had a cappuccino in front of them, and Adi picked up a brown sugar cube that was by the side of the cup. Gia expected him to put it in his drink but instead he popped it into his mouth and began to chew it, grinning back at her, which made her laugh.

Gia glanced around at the starry flags and banners. "It is certainly colorful," she agreed.

"I just saw my best friend from school, Rohit," Adi told her. "He lives here because he's gay and his family won't have anything to do with him. At school he tried to please them, was captain of the lacrosse team, now he's got bleached-blond hair and a boyfriend called Justin."

"He must be happy, if he can be himself."

"As happy as anyone can be without their family."

"I do not have any family," Gia said. "Well, I have an uncle, but I am going to meet him for the first time tomorrow morning."

Adi regarded her for a moment, staring deeply at her as if she fascinated him. It made her a little uncomfortable, although she also enjoyed it. "Why are you here, Gia, in San Francisco?"

It was an interesting question; a *good* question, she supposed. Not, "What do you do?" or, "Where do you come from?" Not even, "When did you get here?" But *why*. Maybe that was the only question that mattered.

"It was 'be here or be homeless,'" Gia answered. It felt like an honest answer when she started to say it, yet, by the time she finished, it felt like a half truth instead.

Either way, her answer seemed to have intrigued Adi, who leaned slightly across the table, as if she had garnered his undivided attention.

"Wow," he breathed, "you are *in*teresting."

No, she wasn't, although she loved the way he emphasized just a part of the word. Gia spoke to keep from blushing. "You made me laugh this morning, and I kept remembering you all day." That was kind of a lie, she hadn't had much time to think of anything but work all day. This was it, wasn't it? This was flirting. It was like lying but not feeling guilty about it.

"All day?"

She nodded. "Mmm."

"I'm going to do something spontaneous and stupid now."

That made Gia think of the two people she had seen from the window of the tram, the young woman and young man standing by one of the roadside seating areas. Adi leaned forward and put a hand softly against her cheek.

"I like you, Miss Gia," he said, as he gently brushed his lips against her.

"Oh," was all Gia could manage, as she bowed her head in confusion.

"Am I making you uncomfortable?"

"No," she murmured.

He leaned forward again, and this time he lingered, and she parted her lips to him. Finally, giving in to all her pent-up longings, Gia slipped her hands around his neck and kissed him back.

CHAPTER 11

Mohammed felt conflicted as he walked through the unfamiliar San Francisco streets on the way to his first-ever breakfast with his niece. He had been forced to park his taxicab in an expensive parking lot, as this area was not where he usually drove for a living, and he did not know it well, preferring to keep most of his business to the other side of the San Francisco–Oakland Bay Bridge, with only occasional early morning airport runs for extra money, mostly on the weekends.

He was a dowdy, unimpressive-looking man—he knew this—not quite yet in middle age but certainly looking it. He had been a dowdy youth, yet that hadn't seemed to matter when his mind and his academic achievements had been what was noteworthy about him. That was years ago, another life.

A potbelly that had attached itself to him in his early thirties like some foreign creature from a science-fiction movie had fortunately only grown a little bigger since then, although it stubbornly refused to leave during the sporadic bouts of dieting—mostly his wife's idea—and his infrequent attempts at exercise. His hair had been slowly receding since before the potbelly had appeared, even though an unattractive fuzz still stubbornly clung in patches to the top of his head. His thin but unkempt mustache was occasionally joined by some facial stubble. Although, today, he had shaved the stubble off.

Mohammed turned a corner and was relieved to see the Stacked! Pancake House a little farther down the street. He had lived just across the bay from San Francisco for more than twenty years, yet the heart of the city was mostly a mystery to him, only ever visited for reluctant bouts of shopping and for the rare weekend getaway from Oakland. He hoped that Gia would already be inside, because he didn't like the idea of sitting on his own at a table in a pancake house—or, for that matter, any sort of restaurant. He did not sit easily in public places on his own, except in his taxicab.

Still, at least this first meeting with his niece was not at his house, he should be thankful for that. For all his desire to see her in the United States and safely out of the orphanage, her arrival was in other ways making things difficult—dredging up the past. The past had been a little easier when he dealt with it on his phone in a different room from the rest of the family.

He climbed the steps and looked through the window, those complicated thoughts drifting away from him as—despite the fact that she looked very different from even his most recent photos of her—Mohammed instantly spotted Gia.

"Look at you," he said, "you are a grown woman." He spread his hands, indicating her new trendy outfit, which included a dark-green woolen dress and shiny ankle-high boots. "And so stylish."

Gia, who had stood up to meet him, blushed a little. "Thank you, I bought it just yesterday from Ma-cy," she replied. "It is so good to see you, Uncle." Her accent was somehow more jarring here, in person, than it had ever been over the telephone. All the same, he found himself drinking it in. "I am sorry I could not come over to your house, but work is so busy already."

Mohammed waved her apology away, and they sat back down, Gia tentatively signaling the waitress to get her attention.

"Yes, you must tell me all about your job," Mohammed said enthusiastically. "How did you even get it?"

The grin that had been plastered across Gia's face faltered slightly, and she gave Mohammed a curious look. "You did not apply for me?"

she asked him. "I assumed you must know Sonia Shah or have had something to do with the agency."

Gia's answer left Mohammed a little mystified. What would he ever know about some expensive wedding-planning business in the middle of San Francisco?

"Or Ranveer Shah, her husband?" Gia pushed.

Mohammed shook his head, still completely mystified as to what the girl was talking about. "I only wish I had been so useful, Gia," he told her. "I wanted so badly to help you when you called me. I was so worried about what might become of you outside of the orphanage. But I am a taxi driver, and I do not have influence with anyone important enough to bring you over for work." Mohammed hung his head shamefully, remembering clearly how painful it had been to hear Gia in such distress on the other end of the line, knowing there was almost nothing he could do about it.

"I was not able to find the spare money for a plane ticket to get you here," he went on. "I have a very clever son who I do not think I will be able to put through college."

Gia gave him a weak smile, chewing her lip and shaking her head slowly. Her eyes seemed to focus on some distant point. She was a pretty young woman, he thought, pleased by the idea of that.

An awkward silence descended between them as Gia appeared to remain thoughtful, until the waitress came over and Gia picked up the menu.

After a moment of studying it, Gia looked up at him. "Do you like pancakes?" she said with a wry grin.

Mohammed smiled back. "Luckily, I do," he quipped. "As long as there is no bacon, of course."

"Can we have the sharer stack, please?" Gia asked the waitress. "With only-only maple syrup." Listening to her speak made him realize how rounded and Americanized his own accent had become over the years. Like someone had taken a file to it.

"Already ordering like a pro, I see," Mohammed commented.

His words made Gia's eyes light up, which made him feel like a better person. Nieces, apparently, could be addictive. "I saw pancakes on a commercial on television, and I have been wanting to try them, and I went to my first restaurant last night, Uncle," she told him, "with some work friends. And I drank pro-secc-o," she added with the air of someone who had done something either incredibly naughty or extravagant. Barely a moment later, her smile began to fade, and Mohammed thought he knew why. He reached across and squeezed her hand.

"Hey," he said to her, "you deserve to be here, okay? You must not feel guilty. If anyone should feel guilty, it should be me. I should have found a way to bring you over years ago."

Gia shook her head, as if in disagreement, but gave him that lopsided smile again, meeting his eyes briefly. It felt like there was a shared knowledge between them—how this was at once such a happy occasion and yet a little sad. It was something they shared, if even for slightly different reasons, and it was a bond no one else would truly understand.

They fell silent again, and, less than a minute later, the pancakes turned up. Gia took a photo and posted it—#BreakfastWithMyUncle, she told him—and they tucked into them, Gia brightening again.

"I met a boy," she told him out of the blue.

Halfway through his second mouthful of pancake, Mohammed started to choke a little. "How long have you been here?" he asked her, trying to keep his tone light and jovial but probably failing. It wasn't like he even had any of his own daughters to feel protective of in this way. Then again, maybe that was why something very macho was suddenly happening within him.

Gia shrugged but had the good grace at least to look a little bit guilty about it. "I know, I will be careful, Uncle. But boys were not an option in the orphanage, and I am twenty-one years old." She gave a little chuckle. "So maybe it is that I am eager and compensating."

Mohammed appreciated her conciliatory tone, although she had him with the awkwardness of her delivery. He wanted to get up and hug her right there, perhaps pretend that he had met his niece when she was at a more innocent age—six or eight, maybe ten at the most. "You can enjoy some happiness, Gia," he told her, still not entirely at ease with the idea that she might be playing catch-up. "You're allowed, maybe more than anyone. But just remember that boys are not always something to bring happiness. Take it from someone who used to be one."

Gia seemed to pick up on the way he was being protective and smiled affectionately back at him, twisting her head slightly to the side and turning up the corner of her mouth. That look melted his heart even further, and he wondered briefly whether she knew that. Bright little thing.

After eating until he was stuffed too full for the early hour—and Gia seeming to do the same—they had still only managed to work their way through half of the stack of pancakes before finishing and leaving. Gia tried to pay, and Mohammed got appropriately offended, telling her to put her money away or risk insulting her uncle. The girl did pout a little darkly at him and insist that she would be treating him next time.

Now, as he walked her back to work before returning to his taxi to begin his own working day, there was an easy and relaxed feeling about the way they sauntered along together, so quickly at odds with the early moments of their meeting at the pancake house, and it was the most peaceful moment he had known since getting into his taxicab that morning.

"I will come to meet the rest of the family soon, I promise," Gia said. "Once this Jimmy Singh-Tasha wedding is over, I will have some free time on the weekend."

Oh well, there goes that peaceful feeling, Mohammed thought to himself, feeling guilty even as he thought it. There should be nothing more normal than Gia wanting to come and meet the rest of her family. She had so little of it. Anyway, what did he expect, that Gia would ask to come over and that he could put that off forever? "I should think they

79

will give you time off and some bonus pay," he said to her, deflecting a little. "From what you said, it sounds like you saved the wedding."

Gia shrugged, clearly not having such positive thoughts about the story she had told of her first day in the office. "All I did is find out why this poor girl, Tasha, should not be marrying that man, Jimmy Singh."

They were almost at the building now, and Mohammed reached out and placed a hand on his niece's shoulder. "I think I agree with your boss on this one," he told her. "You cannot live their lives or make their choices for them. This shows that you are a good person, Gia, but you cannot make the rest of the world be good too. Believe an old man on this one."

As much as he had been pushing away the memories all morning, Mohammed felt that old familiar pull, like a black hole in his heart. He had once tried to talk two people out of getting married because of what the rest of the world thought. Perhaps he was being a hypocrite right now, yet what could old people do but relay the sum total of their experiences to the next generation?

Gia turned and hugged him tightly, punching the breath out of him with the unexpected ferocity of it, and he, too, fell into the embrace. Some of the breath that left him seemed like it had been stuck deep down inside for a couple of decades, escaping with a sort of inward hiss.

"Goodbye, Uncle," she said, and Mohammed realized that she was crying.

"I'm so glad that I have finally met you," he told her sincerely.

"And this is only the start, right?" Gia said, wiping her eyes and smudging her makeup a little. He caught the need in that question.

"Too right." He stayed and watched her go into the building. Throughout the morning, Mohammed had had little moments of pure joy and watching her disappear into the impressive office building—a hulking cliff of steel and glass—was one of them. They were tiny moments where this young woman's arrival and the memory of who she was could be completely uncomplicated. But they were only moments, bumping up against the anxiety lodged in his brain, like a Roomba stuck in a corner.

He turned and saw a chic-looking woman in her early fifties, wearing a pale-pink pantsuit walking up the street from the opposite direction. He was caught off guard—why would he not be?—and the moment of recognition was a long one, like he was trying to force his thoughts through a small gap. If he had not spent most of his morning deep down the tunnels of that memory, perhaps he wouldn't even have recognized her.

"Is it . . . ?" he breathed to himself.

She must have heard and looked up from her phone, now only several meters away. A to-go Styrofoam coffee cup fell from her hand, and she didn't even seem to notice it drop.

"I did not know . . ." she began, her eyes wide with shock, a brown fist pressed to her mouth, "that you were here." Then she rushed straight up to him, her hands reaching out as if they might somehow find themselves around his neck, squeezing hard.

Oh, how the universe was playing with him. He did not hate this woman, and yet if he could have rubbed a lamp and been granted three wishes, he might have spared one of them for never seeing her again in his life. And yet, of course, he'd never thought that he would.

"You must not say," she said to him, her voice almost a screech. "You must not!"

CHAPTER 12

"Come, come, come!"

Dolly berated Gia as she arrived back at the wedding venue in Yuba City to find the designer hovering in the hallway that led out to the large garden where the rehearsal ceremony was being held. "Tasha is here, and I am not at all ready." What she did not say, but Gia deduced from the shadows under her heavy, languid eyes, was that the two-hour drive from San Francisco to Yuba City had tired her out. The designer's face brightened, however, once she laid eyes upon the gauzy gold-and-silver ribbon that Gia had brought back with her, face lighting up like a creatively inclined child receiving their first art set at Christmas. "This is perfect, though, well done. You have a receipt, yes?"

Gia nodded distractedly, having caught sight of Sonia through the doorway out into the garden, now fussing with the arrangement of the gold Chiavari chairs with her customary authoritative air. Sonia was speaking to Tasha, smiling rosily and nodding her head benignly, her pixie-cut hair moving like silk around her face, not a hint that there was anything wrong with this picture, the one where she knew all about the bridegroom's secret lover. How could she lie like that, knowing that the woman's husband-to-be had a mistress he was likely never going to give up? How could she pretend like nothing was wrong?

Turning away, so as not to be staring, Gia absentmindedly checked her mobile phone for at least the fiftieth time that morning. She and Adi had swapped numbers the previous evening and she had messaged him first thing, before meeting her uncle, but had not heard anything back as yet. Every time she looked and did not see a message from him, it set off horrible butterflies in her stomach. Was it something she had done or said? Or, not done or said? She worried at it, gnawing at her lower lip like a mouse nibbling at a nut, until she realized she was being ridiculous, so she turned her thoughts back to being annoyed with her boss.

Sonia was forcing Gia to keep Jimmy Singh's terrible secret from Tasha, and every time she thought about it, she trembled a little more inside with indignation. *It is wrong!* Ringing up a secretary and pretending to be someone else was one thing, but how could she keep hidden a secret that might affect the rest of this young woman's life?

Gia watched as Sonia leaned forward and touched the bride-to-be's arm with such familiarity. It was that casual gesture that finally lit a flame inside Gia.

"Can I get an interview with the bride now?" It was Chad, who had appeared over Gia's shoulder to call out into the garden.

"Now?" Sonia called back. "We are to start the ceremony soon."

"Better now than after," Chad insisted. He seemed almost like a serious, regular person when he was actually on the job. Almost.

"One more minute," Sonia replied, putting up her index finger as Tasha's cousin passed her carrying two marigold garlands and she stopped the boy so that Tasha could quickly inspect them.

Catching a glance from Sonia, Gia decided to look busy and snapped a shot on her phone of Tasha's fifteen-year-old cousin moving awkwardly toward the spot where the ceremony would be held. #FakeBrideGroom, although she didn't *actually* use that hashtag. The boy was to stand in for the bridegroom as Jimmy was still in New York—and Chad had made a comment on the way up from San Francisco about the rehearsal and the fact that Tasha would be "marrying" her young cousin during it, positing that it was just like some *actual* Yuba City weddings. Dolly had snorted with suppressed laughter and smacked him on the arm. "Stop with the ribbing," she had chastised, but by then Chad was on his soapbox.

"That's small-town rural America for you," he had gone on. "Endless rows of brown crops and country cafés with cheesy names like Ho-Made and Plain Dealing," he had added over his morning container of boiled eggs and spinach, which had stunk up the company van. His ensuing cackles had sprayed bits of hard-boiled egg yolk over the dashboard. Dolly was driving, with Gia wedged in between them on the middle seat. She had eyed the tiny bits of flying food, trying to keep any of it from landing on the dress she had bought the day before, which had cost more—she had done the conversion math on an app on her phone—than the total Gia had previously spent on clothes during her entire life so far.

Finally, Sonia let Tasha move off as she herself strode away to discuss where the *mandap* would be erected. As Tasha climbed the steps of the veranda from the garden, about to enter the coolness of what was a rear parlor, Tasha and Gia were about to be alone in the same space for the first time that day. For what might be the *only* time that day. Her traitorous mouth betrayed her and failed to keep itself shut.

"Tasha-Tasha," she babbled nervously as the woman passed into shadow. She was wearing a peacock-green *salwar-kameez* with gold *zari* stitching that was gathered in pleats at the waist and flowed freely below, *anarkali* style. Tasha turned toward Gia, and the flawlessly made-up face, her picture-perfect Bollywood image that Gia had dreamed of for herself when alone under her thin sheet at Mercy & Grace, took away whatever bravery or foolishness had been working within her moments before. Tasha frowned, taking in Gia's still-compressed lips.

"What?" Tasha demanded, a slightly hysterical edge to the way she asked, almost as if she knew what Gia had to say.

"I'm Gia."

"Yes, I know." Her voice was the audio version of an impatient eye roll.

"I . . . I . . . I . . . need to tell you something." She was faltering and making herself look like an idiot, which might be for the best, as humiliated as she was beginning to feel, her cheeks beginning to burn hotly.

Then Tasha did something unexpected, placing a hand lightly on Gia's chest and then walking toward her so that Gia was, in effect, pushed back through the nearest doorway into a powder room lined with faded flowery wallpaper depicting overgrown cabbage roses that seemed to be straight out of the nineteenth century. It was in keeping with the whole building, which looked as if it was used in a film about the American Civil War.

Tasha nodded her assent with only the slightest look of trepidation. "Go on then, Gia," she said, "you had something you wanted to tell me."

She already knows, Gia thought. She could see it in those eyes that were bravely trying to face up to the truth. Tasha smelled of gardenias and family, and lazy Sunday lunches with a hot pot of *rajma chawal.* It was alluring and, so close to her, Gia felt like she could not refuse her. What was the harm if she already knew? *Great harm to you, Gia Kumari.*

"What do you know?" Tasha asked. Despite the office jokes about the simple farm people of the area, this woman was far from stupid.

Uffff, Gia, what the hell are you doing? You do not owe this woman a thing. Yet, the urge to say something was so strong. Why? And then she knew . . . It was Sister Agatha's voice in her ear, reminding her to hold on to her values.

"Is it about Jimmy?" Tasha's voice cracked.

"He has a girlfriend," Gia blurted out, before the words trying to stay afloat in the maelstrom of her mind lost all coherency and were pulled down into the blackness. "A Caucasian girlfriend," she went on, the feeling of relief enticing as she stammered out her secret. The nuns had called it "confession," although she had never taken part in it before. "He has been seeing her for years, but his parents will not let them marry."

Gia's eyes had been locked on the black-and-white porcelain-tiled floor to avoid making eye contact with Tasha, but a muffled sound from her pulled Gia's gaze upward. Tasha was pulling slowly and spasmodically at the long ends of her highlighted brown hair, vacantly gazing out of the tiny window that provided the space with only a murky light. A single tear ran through the mascara, her cheeks blotchy, but she dabbed her face with a tissue she pulled out from a hidden pocket in her dress and sniffed.

"Tasha?" Gia tried after a moment. Tasha looked down at her, then leaned and kissed her cheek, again filling her nostrils with that intoxicating scent.

"Thank you for your honesty, Gia," she said as she straightened, then turned and left the bathroom. As she turned to the right, her navy *dupatta* trailing in her wake—in the direction that Chad would be waiting to do an interview with her for the wedding video—the empty space revealed Sonia standing in the hallway, her arms folded, her gaze withering and imperious.

Tasha didn't break her stride. She passed Sonia without a word, and Sonia didn't glance at the bride, either; instead, she pointed toward the front of the house and spoke only two words to Gia. "Get out."

"Do you want to explain yourself?" Sonia asked as she climbed into the driver's seat in the Golden State Weddings company van to join Gia, who had been awaiting her fate for fifteen agonizing minutes. In that time, thoughts had shot back and forth in her mind like whips, alternating between groveling to Sonia Shah and a rabid fear of being put back on a plane to Delhi the following day.

Gia didn't say anything for a moment, instead holding her mobile phone—her gorgeous, company iPhone—so hard between her two hands that she was in danger of crushing it. "She-she kind of dragged it out of me," Gia began, sounding weak in her own ears. She hated sounding that way, so put a little conviction into her next words, even if she could not meet that steely gaze. "But she has a right to know. It is the rest of her life we are talking about."

"It was not your call to make, Gia," Sonia replied, her words a freight train running over Gia's reasoning. "Tasha is not the only person you have a responsibility to."

Gia looked up and managed to meet Sonia's eyes, which were sadder than she would have expected. Was it the sadness of having to send her newest employee back to India on the next available flight? *Oh, please, no. I've been so stupid.*

"You have a responsibility to me," Sonia went on, "to Dolly, to Chad . . . to yourself. Your responsibility is also putting food on your own table, which is much more difficult when you do not have a job. I thought that you of all people would appreciate that, Gia, more so than my American-born employees."

"So, I am to be sent back?" she asked, looking down at the phone again, now massaging it between her fingers as if holding a treasured object for the last time. Which could well be the case. There was a lump in her throat, but she was managing, so far, not to cry. In fact, the survivor in her was already planning. She should have spoken to Mohammed that morning about his work. Wily Sister Agatha would always have told her to have a backup plan.

"If Tasha had called the wedding off," Sonia answered, "then that is exactly what would be happening."

Gia's head snapped up. "She has not?" It should be good news, yet she felt disappointed. She had stupidly risked so much, and the woman did not even care.

"No, she still wants to go ahead."

"But . . ." Gia was genuinely stunned.

"But-but-but!" Sonia interjected, perhaps mistaking Gia's confusion for some sort of stubborn moral persistence. "Let's just leave it at that and agree that Gia Kumari does not know everything about the world or what the people in it want."

Yet, Gia could not let it go. She was as jaded as anyone about the world and what lay in it, but weddings, above anything else, were supposed to be pure and magical. "But it is a lie!" Unbidden, Gia found herself again thinking of those slightly rough lips that had tasted of coffee and salt pushing wetly against her own the previous evening. Adi was her first real kiss, the first that counted, and she had been tasting and reliving it all morning, even as she got more irritated as she waited for him to reply to her message. She needed to believe right now that things like love and marriage were honest and genuine. "Love should not have secrets."

Sonia shocked her then, reaching across with a twisted smile and squeezing her knee. "Welcome to the wedding business, Gia," she said, looking up and meeting her gaze. "Now, do you still want in or not?"

Gia hung her head a little numbly, feeling a little like she was in the Mother Superior's office at Mercy & Grace Orphanage after being caught hopping over the back wall after lights out. The adults in the world—which always seemed to be anyone older than Gia—ultimately had you nodding and agreeing with them in the end, whether you were in the right or not. And yes, she still wanted it more than anything else. More even than yesterday, now that she knew how close she'd come to losing it. Stupid, naive girl.

Sonia took in a deep breath, her chest filling up like a peacock's then settling back again. "Good, but this is your one and only pass. Don't you ever, *ever* go behind my back again, understood?"

"Yes, Sonia."

Sonia pulled out her phone and looked at the time, then sat there for a moment fiddling with it, massaging it in the same way that Gia recognized as something she often did. "Not all lies are bad, you know," she said after a moment. "Jimmy Singh's lie is a bad one, I'll agree with you on that. But life is full of big lies and little lies, Gia. Lies that are for the best or can't be avoided. Lies to smooth the road for everybody." She was looking out of the windshield of the van now, her face dimmed like an extinguished candle. "I admire your morals, Gia, I really do. But this is not a life where you can afford them."

She sat up straight, stuffed the phone away again, and turned to Gia. Her smile was suddenly radiant, teeth like pearls, and Gia was for the first time struck by how attractive her new boss's face was when every trace of a frown or scowl was gone from it. "Anyway, I've been thinking about tasks for you. Things suited to your talents . . . and I think you're going to like this."

CHAPTER 13

The sign read SNOW LEOPARD TOUR & TRAVELS; Saumya recognized some of the pictures of exotic destinations on the sign, although not all of them. Behind her, an ornately carved sculpture of the elephant-headed deity Ganesha at least as big as a man stood sentinel over the entrance to the temple. God of new beginnings, remover of obstacles—the presence of Ganesha looming large behind Saumya as she waited for her sister should be a good omen, should it not? She was almost there, to a new life.

Saumya turned back to the travel-company sign and sighed heavily, a bound-up pressure escaping her chest, a little like air through a valve. She gave it a closer inspection, ignoring the tightness that was invading her every muscle. Saumya recognized panic approaching—three months pockmarked by the knowledge that the pressure behind her eyeballs was panic, not tears—and tried to force her mind away from it.

The Eiffel Tower: she knew that one. *Everyone* knew that one, it was so distinctive, and Paris was a byword for cosmopolitan adventure, synonymous with style . . . with *escape*. Even a girl from provincial Ayodhya knew that. A nasty pang twisted inside Saumya's stomach as she thought of the hometown she might never see again. She hated it, she hated almost everything there, but still the pain seared her insides.

Saumya clutched a nearby railing as it became apparent that the pang in her stomach was also something acutely physical and nausea swept over her in a rush. She gulped down several lungfuls of the frigid mountain air that swept in across from the foothills of the Himalayas and glanced across the rooftops to the tree-covered peaks and troughs beyond, doing her best to take her mind off the tumultuous sensation in her stomach. She had never been anywhere like this. Leaving Ayodhya had been a jagged panic, as by then even Saumya's own brothers had been hunting her down, desperate enough to betray their own blood in the hope of . . . what? Was it redemption from the Hindu vigilantes who were their neighbors in a city dotted with mosques, temples, and churches that they were seeking? A way to convey to the goons who had come wielding knives, chains, and aluminum baseball bats that no one (not even a sister) was exempt from the bloodlust they craved in the name of nationalism? Should not love be both bigger and smaller than that?

Everything had been a blur, and Saumya felt like a pebble caught up in the fast-flowing waters of the Ghaghara River in flood. It was as if the mob had cast her into the river waters on the day of the wedding and she now floated helplessly at the mercy of its currents.

Except that she had flowed northward, somehow working against the current, back toward the mountains. For now, here in Shimla, the pebble had settled for a moment, the people of this small mountain town like the ever-flowing waters of the river slipping around her while she stood staring at the billboard, their own lives moving inexorably forward while the life she had known had come to a stop. The pebble teetered, could at any moment be swept left or right.

There was a cable car on the poster, colored a deep red underneath and with a white cross on it. Next to that was a half-ruined circular building made almost entirely of arches. Saumya did not recognize either of them but the picture above the circular building was familiar, even if she did not know *exactly* where it was taken. The picture had Mickey Mouse in it, and Minnie Mouse . . . Donald Duck too. They were gathered in front of a fairy-tale castle in what had to be Disneyland. They were waving, they were beckoning. *Come with us and escape, Saumya; come with us and escape this fate your sister has planned out for you.*

"It's all arranged," Bindu said. Saumya had not noticed her sister approaching; she had been staring intently at the big poster, at people in costumes likely half a world away. "We should get going straightaway," Bindu went on. "The van from the convent will meet us close to Scandal Point in about thirty minutes. If we hurry, we can eat something together before you go."

Saumya barked out a harsh laugh that brought another small wave of nausea with it. "Scandal Point!" she gasped. She knew about Scandal Point, everyone did—it was a major hangout place and shopping center for the people of Shimla. Locals were quick to tell it had gained its name because in the colonial period, the Maharaja of Patiala had defied a ban by the British for people to ride horses on Mall Road. What is more, he not only rode his horse up to that point, but at that juncture swept up onto the horse's back the daughter of the British viceroy before riding off with her into the hills. Scandal used to be more romantic.

Saumya turned and eyed the poster again, then flicked a glance at the ancient granite statue of Ganesha. *New beginnings.*

Bindu's brow creased in sympathy, and she reached out to touch her sister's arm. *"Didi—"*

"I don't want to go," Saumya blubbered, tears filling her eyes. "I . . ." Her knees felt weak, and she grabbed the railing again to steady herself.

"And what other choice do you have?" her sister snapped, the apparent sympathy gone in an instant. Saumya saw the tiredness in her sibling, the strain, the worry of a woman who still planned to go back to Ayodhya and face everyone there, so a small spear of guilt thrust its way through the self-pity that had been overwhelming Saumya almost constantly since the day of the wedding.

"Stay with me," she tried quietly, more for the pleasurable feeling of saying the words—to live for even a fraction of a second within the possibility they held—than for any belief that her sister would do such a thing. She, after all, had not tried to marry a Muslim.

Bindu burst out guffawing in that whole-body, unabashed way she had, throwing her head back, the simple brightness of her laughter blowing away the harshness of the moment before like a fan blowing smoke from a room. "The life of a nun is not for me, *Didi*. Anyway, I don't think they would take me, as it was hard enough to barter a way in for you. They don't seem as desperate for new sisters as everyone makes out."

"I'm not—" Saumya started to protest, but her sister stopped her by taking her hand.

"I know, I know. Six months, yes? That is about how long it will be. Then we'll see where we are after that."

Saumya nodded meekly, the pathetic remnants of any fight she had left draining out of her, and she took a last lingering look at the travel poster before the two sisters crossed over to another set of steps that led up and toward Mall Road, where street vendors had gathered to sell *papri chaat* and *muri*. Halting to catch her breath, she watched as the *muri walla* mixed green-mint chutney, chopped tomato and onion, raw peanuts, and the puffed rice in a tin. He shook the jar of spices upside down. Then he poured the *muri* in a bowl made of newspaper and handed it to his customer. Around the corner was a Banta soda stand covered with blue tarp whose owner had not yet arrived. It was too early in the day for people to ask for a cool drink. By afternoon, tourists would be lining up for the exotic drink, relishing the sight of a shock of gas springing out of the bottle when the round marble seal was taken off.

The clock at Christ Church struck nine times. The city of Shimla, capital of Himachal Pradesh, clung to the slopes of great wooded hills and mountainsides behind and around them, a mishmash of old and new, of beautiful and ugly, of simple and complex. A one-time colonial paradise.

Saumya had to admit there was something reassuring in a city wrapped up in trees on the side of a mountain. So unlike the much flatter, open landscape where she was from, it seemed like Shimla had a million places to hide. Living in a convent with nuns filled Saumya with a sense of dread, yet, if nothing else, she felt safe here among the biota of this sleepy "hill station" for the first time since the mob had come.

CHAPTER 14

Gia was at work early. The couple of days since the rehearsal had flown by, and this was the day of the Jimmy and Tasha wedding—despite Gia's best efforts, some might say. Gia and the entire wedding company were leaving in a few hours for Yuba City.

Since the last time she'd been there, Gia had gone from thinking she was getting fired to getting what felt like a promotion, as she now handled Golden State Wedding's social media accounts. Sonia's idea was that, on the day of a wedding—and with the permission of those involved, although so far Sonia seemed good at getting that without actually appearing to ask—the whole event would be streamed live across the company's social media accounts. This new responsibility weighed heavily across Gia's shoulders, even as her insides churned with nervous excitement.

And yet, just when she should be fully focused on this great opportunity, she was distracted. The fingertips of her right hand slipped down to rest on her stomach, just below her belly button, at the memory of a pair of lips resting there.

Adi had finally called after their first meeting—although it had taken him nearly three days to do so. Maybe Gia had been naive in thinking that, after sharing a kiss with a boy, he would message her straight away the following morning, their WhatsApp missives falling instantly into the same fun, coquettish banter that they had shared in person the night before. When he didn't contact her at all the following day, Gia had begun to expect that he would not do so at all. And that had hurt. It was like some cruel twist to flirt, kiss, feel that spark in another person's company, and then—the American saying was, she believed, to be "ghosted." It hurt worse than the indigestion caused by scarfing down her only meal of the day too quickly, which had happened more than once in the orphanage.

But when he did finally get in touch, Adi hadn't merely messaged her, he had *actually called her*, and when she heard his voice again—smooth and rich and sounding like the West Coast of America as she was already coming to understand it—all doubt and annoyance had melted away. "Have you seen the Golden Gate Bridge yet?" he had asked her.

She hadn't.

"Meet me at the plaza beyond the Round House Cafe."

"Shall I bring-bring anything?" Gia had winced at her own turn of phrase. She sounded like an old-style telephone; there had been one on the desk in the Mother Superior's office that buzzed just like that.

"Just yourself. And don't eat dinner before you come."

They had met the same evening. The bus had pulled up at the stop for the Golden Gate Bridge Toll Plaza, and Gia looked doubtfully at the wet, silvery mist as it hung over the bridge, filling the empty space around the suspension cables, the rail guards, and the bridge's towers, making it seem insubstantial in the fading light of the early evening. She had taken the bus from Market Street after work and, most of the way, had second thoughts about the whole thing. And yet she'd carefully prepared for the date, spraying her armpits with the Yardley Precious Petals deodorant that she had bought at Delhi's Indira Gandhi International Airport, putting gold hoops in her ears, and brushing her raven-black hair until it shone, all in the restroom before she left work.

She'd worried about seeing Adi again. What if it was awkward and not the same as it had been when they had initially clicked at the café in

Castro? That night had been magical, and now she felt pressure for this one to be better. It felt like it was a responsibility—to be interesting, to make sure they had the same chemistry. Dating was stressful!

The mist-shrouded Golden Gate Bridge was a hulking presence to her left as she walked down and past the distinctive Round House Cafe and on toward the small plaza where Adi had asked her to meet him. Despite the weather and the fading light of afternoon turning toward evening, people still hung about, disembodied heads sticking out of the mist and taking pictures as if they were tourists. They were probably just taking pictures for their Instagram accounts, Gia thought. Everyone was a tourist if they had a smartphone and a social media account, even in their hometown, and Gia followed an impulse to join them, the action of snapping something with her phone and posting it to Instagram a calming distraction. Her breathing had been getting quicker and shorter ever since leaving the bus—and it wasn't only the exercise.

She typed #WaitingForLove below the picture of the great behemoth of a bridge poking up out of the sea fog. Could she get away with that? She hadn't connected with Adi on Instagram or Facebook or anything else but WhatsApp, but fear still got the better of her, and she deleted the hashtag. She put #GoldenGate instead, deeply disappointed with her lackluster alternative.

Gia looked over at the landmass across the stretch of water. "Saus . . . Sausal . . . Sausalito," she finally managed, recalling the strange name that Dolly had told her earlier in the day. Sausalito was where Sonia lived, a small city hidden just out of sight beyond the bridge. Dolly had volunteered this information without any preamble or encouragement, happy as always to talk about their boss, who was like some mysterious enigma to the designer—her favorite subject.

Sonia was interesting to Gia too. After all, she'd plucked Gia from a bad set of options in India and brought her to a new life full of possibilities. She should *love* Sonia, but the woman was something of a cold fish most of the time. The only time she'd been animated, oddly, was when she'd been chewing Gia out in the company van. It was this, more than anything else, that made her intriguing in Gia's eyes.

Out of the corner of her eye, Gia spotted Adi walking across the plaza toward her from the direction of the bridge, with what looked to be a wicker picnic basket dangling from one hand. He had on a tight-fitting, short-sleeved T-shirt that showed off his firm, muscular arms, and seeing him brought a rush of desire and excitement.

Gia remained dry, but the light, misty rain looked to have done a good job of soaking Adi and caused his thin white shirt to stick to his skin. His hair, which she remembered being quite thick and unruly on top, had been flattened down by the rain, making him look—at least as Gia fancied it—a little like some model on a photo shoot. Although perhaps someone else might have just thought he looked bedraggled, wet, and sorry for himself.

"I cannot believe the weather," Adi said as he reached her. "This was not predicted at all. I saw this sweep in from the ocean not even half an hour ago."

Gia looked between the picnic hamper that he was clutching and Adi's face.

"I'm sorry, so rude," Adi said, appearing to catch himself. "Hi." He stood there and waved a hand at her awkwardly, the picnic hamper making it difficult for the two of them to decide whether they should hug or shake hands, or whether Gia should just wave back. Which, in the end, she did. It was weird.

Adi continued trying to explain. "I thought an evening picnic with the sun setting behind the Golden Gate Bridge . . ." The man was rambling a little, not nearly so confident as he had seemed the night she met him. It was one part confusing but two parts reassuring, because it was endearing and put her at ease.

"It is a lovely idea," Gia told him and put a hand up to indicate the weather. "We should eat, anyway. This is not rain. You have not seen rain until you have been caught out in a downpour during the monsoons."

Adi smiled at that. She had begun to notice the other night that he seemed to like it every time she mentioned India or anything that was culturally specific to where she had come from. Yet Gia had found herself unwilling to talk about the orphanage and the realities of her life growing up. She was not totally sure why, and she did not know if she was angry with herself about it. She didn't feel shame about who she was, where she came from . . . but still. Whatever this flirtation was going to end up being, she *so* wanted to spend more time in Adi's company and felt on guard against anything that might ruin it.

Appearing to recover some of his poise, Adi held out a hand to her, and she took it, delighting in how the small innocent skin-to-skin contact felt like the most extreme of sensations. It was like a new and delicious flavor bursting in your mouth, very much like the first time she had tasted cassata ice cream in the orphanage. (A rich benefactor, Mrs. Kapoor, dressed in a translucent pink-chiffon sari, with pearls at her neck and ears, had passed them around on her son's birthday.)

They walked down some steps, hand in hand, exiting the plaza, and were quickly on a path surrounded by low, scrub-like undergrowth that took a meandering course toward the water. Gia had held hands before, mostly with other orphans during group trips outside of the orphanage, and never with someone she desired the way that she desired Adi. He was handsome, and Gia was still a little incredulous that he was glancing over at her the way he was right then. Every time their grip shifted the resultant movement of skin against skin brought a sensation that threatened to steal the breath from her chest. It seemed impossible that he should like her, and, as the low sun finally poked out from behind clouds and the rain started to lift and move away to the east, casting the Golden Gate Bridge in a light befitting its name, Gia felt like she was in a fairy tale.

Hours later, Gia had reclined on Adi's bed in his Castro apartment. She still wore her little black dress that had dried while they ate and watched the distant sky turning pink to purple behind the bridge. Then the night took over and the bridge lit up. Now Adi, minus that form-fitting shirt, crawled onto the bed and filled the space above her. "Is it too soon?" he asked.

Gia shook her head in the half light of a street lamp shining through the window. For her, this was long, long overdue. She had always been a good girl where boys were concerned. The orphanage was not a place where it was easy to misbehave with boys, yet some of the girls had still managed it. As Adi moved down and began to kiss the exposed parts of her skin, his lips sliding farther to that area just below her belly button, it seemed to Gia that the wait had been worth it.

And then he had ghosted her again.

Sitting in the office, needing to finish the Twitter tease tweets hinting about the wedding that would start later that day, Gia's right hand now snatched itself away. They had been intimate two nights ago—it was now Saturday morning—and she had not received a single message from Adi since, despite having sent three of her own. What she felt ill-equipped to know was whether sending a fourth would somehow seem desperate, or like she was some crazy stalking woman. Would that turn her into a needy, clingy person in all of this?

Gia felt angry and inadequate all at once. No one had ever made her feel like Adi had made her feel two nights ago. No one had ever known her the way he had known her, yet she clenched her fists at the thought of how angry and used and cheap he was making her feel.

"You alright there?"

"Huh?" Gia looked up to find Chad frowning down at her, a giant apricot in his hand and a little juice running down his chin.

He nodded to the mouse in her right hand. "You do realize that's a mouse, not a stress ball, yeah?"

Gia was gripping it so hard that the blood seemed to have drained out of her knuckles. "Just . . . you know. I am think-thinking of what to say."

"Well, don't take too long. We're heading out in twenty."

Hai! Gia had zoned out so much that she'd lost track of time. This was no good, she needed to get these posts out and be ready to go. She returned her attention to the little text box in front of her, which still showed 140/140 characters available. *Get it together, idiot. Don't mess things up for the sake of some boy who won't even message you.*

Her attention had only been back for about thirty seconds, though, when it was taken away again as the main door to the office opened. Gia wasn't quite sure that she was seeing correctly at first, and she did a sort of double take, looking up, down, and up again. *Nope*, it really was him. Adi had come to her place of work.

As much as her spirits lifted and her two days' worth of doubt evaporated just like that, Gia was also suddenly getting a severe case of the "careful what you wish for." Sonia would no doubt be furious to have her new-but-already-on-a-last-chance employee visited by a boy, especially on a busy, important day like this. She felt her cheeks begin to flush hotly and wondered whether to get to her feet and try and head Adi off—perhaps she could quickly get him back outside of the office before Sonia, who was shut away in her own dimly lit office, even noticed. Then they could have their wonderfully romantic moment out in the corridor because she probably didn't have time to take it all the way outside.

What Gia didn't realize was that, until she stood up, Adi hadn't even spotted her. His eyes went wide as he did so, a smile passing briefly across his face to be replaced by something else. Shock, perhaps? Which was weird. Actually, it was a little more like horror.

Gia heard a door open to her right and looked up to see Sonia striding out. Her eyes were fixed on Adi. Damn it but if that woman didn't have senses like a hawk. Sonia smiled, though, then opened her arms, and—with an almost imperceptibly quick glance over at Gia—Adi lightly embraced Gia's boss and gave her a light kiss on the cheek.

As if remembering herself, Sonia turned to Gia. "You've not met Adi yet, have you?" she asked Gia, then glanced back to Adi. "This is Gia, our new employee. Gia, this is Adi, my stepson."

CHAPTER 15

NOW

"There was a boy once," Gia told Dolly as the two of them took a quick break ahead of the marriage ceremony in Yuba City, finding a spare moment since the *baraat*—the groom's party—was running late. They were sitting on the front porch of the converted Victorian mansion where the ceremony was to be held, the type of porch that deserved a swing seat or a resplendent rocking chair. Instead the wicker chairs they sat on were wooden and painted white with worn, flowered cushions.

"Only once?" Dolly teased. Instead of a length of straw, as might have seemed appropriate on such a porch, the two women were sucking on red-and-white-striped candy canes, and they were doing so far too noisily.

Gia blushed. Until Adi, it *had* only been once and had resulted in no more than a couple of times clumsily making out, not that she was going to tell Dolly that. She went on, pushing past Dolly's comment. "His name was Arjun. I have always been a good-good girl," Gia went on after another lip-smacking suck, "but Arjun persuaded me to sneak into a rock concert. It was on the other side of town, and we walked for miles only to find that it was the wrong night. The concert was the next night."

"Oy!" Dolly took her candy cane out of her mouth and examined it thoughtfully. "Why are men so useless?" The scent of star jasmine came stealing up from the vine clinging to the trellis on the wall. The sweet basil in the flower beds below the porch sent up a spicy richness, the smell mingling with the sugar-sweet aroma of the candy. The sun beat on open fields, machines creeping across them like giant metal critters in the distance. It was a beautiful day for a wedding, although Gia was starting to wonder whether Jimmy was even going to turn up.

A man with a red bandana looped around his head was watching them from far out in the fields, just before the rice stalks bumped up against a row of bushy trees. Gia waved at the worker, and he nodded.

"We still heard music coming from inside, though," Gia went on, continuing her Arjun story, "so we climbed until we found the fire door that Arjun knew would be unlocked and not alarmed. His secret way in. We hid in a space near the roof and watched the band rehearsing for their . . . What is it you say?"

"Gig," Dolly answered and Gia smiled.

"Gig," Gia agreed, enjoying the feel of the word on her tongue, especially with the sweet taste of the candy beneath it. "Weddings are like gigs, I think."

Dolly stopped midsuck. "You've lost me, I thought this was about a boy."

"No-no," Gia waved away Dolly's misunderstanding. It had started about a boy, but now Gia was finding something deeper and more meaningful to speak about because she was in a strange, reflective mood. Which, ironically, was because of a boy. "I mean that the rehearsal we had the other day, it is just not the same as the real thing. It is intimate, but it is not . . . magical. The people bring the magic."

Dolly, who was wearing a *salwar-kameez* in blue chiffon with embroidered pink flowers and round puffy short sleeves, let out a little cackle of agreement. "You are a romantic today, Gia. Is there a boy behind this?"

Gia felt herself flush and kept quiet as Dolly looked at the square-faced watch on her slim wrist. "It's going to get a lot less magical if

Jimmy doesn't turn up soon," Dolly observed. "Tasha was furious and saying something about calling it off."

Gia drew in a sharp breath, unable to stop herself from doing so. Her feelings about this wedding were still complicated. She couldn't agree in her heart with the fact that it was going ahead with what she—and, indeed, the bride—knew about the bridegroom, yet having been involved in the weeklong preparations had certainly invested her in it. She *wanted* it to be all okay, if it could be. More than that, any last-minute jitters by the bride might turn certain eyes angrily back toward Gia.

"Oh, nerves and bluster," Dolly said with her candy-red mouth, likely noticing Gia's expression. "She's going ahead with it, despite your best efforts," she added with a mischievous smirk. "That Singh money."

Gia looked down at her phone, which, as always, was in her hand. "I thought Sonia was going to fire me." Her Instagram app was open, and there was a shot of the waiting guests sipping tall glasses of *am panna* and mocktails on it—no alcohol or meat was to be served in observance of the Sikh *anand karaj* ceremony. "I don't want to lose my job."

"Well," Dolly said, heaping a whole bucketload of irony into her voice, "tip for the new girl . . ."

She left the words hanging there, and it felt somehow cathartic for Gia to finish the thought, like the first step of a multiple-step program back to being a model employee. "Don't go behind the boss's back and try to ruin the wedding."

"Ah," Dolly exclaimed, waving her candy cane about for emphasis, "Sonia wouldn't fire you now, anyway, even if the bride did pull out."

Gia looked at Dolly, her gaze falling to the distinctive birthmark at the top of her neck. "But she said that I only kept my job because Tasha was still getting married."

Dolly rolled her eyes. "For such a smart girl, you can be dumb sometimes. Sonia had to scare you, because what you did was not acceptable—however morally right it might have been. Either way, don't screw up so big again, and you'll be just fine."

Chad appeared at the front door to the house, his bulky camera held rather precariously in one hand, a huge, half-eaten carrot in the other. "There you are," he chided Dolly. "Sonia wants you in the garden; Jimmy's two minutes out, and Tasha's found some detail to panic about. There's a vein pulsing in the boss's forehead, and you're out here sucking . . ." He turned his nose up at their sugary treats. "That crap."

"Alright," Dolly shot back, "calm down, Bugs." Despite the deflection, she did hurry to her feet.

"You want to stay and get a shot of the groom arriving?" Chad asked Gia.

"No," she replied. "I'll take a short-short video of Tasha when she comes into the garden and put it straight onto the story. That's the money shot."

Dolly laughed, and Gia assumed it was at the American turn of phrase she had used, while Chad nodded his head deferentially. "You know your stuff, social media girl," he said.

Gia grabbed her clipboard and hurriedly followed Dolly back through the house, the anticipation and excitement building within her like mercury rising rapidly in a thermometer. It wasn't *her* wedding, yet there was an element of performance about the whole thing, now that the *baraat* was on its way and the bride's grand entry was only a couple of minutes out. Loping outside to where the ceremony was to take place, Gia admired the red-and-gold wedding wonderland they'd created on the grounds. The *pheras* were to take place at the raised marble pagoda situated at the center of the freshly mowed lawn. *Ragis* who would be singing wedding hymns were seated to the side, under an arched *mandap* sprinkled with gold glitter and swathed in garlands of orange-marigold flowers intertwined with mounds of pink roses and creamy frangipani. Guests mingled beneath ancestral black walnut trees—men dressed in achkans and *churidaars*, and Western-style clothes, and women in traditional silk saris of all colors with heavy gold jewelry. Chefs at open-air counters were basting skewers of tandoori paneer and cauliflower kebabs with marinade. The sky was bathed in the orange glow of the midday sun. The air—sweet with the fragrance of the freshly cut flowers mixed with the strong perfumes the women were wearing—contained an aroma that Gia inhaled deeply. *It has all come together,* she thought, anticipation buzzing within her so greatly that it felt like her chest itself was vibrating. *This is the moment.*

Sonia was waiting for them, looking imposing but not exactly angry. She waved Gia off to one side with a magisterial sweep of her arm—a spot where she could stand and film without spoiling the view of anyone important—and pulled Dolly toward the front, immediately engaging the designer in furious conversation about something that must have fallen from perfection since Dolly had left for her break on the porch.

A few minutes later, the groom's party arrived. The *baraat* was a royal procession. Jimmy Singh, dressed in a gold-embroidered sherwani and a red turban with a *sehra* that covered most of his face like a veil, rode upon a long-legged mare whose tail and mane were braided with flowers. A twenty-piece band led the way, blowing trumpets and beating drums. Jimmy's mom and the rest of Jimmy's cousins danced joyously in front of the band. Reaching the entrance of the historic property, Jimmy dismounted awkwardly from the horse, gripping a gilded sword in his right hand. The bride's party welcomed the *baraat* by beginning the *milni* ceremony to rousing cheers as the bride's male relations garlanded the groom's male relatives and presented them with gifts.

Standing in an inconspicuous corner of the garden, Gia found herself glancing across to look at the Singh family. She had been doing her best to avoid ending up too close to the elder Mr. Singh at any point. She had this itchy feeling between her shoulders that they would somehow know she had pretended to be Mr. Singh's secretary and would call her out about it in front of everyone else at the wedding. It was ridiculous, of course, the sort of consequence that Gia the girl from the orphanage would hardly have considered, yet her life in America was already making her more nervous about such things. She had found more than one tightrope to walk since being here.

In all her life up until now, Gia had never laid her eyes on anyone who was anywhere near as wealthy as Mr. Singh, not in person. On the one hand, he was an unremarkable-looking man with mousy-gray thinning hair of slightly below average height and slightly above average waistline. He was dressed a little dourly for a wedding, in a simple, largely unadorned, charcoal-gray kurta. On the other hand, he was somehow utterly terrifying. Maybe that was a little to do with the way he seemed hardly to smile, even though it was his son's wedding day, but he also seemed like the kind of man who wore his wealth and influence like a weapon.

Tasha, her golden-brown hair decorously covered with the elaborate gold *pallav* of her bridal outfit, entered just as the rhythmic beat of the *dhol* filled the venue with Punjabi bhangra music. She had elected to wear a sequined, *rani* pink *salwar-kameez* for the wedding ceremony, instead of the traditional red favored by most Sikh brides. Her scarlet and cream ivory wedding bangles tinkled with the sound of the gold-plated *kaliras* hanging from them. She walked with short, deliberate steps from around the side of the house to appear underneath a long and elaborate *phoolon ki chadar* that had been handmade by Dolly. She had chosen to have eight of her girlfriends support the canopy of golden mesh and flowers—rather than having her male family members, as was custom—and lead her to the *mandap* where Jimmy was already seated. Whatever else, this was Tasha's wedding.

Gia eagerly brought up her phone, her heart racing at around a hundred miles per hour, knowing that she had never filmed something quite so magical in her life, that she had never been in a moment that felt so perfect, and every other thought and complication slid away like melting snow falling from a rooftop.

"Gia," Tasha called out, "where are you going?"

Gia was halfway across the front garden of the wedding venue when she heard the bride's voice. Day had long since turned to night, the guests had almost all left, and, as magical as the whole event had been, Gia was beginning to yearn for her bed and a little solitude—a concept that had quickly gone from pleasantly novel to unsettling to strangely comforting. The cleanup was not yet over, however, and none of them could leave until the venue was spotless. It was going to be a long night.

She turned and plodded over to the porch, where Tasha was sitting with one of her girlfriends, and Gia thought of the fact that she had not seen Jimmy for at least the last half hour. With night falling, the front of the old house had become a myriad of flashing colors as a cloud of fireflies danced over their heads and lights twinkled from the branches of the towering trees in the garden. The long front porch had been wound around with fairy lights, and Tasha's face—now sitting in the same seat that Dolly had been sucking a candy cane in earlier in the day—was only dimly visible to Gia as she approached.

"I am going to the 7-Eleven across the street for trash bags," Gia answered. "It's only a five-minute walk, isn't it? Left at the end of the lane?" Gia had not spoken a single word to Tasha since they had been together in the restroom at the rehearsal. The bride wore a lazy grin, no sign of animosity or awkwardness. She cradled a glass of champagne in one hand, a half-empty bottle of Dom Perignon on the steps, and her friend passed her what looked like a cigarette, then Gia caught the distinctive smell of cannabis as the smoke floated out from under the porch.

"Yay!" Tasha punched the air lightly but drunkenly with the hand that now held the joint. "Tra-shhh bags." She turned to her friend and nudged her arm. "Gia is a trouper, a real gal. She told me about"—her head lolled for a moment—"you know, the mistress."

The friend nodded, her honey-blonde hair swinging around her shoulders, and looked at Gia, who was beyond stunned that Tasha had told her. Perhaps, she thought—although she had been actively trying not to wonder—Tasha might have told her parents. Yet she was utterly shocked that Tasha was brazenly discussing it here, on her wedding night.

"You thought I wouldn't go through with it," Tasha said, pointing the joint accusingly at her, "I can see it in your face."

"I—"

"But what else is a country girl to do?" Tasha went on, apparently not too desperate to hear Gia's opinion. She turned to her friend. "Isn't that right, Bri?"

"Only way out of this godforsaken backwater," the friend called Bri agreed with a sweeping gesture at the sprawling acres of farmlands now invisible in the night-blackened distance—during the day barren and desolate, showing only the rows of dwarfed brown stumps, with here and there a patch of emerald wheat or green pastureland. She made it sound like a practiced, well-used response, then took the joint back, although the sozzled bride hadn't even taken a drag. "I'm jealous, Tash, so jealous. I wish I could move to a place where Starbucks is at every corner instead of an hour away at the nearest mall."

Tasha grabbed the rail at the front of the porch and hauled herself up to look straight down at Gia. "You've got to take your chances, Gia," she lectured, "you never know if they will come again."

Gia nodded; no one had to tell her that. All the same . . .

"Life is compromise, Gia, and I can't wait to get out of this hell hole and up to New York," Tasha went on. "I don't belong here with the peaches and the walnuts." Unseen by the bride as she unsteadily waved her arm back and forth, back on her seat under the porch, Bri's dozy smile was fading.

"Better get those bags," Gia said and backed away with a wave from the bride. *Yes, Tasha,* she thought, *but how much compromise is too much?*

Shit, this is weird.

Adi's first message to her since they had slept together. A sensitive, insecure girl who had never slept with anyone else before might be insulted. Luckily, Gia was only one of those things. Also, exiting the 7-Eleven, trash bags under her arm, Gia was too tired and numb to have the energy to be offended.

I can't believe we didn't figure it out before. He added in a second message, while Gia was still trying to think of her response to the first. Yes, it was all very weird and complicated, and Gia hated the way that Adi hadn't messaged her until now. She should tell him that they should not see each other anymore, ask him never to speak of it to Sonia. *This* was the best thing to do. But she didn't want to.

It felt like fate when I saw you in the Castro. Gia's middle finger hovered over her phone screen. She hated those words; she hated the weakness of them. The need.

She pressed send anyway.

CHAPTER 16

THEN

There were three types of clouds visible from the convent window that Saumya was currently sitting in, her back against the cold stone, looking out at the green-topped lower slopes of the Himalayas. The first type was high above her, flat, gray stratus clouds that imprisoned everything, occasionally revealing a crisp, blue sky below them. Then there were the cumulus clouds below her; thick puffs of cotton-wool white that were stuffed into the depths of the valleys, sometimes so much so that only the peaks of wooded hills and mountains poked through the middle of it.

One particular foaming bubble of cumulus cloud could be seen right beneath her, and it seemed to Saumya that she could jump from the window and land in the middle of it like it was a soft duvet, or a huge, misshapen bale of white-colored hay. Of course, she knew better than that, although there had been times in the first few months after arriving at the convent that the idea of jumping from this window—and that short fall into oblivion—had seemed better than the reality of her existence.

She had been so consumed with survival after the disrupted wedding, overwhelmed with the terror that the mob might find her, and caught up in the escape to Shimla. Arriving in the convent, which was the embodiment of stillness, of stasis, of life's perpetual motion coming to a halt, Saumya had finally been able to reflect on how her own life and all the expectations that she had of it had suddenly come to a standstill.

It hadn't been pretty and had almost finished her off. Were she to be poetic about it, perhaps Saumya would say that the baby inside her had saved her life, although the more prosaic truth was that there were moments when her own despair had simply not even taken the responsibility for another life—even one that was all that was left of Hassan—into account. Not that she would *ever* tell anyone that.

The final type of cloud to be seen out of the window was just a misty feather that could be found at Saumya's eye level and came from within her. It was an instantly condensed cloud of breath, which floated off and away as it left her, escaping into the frigid morning air of early winter. Saumya watched her breath as it slowly came apart like entropy in action. Before its inevitable end, it was at least momentarily free from the wretched stone edifice in which she had been imprisoned, the place where she was serving out her sentence for daring to love the wrong man.

Hassan had been a good, decent man first, and a Muslim second. More than that, Saumya was a grown woman, she had kept telling herself that, yet she now remembered how, shortly after discovering she was pregnant, she had felt like a child as she'd waited under the narrow veranda at the front of the family home in Ayodhya. The veranda had been threatening to collapse for several years, every time the monsoon rains arrived with a vengeance. In fact, she could see where the rough wooden pole—holding up the veranda's roof next to where Saumya sat slumped on the jute cot right where her mother, lips stained red with chain consumption of *paan*, often reclined in the afternoons—had been stapled back together only the previous summer. A part of her wished that the structure would just let go and bury her under the corrugated iron roof, and perhaps some of the front of the house. It would solve a lot of problems for everyone.

She didn't mean that, *hai*, she did not mean that at all. Saumya had a little life growing inside her now, a part of Hassan who she was responsible for and who she wanted to protect. Someone she could not wait to meet. Although this little fetus that was only the beginning of an idea, which might then one day be a full person with their own hopes and dreams and personality, was right now the cause of great distress within the Pandey family. Saumya, for one, had never been so scared in her life.

She remembered how she could hear them inside the puja room, arguing. The gods of her childhood lived in a dark room, breathing sandalwood incense. Photo frames of Saraswati, the goddess of learning; Hanuman, an incarnation of Lord Shiva; Ganesha, the creator and remover of obstacles; and, Lakshmi, the goddess of wealth, lined the puja room walls. Every morning, *Amma* dotted the photo frames with wet sandal paste and vermilion, lit white squares of camphor, and circled them twice around each photo, muttering unintelligible Sanskrit chants.

Every Sunday, her father had performed *aarti*, chanting a hymn while one of the kids circled the *diya* clockwise before the gods to show respect and ask blessings, and another rang a small handheld bell. She had always looked forward to her father's pujas, not for any spiritual reasons but because of a sweet tooth. If her two older brothers and Bindu and she behaved, Papa let them have the leftover *prasad*, which was given as a sacrament. She could picture her father now, who was every year becoming a thinner, more worried-looking man with more gray in his toothbrush mustache and less hair on the top of his head. This was not doing him any good. Her mother, the stern matriarch who nonetheless had such love for her two daughters, had tried to find a sensible outcome to the madness Saumya had suddenly brought down upon their household. And then her two brothers. Mostly Jeet, the oldest child who had an opinion on everything that happened within the family and who, Saumya had to admit, was the most likely to do the Pandey name proud.

That day as she'd stood on the veranda, she could hear Bindu too. It was hard to make out all the words, only snatches and the general tone (Jeet, sharp and high pitched. Her mom, conciliatory. Her sister, assertive.) of what was going back and forth, but it seemed that little Bindu—the younger sister who was supposed to look up to *her*—was the only one really standing up to Jeet. Every family had its politics, and, until a few months ago, Saumya would have felt secure about her place within her own household. She was the steady, reliable one with an eye for design and presentation—some might say *overly fastidious*, and she never minded that. Bindu had been better with boys, and Saumya had always secretly hoped that marriage might pass her by and that she might be free to work, to indulge her passion in a way that made money. Now, all of a sudden, she was the disgrace, the ruined, sullied daughter who had gotten herself "knocked up" by a Muslim. *She*, of all people, had turned out to be the problem that they did not know what to do with.

The argument had gone on forever, and Saumya grew tired of hearing only tantalizing bits of what was being said—only enough each time to increase her worry and to make her stomach churn a little faster. Like the chastised child, she'd dared not move from the seat in which she had been placed to await her fate, so instead she tried to tune them out, taking in a deep breath and closing her eyes, listening but at the same time feeling like she was reaching out to see what was happening in the world around their humble family dwelling on the outskirts of Ayodhya.

Distantly, a truck had revved its engine, while somewhere closer by a pack of stray dogs barked as if in competition. Then something creaked for a moment—a door or a gate perhaps, opening or closing. And then, cutting through everything else, she'd heard a bird call. The call was a familiar one, and yet, in another way, she was sure she had not heard it since she was a little girl. "Cuck-oo," the bird went, "cuck-oo." After the first few moments of unadulterated joy that Saumya felt at hearing this sound, the tone of the bird call seemed to change for her.

She heard it in a way that was half-imagined, yet in another way it was oh so clear. "Hus-sy," the cuckoo had called. "Un-clean."

And yet, after the initial shock of having these words pass through her brain, Saumya began to realize that the cuckoo was not mocking her. It was telling her that these things were just names, it was talking about possibility—that lust and love and desire might be things to be embraced. "Cuck-oo," went the bird who pleased itself, who laid its eggs in other birds' nests and was then gone, free to live its life. All Saumya wanted was to be true to her love and to the life inside her. How could such a desire ever be selfish? How was it that it could have everyone so angry and animated inside the Pandey house?

Then the voices emanating from the main room that opened onto the veranda had stopped. Saumya opened her eyes just as the front door opened and the rest of her family tromped out. The veranda would not hold them all at one time, and it creaked dangerously under the weight of those who tried to cram onto it rather than go down the steps and stand in the front yard. It was not so much a yard, really, as it had no fence or gate, but was more a parched, scrubby partition between their house and the road.

These people, Saumya remembered they looked more like a jury than her family. "We've decided," Saumya's father had said, as if it were he who had led the discussion, probably invoking the blessings of the Hindu gods in winning the casting vote, "that you are going to have to marry him."

Saumya grinned now, remembering how she had almost fallen from her chair in response, stunned that their great, weighty judgment had been exactly what she wanted.

"Are you going to jump or what?" came a sharp but familiar voice from behind her, pulling her harshly from her reverie, from the joy of that moment that had not led to any joy at all. Which, in fact, had led her *here*, to this convent tucked in the Himalayas. "I do not have all day."

"Is not suicide a sin?" Saumya asked, although she did not turn around to address the voice. Instead she watched as the wispy breaths from the words she had just spoken drifted out into the open abyss beyond the window. *Suicide*, three syllables of condensed breath slowly stretching out and enjoying a glorious moment in the sunlight that had just broken through. It was so cold up here, and she was dressed in what was barely more than a thin shift, yet Saumya had stopped feeling the cold some time ago.

"It would not be your first sin, young lady," came the wry and slightly caustic response from behind Saumya. "Although at least it would be your last."

Saumya laughed at that—a bitter, mocking laugh—and turned to address the speaker, who was a muscular-looking nun, dressed all in white and wearing rimless glasses. Grim and unsmiling, she pointed at the watch pinned to her habit.

"Come, your chores have been waiting for you while you have sat here daydreaming," Sister Mary told her, looking Saumya up and down in that disapproving way she always did. A casual observer might have thought that Sister Mary could not stand Saumya—and perhaps she could not—yet Saumya counted the sour old maid as the closest thing she had to a friend in the convent.

"They are not going anywhere," Saumya shot back habitually, although she spun on her backside and let her bare feet down to the floor. "But they would be welcome to if they liked."

"Is it not bad enough that we must feed you and clothe you," Sister Mary complained as they walked, "that you should also get lazier every day?" She looked upward at the stone ceiling of the corridor, as if for some cosmic sign, and shook her head. "All the strength that the Lord sends me I must save to deal with you, my girl."

"Is this why you built the convent all the way up here in the mountains, so that he would not have so far to send his strength to you?"

"And to you," Sister Mary shot back. "He sends his strength to you, as well. Even if you are a dirty sinner. Even if you sit in that window and consider things that you should not be considering. Terrible, selfish things."

Saumya glowered at the floor as they walked. She had not been thinking those things, yet Sister Mary had a way of making the sins of Saumya's past feel like the sins of her present. "I thought you didn't care."

"I didn't say that," Sister Mary quipped, although her tone did not betray any particular offense. "And whether I care or not, it does not make these things any less terrible or selfish."

They arrived at a kitchen that was devoid of any nuns or other staff. A cracked terra-cotta-colored stone floor had a water-filled wooden bucket and a scrubbing brush in the middle of it. "I wasn't going to, anyway," Saumya muttered sullenly, feeling like a petulant child as she did so. "I'm . . . past that."

"Good."

"Now I'm just angry."

A faint, scornful smile twisted Sister Mary's lips, her raised unibrow accentuated by the white line of the surrounding veil. "And what are you going to do? March back down to Ayodhya and exact your revenge upon the Hindu activists? Why don't you just get revenge on half of India while you're at it?"

Saumya poked her chin out, met the sister's gaze, and forced all the fire and bitterness within her into the look she threw back.

"Do you know what the best revenge is, Saumya?" Sister Mary asked.

"If you say living—"

"Being better than them."

"What?" Saumya retorted sharply, throwing her arms out wide. "Up here in the mountains, where only God can see me being better? No, thanks."

Sister Mary laughed—a loud, open, barking sound—grabbing her sides and screwing up her face. Saumya even thought that she saw a tear escape. "Oh no, you'll be out of here and on your own soon, girl," Sister Mary replied, still chuckling through the harsh words. "I think our savior will return before you are ever allowed to take your vows."

Saumya tried but failed to feel insulted. "I'm just a guest for a few more weeks, huh?" she growled, unable to stop herself from casting an eye down at the large bump in the middle of her shift.

"That's about right," Sister Mary nodded. "And then you need to leave here and become something amazing, Saumya," she added, using her name in a way she almost never did, "that's what I mean by *better*. Become famous and rich and powerful, and let all those small-minded"—Sister Mary glanced quickly left and right to check there were no other nuns around—"bastards in Ayodhya know that you are better than them and their prejudices."

Saumya could not help but give up a small grin at the sister's foul language, which seemed so alien coming out of her mouth. The grin might even have been a chuckle, if she could have felt anywhere near as hopeful for her future as Sister Mary was. "I do not even know where I might go when I leave here," she said gloomily.

"Well, you had best get to thinking about that when you are sitting in your window or doing your chores." Sister Mary pointed, and Saumya followed the sister's finger to her own belly, gently moving the fingers of her left hand across the bump as the sister spoke again. "Because once that child comes out, we'll have done all that we agreed to do for you."

CHAPTER 17

NOW

Mohammed was fussing, he knew that he was fussing, and had been doing it all morning. Not normally the most helpful with tidying the house, he had been working his way back and forth in the family room and breakfast nook of their single-story home in Oakland. The thing was, no matter how much tidying he did, their home was going to look just the same: tired, run-down, the home of an illegal immigrant and a cab driver.

He popped his head into the kitchen. "How's it going?" he asked his wife, Farha, who was tending a bubbling pot that was giving off a strong scent of coriander. His nervous stomach grumbled.

"The same as the last time you asked," she replied testily. "Now, will you stop fretting? You would think that this girl is royalty. If she has come from an orphanage in India, I'm sure that our food and our house will be perfectly good enough for her."

"She is living in an apartment over by the hospital," Mohammed pointed out. Where Gia lived was a much nicer area than where they lived, but then almost anywhere across the other side of the bay was.

"Well, I'm very pleased for her," Farha told him acidly.

Mohammed decided not to push the point any further—he had been living somewhere around the edge of his wife's goodwill all morning.

"Are you going to give her that picture?" Farha asked just a little too casually.

Mohammed nodded warily, wishing that he had ducked back out of the kitchen a little quicker. "I got a frame," he informed her with forced cheeriness.

"How come you've never shown those pictures to your own sons before today?" she asked, getting straight to her point. "Or me?"

Mohammed waved a dismissive hand and backed out of the kitchen. "I told you this before," he called back. "Our life started here. Hers . . ."

He left the thought hanging, which was sometimes a good trick with Farha, but then heard the utensil she had been holding clatter to the counter, and his wife followed him out and into the family room apparently not wanting to let go of it. "It's not fair, Mike," she said, using the American name that he had adopted when he first came to the United States and that almost everybody called him. With Gia, he had chosen to be "Mohammed," the name that he had been born with and had carried for over half of his life. There had been an odd sort of freedom in doing so, although a selfish one, he had to admit. "You've shut your own wife and children out all these years, but you are letting her straight in."

"Not today," he said to her in a hoarse voice, "please."

His plea seemed to work, and he saw his wife's temper cooling. "If not now, then when?" she sighed, a half-hearted parting shot, but then she looked up at the clock and changed the subject. "Is it not time you should be picking her up from the station?" she asked.

Mohammed looked at the clock, too, then across to the hallway that led through to his two boys' bedrooms. "Just make sure the boys are ready, okay?" he told her. "Zayn was still in his pajamas the last time I checked."

As he drove the cab toward the station, Mohammed thought of how much easier it had been when he had met Gia for breakfast in the city, only the two of them. His wife and children represented one world, while Gia represented another, and he was not so sure that he was ready for these two worlds to come together. Scratch that, he wasn't sure they *ever* should. Of course, Gia was rightfully curious about the rest of her family, and he had no right to keep her from it. Nonetheless, all day Mohammed had been possessed of this eerie, shivery feeling that the past was reaching its bony hands out for him, like it wasn't done with him yet.

"I told you that you did not have to come and pick me up," Gia scolded Mohammed as she opened the car door at the station. "I could have got the bus from the station; I am getting very good at using the public transportation around here."

Mohammed swatted away her protest. "I pick people up for a living. I cannot drive my own niece?"

Gia grinned affectionately and then settled into the seat and reached for her belt. The way she smiled at him, showing the gap in her front teeth, filled Mohammed with warmth and, for the moment, chased away his doubts like the light chases away the darkness.

"I'm looking forward to meeting my cousins," Gia said once they were underway. "Zayn and . . . Hassan?" she checked.

Mohammed had named his oldest son over sixteen years ago, yet still a small shiver went down his spine as he heard her say the name. All he did by way of reply was to nod and let her know that she was correct.

"So much new family at once," she said enthusiastically.

"I warn you that your cousins are lazy, American-born boys," Mohammed said, inwardly chastising himself for his lack of loyalty even as he said it. "But I love them anyway," he added.

"I must admit that I'm looking forward to having a home-home-cooked Indian meal too," Gia told him.

Mohammed nodded his agreement. "My wife is a good cook," he told her, feeling a little bit more loyal as he said it. "It is why I married her."

Gia laughed. "Then maybe she can help me. I find myself afraid of my kitchen, and I'm spending too much money on takeout food." The smile faded just a little. "Sometimes I feel guilty about how much I'm spending here. Money is . . . not the same."

"Is work still going well?" Mohammed asked her, intentionally changing the subject.

That seemed to bring Gia out of her temporary malaise, although the grin she gave him was a sheepish one. "I nearly got fired," she admitted, and Mohammed almost choked on his own surprise.

"That's . . . What?"

"I . . . how do you say it?" Gia said, reaching for the right phrase. "That is it: I stood up from my principles."

Mohammed cackled; the scoff of the longer lived and wiser of the two. "*For* your principles? Well, that will be your mistake. Silly girl, I wouldn't do that again."

They both laughed, and afterward settled into an easy silence for the rest of the drive.

"Thank you, Aunty," Gia said politely to Farha as she finished the last of her food. "This is the best meal I've had . . . Well, in a very long time. I mean it."

Mohammed was pleased to see his wife smile appreciatively. The way to Farha's heart was most certainly to compliment her cooking. Gia moved to help with the clearing up, but Farha generously waved her away.

"The two of you should go and talk in the yard," she told them. "The boys can help me with the dishes."

The boys did not look particularly happy about this, but Mohammed was at least pleased that they got up to help without complaint, although the *way* that they got up told a different story, their limbs drooping the way teenagers' limbs often did. Mohammed and Gia headed out to the backyard, with Mohammed casting a doubtful look at the clouds that had rolled in, gray-blue and engorged.

Once they were settled into the white-plastic garden seats, and thinking that he felt comfortable about the way things had gone so far, Mohammed said, "I am glad that we are able to do this. It seems well past time; I wish I could have brought you here before—over to America, I mean."

Gia shrugged as she sipped at her cold drink. "I owe Sonia Shah a lot, I know that." Mohammed saw Gia grimace. Her employer's name had unsettled him again, but he waited patiently for what else she had to tell him. Sure enough, a few moments later Gia asked, "Can I tell you a secret?"

Mohammed inclined his head, feeling the butterflies fluttering in his stomach.

"I'm dating a boy," she told him.

"I remember. Still on, is it?"

"Yes, sort of. But . . . he is Sonia's stepson."

Mohammed choked on his drink, splattering his mouthful everywhere. Gia looked suitably abashed, even before he spoke. "That's . . . Oh, Gia. You've got a nose for trouble."

Gia silently nodded her agreement.

His heart racing, Mohammed searched for how to go on. He wanted at once to reprimand her, to plead with her, and also to tell her all the good reasons that this was a bad idea. "Look, you're an adult, and I'm in no position to tell you your business. But . . ."

"I know . . ." Gia cut in a little dismissively.

Despite the internal horror that was still lingering, Mohammed almost laughed at the way she had said those two words. "That's exactly what your father would say when he was about to ignore me," he told her without really thinking.

Gia looked up, her eyes alert at the mention of her father, a subject that Mohammed had always been reluctant to talk about with her. With anyone. A long moment passed between them while Mohammed silently admonished himself.

"Did he do that a lot?" Gia asked eventually. "Ignore you?"

"Most of the time," Mohammed answered with a distant smile.

"About my mother?"

Mohammed was taken aback, but it was to be expected, he guessed. He could kid himself that he was enough for her, that spending time with her uncle and his family was the only reason that she was here, but *of course* she had come seeking more than a life in America, she had come seeking answers. He had avoided giving the answers she wanted for these last few years of occasional phone calls, but now that she was here, in his world, it made sense that Gia would expect to finally get what she had been after for so long. All the same, Mohammed did what he was good at and changed the subject, although only enough to make it seem like he wasn't really changing the subject at all. "I found some photos from home," he told her. "Your grandparents, your father."

"Yes-yes," Gia said, sitting up eagerly.

"I should have got them out before," Mohammed said as they rose and made their way back inside and into his and Farha's bedroom. He pulled out a box from on top of a tall dresser and took out a stack of photos, careful to only slightly open the top of the box and then quickly close it afterward. He began placing the photos on a low plywood table as they sat next to each other on the bed.

"This is your grandfather and grandmother," he said, pointing to the grainy black-and-white picture with his parents standing outside the family home where he'd grown up. "They . . . they would have died by the time you were twelve, both of them."

Gia eyed him, and he could almost see the questions forming on the tip of her tongue, so he pushed quickly on, bringing out the picture that he knew she would be waiting for. "And this is me with your father." How young the two of them looked—it would have been one of the last photos taken of them together. Like boys, they were, one an image of a dark-haired youth with a shy smile, another of a taller man that was clearly Mohammed, laughing at something, his eyes squinting into tiny slits.

Gia took the photo from him with eager fingers, clearly fascinated.

"Oh-oh . . ." Mohammed said, pulling out a photo that he had intentionally put right at the bottom of the pile so that he would know where it was. "You can have this one of him to take with you."

He handed over a photo of his younger brother that had been taken in the Buddha garden on the outskirts of the city where they grew up. The picture had been snapped only months before his death, and Mohammed could not help but dwell on how much more handsome his little brother had been than him. *You the attractive artist, brother, me the plain academic.* In some ways, both brothers had died shortly after the picture was taken. "Mike" was the man who had arrived in the United States.

"Are you sure?" Gia asked him breathlessly, although he could hear the hunger in her voice. The desire to own her father's likeness.

"Of course," he told her. "I scanned a copy of it, anyway. Well, Hassan did it for me." He got to his feet. "And I bought a little frame that should fit . . ."

Mohammed went back into the family room, looking for the frame that he was sure was in the drawer in the sideboard. Farha came out from the kitchen to see what he was doing.

"Did you see where I put the frame?" he asked.

Farha held it up, and Mohammed reached for it, but she snatched it away, an action that was almost childish in its execution, like she was playing the part of the schoolyard bully. "Remember what I said about opening up to your own family?"

Even though Mohammed did not reply, she let him take it at the second grab. "Grow up, woman," he grumbled ineffectually.

As he turned back to return to his niece, Gia walked quickly from the bedroom and came into the hallway with them. Straightaway, Mohammed could see shock stretched across her pretty features.

"I have it," he said brightly, holding up the frame for her. Why did she look so upset? She couldn't possibly have heard him and Farha arguing.

Gia stopped, looking between Mohammed and Farha as if she hadn't quite heard him. Almost as if she did not know where she even was. "I'm so sorry, I must go," she told him. "My, er . . . My friend from work is needing me. Terribly urgent-important." She was a terrible liar. Gia turned to Farha. "Thank you very much for the meal and all your hospitality." She turned back to Mohammed. "And for the picture. I am sorry to run off so soon."

Farha nodded, her expression as bemused as Mohammed felt. "I'll give you a ride," Mohammed said, noticing the splatter of raindrops against the window.

Gia, however, seemed to be having none of it and waved her hands in a very definite negative gesture. "No-no. She's not far from here. I . . . Sorry. Thank you."

And with that she backed out of the front door in what could be considered an extremely rushed and rude exit, leaving Mohammed and his wife still looking at each other in confusion.

"What the hell were you showing her in there?" Farha demanded after a moment.

"Nothing," Mohammed replied, but rushed back into the bedroom to find the shoebox that he had so carefully closed after removing the photos now open, a handwritten letter on top of it.

"Oh," he said, his finger reaching out and brushing the top of it. "Oh shit."

PART II

PART II

CHAPTER 18

In contrast with the rest of the smart office building in which Golden State Weddings & Events was located, the service corridor and fire escape at the rear of building was exceedingly unimpressive. In fact, the bare concrete facade, along with the odor of piss and the cigarette butts scattered around the entrance, reminded Gia of areas around her hometown. Not in a good way, of course.

She, Dolly, and Sonia were standing near the exit, beyond which was parked a rented U-Haul truck, and Sonia was currently midrant. "This is what you get when you work for so-called friends," she grumbled. "They pay you a small retainer fee and are then surprised every time you tell them that something will cost extra."

Out of the corner of her eye, Gia saw Dolly open her mouth to speak, but Sonia cut her off before she could even get a syllable out. Gia's gaze, for her part, was fixed entirely on Sonia. Perhaps she had the look of a suck-up, one of those employees who hung on her boss's every word, in case it contained genuine nuggets of career gold.

But it wasn't that.

"And then they want to add about a hundred-million things last minute, just assuming that you can magic every single one of them into being like Marvo the Marvelous Magician, or something. I mean, padded-bloody-sumo wrestlers . . . *Really?*"

Sonia paused, so Dolly took a short intake of breath as if ready to speak, but again was too slow.

"I bet he wouldn't be doing this to some damned event firm out of Palo Alto or San Jose," Sonia raged on, before turning on her heel and stalking back toward the building.

How can it be you? How? Bile choked her. In a short amount of time, Gia had gone from idolizing this woman to defying her to finding something else that lay between fear and respect. And yet it was like she had known, perhaps even within minutes of meeting her, that she would never love her. Sonia Shah was too . . . *cold.*

How? How can it be you? Yet every ounce of sense that Gia had within her knew that the conclusion she had come to as she had fled her Uncle Mohammed's house was true. The handwriting on the letter had given it away, but now everything else slotted into place. How many Indian orphans conveniently land an out-of-the-blue internship at a business like Golden State Weddings & Events?

Gia coughed out a bitter laugh that caused Dolly to glance at her. Global Equality Initiative program. Yeah, right. Gia got the job because she and this impressive but unlikeable woman were . . .

The letter had been in the shoebox—a probably decades-old cardboard box, yellowed with age—which held photos and memorabilia. Mohammed had been showing her photos from it, but maybe hadn't expected her to dig further once he was not in the room. It had belonged to her father, she supposed. *Hassan.* His name almost had a taste to it whenever it left her tongue—which it only did when she was on her own, of course. What did desire and yearning taste like? She was sure it was like that. By dying young, he had almost been deified in her mind.

Hassan, I feel like we were one before we ever met, the letter had said. *Although I should be scared, I am not. This child growing inside me is a part of you. I will love it always and we will raise our child together.*

And Gia recognized the handwriting at once—it was so neat and precise it struck Gia the first time she'd seen it, in the note that had welcomed her to San Francisco. It struck her again each time she'd seen it written across memos, purchase orders, and sticky notes all over the office. It was undoubtedly, irrefutably Sonia's.

Everything fell into place that moment at her uncle's. *That* was why she'd been offered the job, *that* was why she'd received the plane ticket, the apartment. Her mother had known where she was. But for how long? And why hadn't she identified herself to Gia?

Though it seemed so impossible, the idea of it—that this icicle of a woman had once been so much in love—the *reality* of it had needed to slowly ferment in her mind all week. A hundred times it had almost come out, yet here she still was, an invisible cork keeping her bottle sealed. Waiting for something, though she didn't know what. For Sonia to embrace her? To look at her in acknowledgment?

In the last few days since discovering the truth, encountering Sonia every day at work had been torturous for Gia. It was as if what little sense of belonging, what little belief and certainty she had allowed herself to cling to had been stripped away. So many years spent as an orphan. Lost. Scared. Alone. Always alone. And this selfish, manipulative woman could have made it better. Years after she had armored her heart and accepted that she had no mother, here she was. How could she ever trust anyone again?

A chilly breeze wafted in as the door was yanked open. Small bumps rose up along Gia's arms.

"Ranveer's bloody friends," Sonia tossed over her shoulder as she left, the words echoing back off the cool, bare walls before Sonia disappeared out of sight.

Gia turned to Dolly, who was letting out a long, slow breath. "I thought money was no object for Mr. Khosla with his daughter's sixteenth birthday party?" Gia asked. A part of her, it turned out, was still present, still cared enough to want to understand the world and the job she had, supposedly, been brought all the way from India to do.

Dolly huffed and spoke as if she was saying something that was plainly obvious. "Rich people say shit they don't mean all the time. Wish I could afford to be that insincere."

"Well," Gia argued, "his daughter did triple the guest list just two days ago, so that would mean more revenue."

"You shouldn't make excuses for him," Dolly shot back, as if taking Sonia's side on the whole matter.

Having met Samar "Sam" Khosla—a spindly man with a loud voice and I'm-too-good-for-this overtones—Gia had no particular affection for him, yet she found herself arguing on the Silicon Valley entrepreneur's behalf. Or, maybe she was only really arguing *against* Sonia. "Mahi invited her whole high school year group," she pointed out, referring to Sam Khosla's daughter—the birthday girl.

Dolly sneered. "She goes to Parker-Robbins," she told Gia. "It's an exclusive private school with probably only about thirty kids in each year group. Anyway, he'll pay—they bought the Full Fabulous Wedding package even though it is a single party." She arched an eyebrow, indicating the three-ton truck that was almost two-thirds full with additional seating and tables. "He sold his company to Apple for, like, a gazillion dollars or something. Sonia just hates the level of disorganization that comes with last-minute anything. Well," Dolly adjusted, "unless it's her own last-minute bit of inspiration. But that hardly ever happens because the woman is the most organized person in the universe."

Dolly's observation about Sonia made Gia glance back down the dank corridor toward where Sonia had disappeared a few moments before. "It must be easy for her to be so organized when she does not have any children." Gia sniffed.

"She has two, actually," Dolly pointed out. "Children, that is. Both grown-up."

Gia's reply was an acid one. "They are not *hers*, though."

Dolly, who was quite capable of disagreeing and arguing on just about any subject quite pleasantly, finally began to look a little nonplussed by the way Gia was speaking. After a moment, though, she just shrugged. "I guess. Let's get in the truck. I'll let you drive if you like," she added with a mischievous grin.

It had the desired effect, and Gia raised her eyebrow, amused and interested by the idea.

"Only kidding, of course," Dolly added quickly. "You should look into getting your license, though, if you're going to be staying here. Did you drive in India?"

Gia blushed. "Well . . . once. I drove someone to the hospital."

"Without a license?"

"Without ever having driven before," Gia admitted. "I was the oldest orphan present, and we were at a park, away from the orphanage, so the nun could not leave everyone else alone. It was really hard."

The two of them got into the truck, and, as Gia settled into the passenger seat, Dolly gave her a light slap on the arm. "You're bad to the bone, girl, bad to the bone."

Gia glanced backward out of the rented U-Haul truck—Chad had already gone ahead in the smaller company van. "Is Sonia not coming with us?" Gia asked. She doubted that Sonia would not be coming to the event, yet a small hope bloomed within her at the thought of not having to be around Sonia all day.

"She's taking her own car," Dolly said. "That silly little electric thing."

Gia decided that she was, after all, relieved that Sonia was coming. She could not imagine her, Dolly, and Chad all overseeing an event of this size, which was larger than some of the weddings that the company arranged—or so Dolly had told her.

Gia had gathered that Sam Khosla, the client, was an old business friend of Ranveer's from Sonia's husband's early days in recruitment. While Ranveer had already gone on to great success as a specialty headhunter by the time Sonia had met him, Sam Khosla—whose heart had not really been in recruitment—had done very little until seven years ago, when he started a company that Sonia did not really understand but that apparently did something very clever with domain-name acquisition.

They had lost touch until Sam Khosla had looked up Ranveer for the first time since his early retirement and suggested a game of golf, and what had previously been one of Ranveer's many fads became his new obsession. So, *of course*, when they were out on the course two months ago and Sam Khosla had said, "Hey, doesn't your wife do events?" Sonia had subsequently been pretty much bullied into accepting the job.

Which explained Sonia's current foul mood.

"Right," Dolly said, backing the truck out of the parking lot, "are you ready for this, Gia? I reckon it's going to be one heck of a day."

Gia nodded, even though—as had been the case quite a lot this week—her thoughts were mostly elsewhere. Little did she know that Dolly was making a huge understatement.

Standing at a vantage point on the terrace, Gia looked out over the football field–size garden of the Khoslas' waterside property, which petered out as it ran into San Francisco Bay, with a couple of inflatable dinghies tied to a wooden dock. The sun was slipping behind low clouds as Gia and Dolly scanned the result of their day's efforts. A huge white marquee had been erected with roses, floating candles, feathers, and bubblegum-pink and cream confetti, with all the decor worked around a "pretty in pink" theme—which, although it was not Sonia's first choice, had worked with a tasteful infusion of rose-gold details here and there.

The birthday girl was Mahi, and her mother—Anita Khosla—had wanted the pink theme. Apparently she had a penchant for pink. She always wore pink clothes accessorized with a pink bag and hot-pink fingernail polish. Personally, Gia thought it was a bit much every time she saw her in the office. But who could argue with the rich and their idiosyncrasies?

Sonia had given them a running checklist of the items that needed to be taken care of: seating charts, the *M* for Mahi ice sculpture, Bollywood and pop-song playlist for the DJ, Indian street food stands, pasta and sushi stations, liquid-nitrogen-churned ice-cream bar, a minimum of two waitstaff to man every station, and fireworks to end the party. Oh, and the sumo-suit wrestling, of course. Close to the stage was a table holding a huge pile of party favors—embroidered purse pouches that had come all the way from Jaipur in India, although Gia was struggling to think of this as the exotic extravagance that everyone else seemed to think it was.

Gia snapped a picture of the table for the Instagram story of the event. #BehindTheScenes. "I cannot believe that there was not any of this here this morning." She beamed. "Just look at what we have done."

Dolly grinned with satisfaction too. "We are in the business of creating miracles, it's true. Did I tell you about the wedding we did where the bride insisted on having white tigers on bejeweled leashes? Some heiress of an Ayurvedic jam empire—" She stopped, pointing to beyond the tent, to where some familiar faces were walking along the garden toward them. "Oh look, Ranveer is here with Adi." Dolly turned to Gia. "Have you met Sonia's son yet? Very handsome."

Panic gripped Gia, like a thousand vultures swirling in the sky. "In the office the other day." *And in his bed before that.* Unprepared for this, she felt an overwhelming need to escape. "I-I . . . um, need to use the restroom, really quickly. You know, ladies' things. Look, the guests are starting to arrive too . . ." She held up her phone for illustration. "I need to get back quick to capture it for the story." With that babbling excuse, Gia rushed off, feeling that she had been far too verbose and sure that she could feel Dolly's suspicious eyes on her back.

Making her way up the slope toward the back of the house, Gia decided that she actually *did* need to go to the bathroom as she headed past the pool and the oversize pool house that stood next to it. She had nearly reached the sliding doors into what the Khoslas called their "snug" room—which was, in fact, vast, two stories high, and with a mezzanine level running along one side—when a familiar figure came rushing toward her from along the side of the house. Gia wasn't quite sure how he had gotten there so quickly, unless he had suddenly broken into a sprint in front of everybody, racing around the other side of the pool to head her off. Yeah, that wouldn't look suspicious!

"What are you doing here?" she demanded.

Her abruptness changed his features at once. "Dad asked . . . well, insisted. He's good friends with Sam Khosla."

"I was going to the restroom," Gia said, wincing at her automatic need to explain herself. His being here was too complicated, and she desperately wanted him to be elsewhere. Ironic, perhaps, after she had been so addicted to him. Addicted enough that she had been able to forgive the two days it took for him to get back to her after they had slept together. She had not seen him for a week since that awkward moment in the office.

But since he'd broken the ice with his "Shit, this is weird" text, they had fallen into a pleasurable back-and-forth exchange, gently dancing around the fact that they had such intimate knowledge of each other yet, in truth, did not know each other so well. That perhaps it was right to slow things down and not see each other for a few days—or this was how Gia had been reading it.

In those few days, Gia had become a slave to the joy of seeing a text from Adi—the rush of anticipation and pleasure that came with opening it, the reading and rereading and teasing every bit of meaning from the few sentences he had written. And all the while, she had dreamed of being with him again.

But now things were reversed. He had not changed and neither had she, yet she wished him anywhere else while he looked at her expectantly, something like adoration in his eyes. She had once wanted that and bathed in it when it came; now she wanted to hide from it. "Is that so," Adi said breathlessly, managing to flash that roguish smile of his, "because it looks a lot like you were running away from me."

Gia snorted the way that liars do. "That is . . . just . . . silly."

"You've hardly returned any of my messages all week," Adi pushed, still keeping his tone light.

She swung a hand out to indicate the huge event below them. "I have had a busy, tiring week, you know," she said, trying to use her own tone to make him feel guilty.

Adi reached out his hand and touched Gia's arm. "I know we haven't been seeing each other because of the whole, you know, my stepmother being your boss thing . . . but I've missed you."

Funny, Gia thought, *because before that you kept ghosting me.* But she didn't say that. "I am working!" she said.

Adi's face fell again. "I wasn't trying to say now. Whenever you're . . . you know . . ."

Gia knew that the expression she had been unable to keep from her face was the reason that Adi suddenly had trailed off. His eyes searched her own deeply, a concern there that should have been comforting but, instead, made her feel sick. Gia felt sure that all her emotions were about to come flooding out, that she would lay her terrible secret bare in front of that kind, wholesome face, but then a loud and sudden shouting came to her rescue.

The noise came from next to the pool, and, after a quick glance at each other, Gia and Adi made their way back down the steps and saw the door to the pool house fly open. With a heavy thud of footsteps, out stormed Sam Khosla—dragging a young man with a shock of black hair and a handsome, triangular face by the arm. Somewhere from inside the building, his daughter's voice wailed, "Daddy, stop!"

Still holding the young man tightly by the upper arm, Sam Khosla whirled on his daughter as she came into view. The look on his face verged on murderous. Mahi was adjusting one of the shoulder straps on her dress in a way that needed no explanation in any language. "This is the thanks I get for all of this," Sam Khosla roared. "The fucking pool boy? Could you be more clichéd, girl? Half of the eligible young men in the district will be at your party today, and you're messing around with"—Sam gave the young man, who had gone as limp as a rag doll, a little shake—"this?"

"José gets me," Mahi screeched back at her father, seemingly not as intimidated by the man's rage as José was.

Sam shoved the pool boy away and pointed toward the rear entrance, the same gate through which most of the things for the party had been brought earlier in the day. "Go!" he commanded, before turning back to Mahi. "Well, now he can understand you from the unemployment line." He pointed a finger at her, his eyes narrowed and threatening. "Mahi, you go and sort yourself out; I want you back out in five minutes to attend to your guests. All smiles, you understand me?"

Seeing José heading for the exit seemed to have taken the last of the fight out of Mahi, and she nodded meekly before turning to walk dejectedly along the side of the pool. She passed Gia and Adi, who were rooted to the spot, Gia feeling like a rubbernecker.

Sam Khosla looked after his daughter but either pretended not to see Adi and Gia standing there, or just didn't care that they were. After a moment he turned and walked back down toward the marquee.

"Did you get that?" Adi asked, indicating Gia's phone, which, as always, was in her hand.

"This is serious, Adi," Gia chastised him. "I should tell someone about this—Sonia or Dolly. This is not good. If this family secret comes out now, the party will be ruined. The guests will only be talking about this scandal, not the beautiful arrangements we've put together!"

Adi lightly grabbed her arm again. "Look, in case I don't get a chance to talk to you later, I wanted you to know that Sonia being your boss shouldn't be a problem." He smiled that reassuring, winning smile. "I know it won't be. I'll make sure of it."

The way he said the words, it sounded like he meant something specific by them, but she didn't have time for that now, knowing that she had to get to Dolly or Sonia and let them know what she had seen.

CHAPTER 19

"Kids these days," harrumphed Ranveer as he watched the birthday girl, Mahi, walk sulkily up onto the small stage at the front of the white marquee. The marquee was packed with party guests, many of whom had been dancing on the dance floor that had been laid out in front of the stage and, like something out of a seventies disco, was spilt into squares that lit up with different colors. The DJ had been playing for almost two hours, and Adi was in the middle there somewhere, although Gia had lost track of where.

"Look how miserable she is," Ranveer went on, "and her father has done all of this for her birthday."

Sonia shushed her husband and pointed to Chad, who was standing a few feet away from the rest of them on a small set of steps, filming the proceedings and the upcoming speech.

"*We* have done all of this for her," Sonia corrected her husband, while keeping her voice low.

Gia had to agree; as far as she could tell, everything about the party seemed to be going well. All the teenagers and their parents—the latter appearing at least as important to Sam Khosla as the kids were—looked like they were having a great time. Gia had watched them separate into different groups at the start of the evening, naturally forming into little tribes—the sporty kids with their buzz cuts and bulging biceps, and the more intellectual ones with plates full of sushi instead of *seekh* kebabs. The silver-haired, arty-farty parents who sported rimless glasses, the business-tycoon parents with their Rolexes and Botoxed foreheads, and Palo Alto's core of Indian social elite (the Aunty Army, as Dolly referred to them) who'd initially gathered to look snootily over the spread being offered before drifting apart into small groups, giving each other air kisses and backhanded compliments. "How was Croatia, darling?" "Great! Did Sid have any fun in Machu Picchu with his orphanage volunteering?" "You know, the kids had never been to a jungle safari before, so we . . ." This was, Dolly had informed her, a potential new source of clientele for the company. The food was good, the drink plentiful, the music just right—and all their hard work was being blessed by great California weather, the setting almost dreamlike under an azure sky that was taking on the color of slate in the twilight.

"You know what I mean," Ranveer said, at least now remembering to keep his voice quieter. "How many children's fathers would pay for such a lavish event? Yet she looks like someone has just slapped her. It must be embarrassing for poor Sam."

Gia noticed Sonia mock her husband's comments while he looked in the opposite direction and then mouth something along the lines of "Poor Sam, my ass." What she actually said a moment later was, "You were here earlier, were you not, when Gia told us about the pool boy?" Her tone was exasperated.

"And I would have thrown him out too," Ranveer replied. "No daughter of mine would risk getting herself pregnant with someone she could never marry."

Ranveer remained oblivious while Sonia continued to stare at her husband with what looked like a certain sort of amazement. "Such a romantic," she muttered loudly. "Don't be so sour."

Ranveer answered overly patiently, like he was generously explaining something obvious. "It doesn't matter how wealthy your father is, the wrong boy can ruin a girl's life. And, anyway, that girl's long face is not advertising the party you put on so well, is it?"

Gia noted how Ranveer had brought the conversation back to Sonia's business. It had the air of a long-used tactic during husband-wife disagreements.

Sonia pursed her lips. "I think the party speaks for itself, thank you very much. And everyone else seems to be enjoying it."

"Especially Adi," Ranveer observed, pointing to where his son was standing in the middle of the dance floor as the song faded out. Even from most of the length of the tent away, Gia thought that Adi looked a little drunk—as well as hot and sweaty from all the dancing he had been doing. The sight of him like that set off little pangs inside her, tiny aches like the ones muscles get when one has flu. They were not thoughts that she should be having.

"A little too much, I think," Sonia told Ranveer in a disapproving mother kind of way.

"Now who's being sour?" Ranveer prodded back. When he went on, there was a note of pride in his voice. "See how he has been the center of attention, my handsome boy." Gia couldn't stop herself from slumping slightly as Ranveer pointed out what she had already been witnessing.

"These girls are all a little bit young for him, don't you think?" Sonia stated.

"I was talking about some of the Silicon Valley housewives," Ranveer shot straight back with a grin, causing Sonia to laugh despite herself and turn to lightly punch her husband on the arm.

Gia had, in fact, noticed that one of the women—who had been dancing close to Adi more than any of the others had—was neither young nor old. She was, as far as Gia could see, just the right age and far too pretty and athletic looking in her fitted jumpsuit with sequins and pearls.

As the music cut, there was a second or so of loud microphone feedback when the DJ handed the microphone to Sam Khosla, who took it clumsily. He turned to the crowd with a slight swagger and a definite flushed look, which Gia put down to the heat of the tent and the quality of the cocktails.

"Thank you all for coming," Sam Khosla said to the gathered crowd after clearing his throat. "I just want to say a few words about my wonderful daughter and how proud I am of her."

Dolly leaned across and whispered into Gia's ear. "The lies we tell, eh?" Gia glanced over at Sonia.

"However," Sam Khosla went on, "she's reluctantly agreed to thank you all herself first."

Sam Khosla's little joke got a few chuckles throughout the crowd, mostly from the parents. He turned to his daughter, and Mahi stepped forward to take the microphone, looking every bit the shy teenager in a watermelon-pink *lehnga* as she nervously twisted the ends of her *chunni* that was draped over one shoulder. Gia briefly wondered if the girl had been drinking, as well, perhaps drowning her sorrows over her lost pool-boy love. She lifted her phone to take a picture for Instagram, then stopped herself when she thought of the likely hashtag that would accompany it. #SadSixteenth.

Mahi glanced back at her father for a moment, who smiled and nodded encouragingly at her. When Mahi turned to the crowd again, her face had hardened and her apparent shyness was gone.

"My dad reminded me today that turning sixteen is not all about fun and parties," she told her peers and their parents, sounding very grown-up. There were a few good-natured noises of disagreement from the teenagers present, while the proud smile that had been lingering on Sam Khosla's face appeared to freeze slightly.

As Mahi spoke again, she did so through slightly gritted teeth. "I'm growing up now, and growing up is about taking responsibility and doing the right thing. And, for an Indian family—even if you are born and raised here—it is about making your family proud and not bringing shame upon them."

The mood in the marquee was changing, and the crowd was now getting the sense that this was not going to be a sparkling or fun—or probably even shyly cute—speech, although a few were still looking hopefully for the punch line.

Mahi took a long, shuddering breath and turned back to her father. "And that works both ways, doesn't it, Dad? Both ways."

With that, the birthday girl shoved the microphone back into her father's hands and stalked off, the hem of her designer *lehnga* trailing behind her as her actions sent a wave of shocked murmurs through the gathering.

Chad chose that moment to suddenly appear right next to Gia, evidently having stopped filming. He was chewing noisily on a stick of celery, annoyingly close to her ear. "Worst Oscars speech ev-er," he said.

Sonia turned and narrowed her eyes at him. "Not funny, Chad." With that, Sonia walked off, and, noticing, Ranveer followed her.

"I wonder what Mahi meant with that?" Gia wondered out loud.

On the stage, the clearly shell-shocked Sam Khosla was doing his best to recover his poise. "Ladies and gentlemen, I give you the mysteriousness of youth." The joke was met with a murmur of nervous laughter, which contained the odd thread of relief running through it. "I'm sure the birthday girl will be back with us soon," he went on. "In the meantime . . . more dancing!"

Gia leaned over to Dolly. "I'm not sure whether to keep clicking and posting."

"Maybe it would be better if we went and found the birthday girl," Dolly replied. "Not sure if that was where Sonia went off to, but we could try and smooth things over if we get to Mahi first; we'll probably be more sensitive than Sonia will. You should come, she might be more likely to talk to someone closer to her age."

Out of the corner of her eye, Gia saw Adi begin to make his way off the dance floor and start to head in their direction. Gia started, her body pulsing with a complicated mix of conflicting emotions.

"I thought we were not supposed to become involved in the lives of the clients," Gia said a little distractedly. The moment she spoke the words, she regretted them, because looking for Mahi was a perfect excuse to get away before Adi reached them.

"It's okay if they're screwing up the event," Dolly told her with a cheeky grin. "Don't worry, you won't get fired for this one, I promise."

All the while Gia could see Adi moving swiftly toward them, and she now realized that it was too late to get away.

Adi looked at Chad and then straight past Gia—not even meeting her eyes—to Dolly. "Where's my mother?" he asked.

Chad thumbed over his shoulder, still munching away on the last bit of celery. "Went that way."

Adi carried on, still not looking at Gia and barely breaking stride. Her world started spinning, like she was spiraling downward into the ground. *Uffff,* why was everything so difficult?

"Come on," Dolly prompted, "let's go find her."

"Wait!" Chad called out. He pointed to the stage and at the same time started to bring up his camera. Mahi had returned to the front of the tent, her father now not anywhere in sight, and she was reaching over and taking the microphone from the DJ again, signaling for him to bring down the music. When Mahi turned, Gia could see that the girl had been crying, the mascara stains down her cheeks clear—even in the low light and from some distance away.

"I saw you, Dad," Mahi said into the microphone as she looked out over the crowd. A gasp went up from the gathering, followed by loud tittering from the back.

Mahi went on undeterred. "I saw you with Ms. Coates," she said.

"Who the hell is Ms. Coates?" Dolly asked.

"Mahi's tennis coach," Chad said quietly, filming again.

"How do you know that?" Dolly asked, seemingly incensed that Chad knew such an apparently relevant bit of information that she did not.

"I listen," Chad replied with a tiny shrug, trying not to disrupt his filming.

Finally, Mahi spotted her father, who was over to the far right, just within the line of the stretch tent. "I saw you fuck her!" she shouted, while pointing at him. "But it's okay for you, you're only married!"

As shocked as many of the onlookers appeared to be, Gia was also noticing that quite a few of them—especially the Aunty Army—were enjoying this turn of events: parents behaving badly. Many were craning their necks for a glimpse of Anita Khosla—dressed in pink from head to toe—who had been standing next to the stage. She had been smiling beatifically until this revelation, at which point Gia saw her features crumple with hate and pain.

Sam Khosla appeared stuck, apparently not sure whether to try and remove his daughter from the stage or turn and flee the tent.

Mahi swayed slightly on her feet for a few moments, then decided that she was finished, turning now rather meekly to hand the microphone back to the DJ before vanishing out the back of the tent.

"She really hates her dad," Gia observed.

"Or maybe she really loves José," Dolly put in a little wryly.

Chad stopped filming. "It would never have worked with José," he said, sounding like someone who had been getting a little bit too involved in a romantic film. "She would always have had to tell her father eventually."

"Maybe she will run off to be with him," Gia mused out loud.

Chad looked behind them, and Dolly and Gia followed his gaze to see that Sonia was marching back toward them, her face clearly a mask of rage. Adi was following several yards behind, his hands held out wide as if trying to stop her, or protest about something, and Ranveer followed a little farther back again.

"You heard?" Dolly said as Sonia got close to them. "It's turning into a car crash." Then Dolly added, perhaps wanting to appear proactive because Sonia looked about ready to murder someone, her already sheer features pulled even tighter. "Gia and I were going to—"

Dolly didn't get any further, as Sonia completely ignored her, instead walking straight past and right up to Gia, so that their faces were only inches apart. "How dare you!" Sonia spat, a slight whiff of the samosa that Sonia had nibbled on earlier in the day washing across Gia. "How dare you!"

Gia was completely caught off guard by this turn of events, then she looked over Sonia's shoulder and caught Adi's eye as he got closer . . . suddenly, the pieces fell into place. Her stomach flipped—Adi must have just told his stepmother about their relationship.

CHAPTER 20

THEN

"Good news, my girl," Sister Mary said as Saumya lay on her back in what was about to become the convent's delivery room, balanced on a rickety old examination table that was likely older than she was. The makeshift bed creaked alarmingly every time she moved. She could not see the sister, who was currently obscured by the huge bump rising out of Saumya's stomach.

"Don't tell me," Saumya cried out, her voice hoarse with suppressed pain, "it's already out."

From somewhere alarmingly close to her uterus, Sister Mary gave one of her trademark mirthless snorts. "Oh no, this baby's going to be taking his or her time, I can tell. You are in for a long day, young lady." Sister Mary sounded like she was looking forward to an extended period of suffering for Saumya. "And I wish you wouldn't say *it*."

"It, it, it," Saumya shrieked through the ever quicker and intense contractions that racked her body as two more nuns gathered down at the "business end" of things. "What are you all looking at down there? This isn't a public event."

"But it is a teaching opportunity," Sister Mary answered dismissively.

"You said there was good news?" Saumya gasped through the bouts of pain, pushing the image she had concocted of the three nuns staring at her vagina from her mind. The problem was that the wretched, whitewashed walls she had come to hate over the last six months were the only thing to look at, and they were doing their very best to give her a panic attack. Instead, Saumya closed her eyes and imagined she was riding the teacups at Disneyland. She had never done that, of course, but it was an ambition.

"Oh yes," Sister Mary answered absently as Saumya felt herself being prodded down below, "the good news is that your sister is in Shimla; she might even be here in time for the birth."

Bindu is coming! That *was* excellent news. Saumya had not seen her younger sister in the whole six months that she had been stuck in this godforsaken hellhole. It was a small source of bitterness that her sister had not been to see her during the whole pregnancy, but she was coming now, and that was what mattered.

Sister Mary's face appeared like a miserable, joyless sun rising over a shift-covered hillock, framed on either side by Saumya's knees. "How are the contractions?" she asked.

"Like the world's best *fucking* advert for contraception," Saumya said through gritted teeth as a fresh one arrived.

"I mean, how far apart?" the sister replied irritably.

"You never said I was supposed to be counting!" Saumya bellowed as Sister Mary frowned at her and disappeared again. "There isn't even a clock in here; what sort of a delivery room is this?"

"Just count," Sister Agatha instructed from out of sight. "It will help to keep you calm."

"Have any of you done this before?" Saumya asked shrilly. She could not believe that she hadn't even thought of that question until now. They were nuns; she had always assumed they just knew this stuff. All-knowingness was an annoying nun trait she had come to realize during her stay. Then again, *they were nuns*, and as a natural consequence of the life choices they made, babies didn't feature much. "Hello?" Saumya tried again, hysteria snaking into her voice.

"*Didi!*" her younger sister burst out when she arrived in the delivery room, while several nuns were still hovering at the end of the table.

Bindu's voice, that familiar term of endearment, took her back immediately—off the wobbling examination table, down the mountains, and to the safety of home, to the memory of when life was simpler. "Look how big you got!" Bindu went on, smiling and clasping her hand.

"Nuns live well," Saumya joked weakly in reply, reaching up and rubbing the huge mound under the shift she wore, like it was a jolly fat man's belly.

"You're not a nun," Sister Mary pointed out, popping up again from out of sight like one of the targets in a game of Whac-A-Mole. *Whack-a-nun* . . . now, there was a thought. Sister Mary was washing her hands, presumably using water from an unseen enamel bowl. There was something in the practiced way she did this that should have been reassuring, yet it had the air of a dastardly villain rubbing their hands together in anticipation of evil plans about to come to fruition. The sooner the baby came out, the sooner the nuns would be rid of that godless little sinner Saumya—that's what they were probably all thinking. For once, Saumya could not help but agree with the nuns.

"I thought we might have spoken more these past months," Saumya wheezed, trying not to dwell on how she had more than once felt like something out of sight and out of mind all the way up where she was in the mountains. "Do you think I might return home; does not *Amma* wish to see her grandchild?"

All the warmth, all the joy fell from Bindu's face for just a moment, and Saumya realized that it had just been an act—a show for her benefit. The reassuring grin returned almost straight away, although it no longer reached her little sister's eyes. "They barely speak to me, *Didi*. I am a focus for their . . . disappointment."

Saumya's eyes fell from Bindu's, unable to keep looking at them. They had shone much brighter once, she was sure of it, and a note of personal shame mingled with her own disappointment. "Still?" she muttered, and her falling eyes caught a mark across the top of her sister's wrist that had not been there six months before, something long and dark and angry. Suddenly, Bindu snatched the hand back and used the other one to pull the sleeve of her patterned *kurti* so that it covered the scar again.

"How?" Saumya asked. Now it was Bindu who would not meet *her* look.

"Jeet," Bindu answered, giving the name of their brother and oldest sibling. Named for the actor who was known mostly for his villainous roles, he had assumed the role of the head of the household. "When I would not tell him where you were."

"Madarchod!" Saumya hissed.

"Young lady!" Sister Agatha hollered, popping upward again from between Saumya's legs. Saumya wished that she had that chain-tethered mallet handy. "I will not have that language."

"Our bro-bro-ther beat . . . *beat* Bindu because she helped me." Saumya clutched her belly as another contraction hit. "He is a *madar-chod* and more."

"And what did you expect to happen while you were here?" Sister Agatha asked her. "That life for your family would go on just fine?"

"No," Saumya breathed out, impatient, although, in truth, it had been easy to imagine herself forgotten, as if she and Hassan might just disappear from the story of her family back in Ayodhya like faded memories.

"He was just scared," Bindu said quietly, almost like she was making excuses for the brother who had scarred her. "He gets the worst of it from the fanatics. Lost his own wedding match, that big dowry, the plans to move to Delhi."

Saumya had not even thought about Jeet's own match being affected. It seemed unfair that she should be lying on a dilapidated table in a hillside convent, with a missing fiancé and a fatherless child on the way, and yet still have to feel guilt, especially for Jeet of all people. But there it was, a twinge of shame, a feeling of utter selfishness, like she must be the most self-obsessed person in the world. "No chance of going home, then," she stated finally, because, selfish though it might seem, Saumya now understood that she had been holding on to that possibility every day for the past six months, desperate to believe she could at least return to some semblance of her old life . . . that time would again knit together the rifts that had opened.

Now she had a fatherless child with no home, because Sister Mary—and not *only* Sister Mary—had been at pains to point out on a regular basis that she would not be staying for long beyond the birth.

"Where will we go?" Saumya bared her teeth and hissed at the nun, an alien sound that ricocheted off the walls. The contractions were much closer than they had been. It would not be long until it was time to begin pushing in earnest.

"Speak after the birth," Sister Mary cautioned, but the sour old nun's voice was pregnant with meaning that made it seem even more bulbous than her own heaving belly.

"Now," Saumya growled, "or I'll hold the damn thing in, I swear it."

A look passed between Bindu and Sister Agatha that spoke volumes to Saumya, letting her understand without a doubt that the two had colluded on Saumya's possible future. It felt like betrayal, as if she were being treated like an ignorant child incapable of being involved in her life's decisions.

"Well," Bindu began, "I've been in contact with a friend in the United States."

"Of . . . Am-merica?" Saumya asked around a sudden swell of pain.

"Yes, that one. I think I could arrange a job for you there. A new life, if we did it soon."

A maelstrom of thoughts worked their way quickly through Saumya's head in that moment: Terror of the new and fear of forever losing the old preeminent among them. Yet the final thought was a peaceful one, and the corners of her mouth lifted upward, even through the pain.

"I could raise my baby in the USA," she breathed raggedly. *What a life it might have.* But then she looked at Bindu again, whose expression had gone taut.

"It would be only you, *Didi.* I could not get the child in too."

Then no, of course not. No way. Although Saumya did not say that, instead she asked the obvious question. "What would happen to my baby?"

"Not now," Sister Mary growled from out of sight, "it is time for you to concentrate, young woman. Give everything you have to getting this child out of you."

"What would happen to my baby?" Saumya screamed. "What are you going to do to my baby?"

CHAPTER 21

NOW

Sonia was standing in front of Gia, their faces only a few inches apart, her brow scrunched like a caterpillar. Her arm came up, as if she was about to order her employee to immediately leave the party—to be out of her sight—and this was the point at which Gia's shock subsided, and she finally snapped.

"How dare you," she now shot back at Sonia. "Not how dare me; how dare *you!*"

Sonia blinked, thrown by Gia's outburst. It only took her a moment to recover, however. "You have been dating my stepson behind my back," Sonia accused Gia, although *dating* was definitely an overstatement for whatever had been between her and Adi. "Deceiving me."

Gia glanced toward Adi, who stood several paces beyond Sonia's right shoulder. He had the look of someone who had just realized how big the mistake he had made really was. He also, ironically, seemed like Sonia's child in that moment, pushed back into his place by the fury of the parent.

"I trusted you, Gia," Sonia went on, "and after you had let me down once already."

Gia was still looking at Adi as Sonia spoke, her heart getting heavier by the moment. She felt betrayed by him, that was true, even though she already understood that telling Sonia was something he had done with the best of intentions, driven by his feelings for her. It had been selfish and dangerous for her career, even if maybe he had convinced himself that he was doing it for Gia's benefit too. She was coming to understand that love could be self-serving like that.

What seemed unfair, though, was that she was the one who must now feel bad for what she was about to say. She felt so sorry for Adi, so sorry for what she knew she was about to do, even fearful of the hurt and confusion that would soon be plaguing those handsome features. And none of this was her fault, not really. It was the fault of the woman in front of her.

Gia's gaze flicked back to Sonia, and she let out a long, low growl as she tried to find the words she needed. The growl startled everyone present—including Chad and Dolly—none of whom had heard even the faintest stirrings of rage from Gia before.

"You want-want to talk about deceit, do you, Sonia Shah? Or shall I say *Saumya*?"

That hit home exactly as Gia thought it might, and Sonia's face froze. Ranveer, who had only just arrived huffing and panting next to Adi, screwed up his face in confusion, his mustache twitching a little like a rabbit's whiskers. "Saumya? Who the hell is Saumya?"

Gia saw Sonia's face shift as she heard her husband's voice, even though she didn't turn around. The horror faded, replaced by a pleading look, although such an expression looked alien on her usually sharp features, the woman's eyes glistening in desperation. Gia was not, however, in a merciful mood and she stepped forward, poking at Sonia's chest.

"And I had almost started to believe that I was good enough to be here," Gia told her and everyone else listening.

"Gia," Dolly said, her face a mixture of confusion and apprehension, "what are you going on about?"

Gia turned to Dolly, now in furious flow, hurt and angry at everything and everyone about her. "You know, I kept thinking, Why me? How did I get so very-very lucky to land the best job in the world at just the right time, when I was about to be turned out into the street?"

Dolly gave a dismissive half scoff, as if willing the whole thing to be insecurity on Gia's part. "I told you not to worry about that."

"Which even makes me wonder whether you are in on it, too, my new best friend Dolly, who was so shocked by the mole behind my ear. Do you know anyone else with a mole just there? Anything you felt you should tell me?"

Dolly shook her head, taking an involuntary step back from Gia, although Gia could not tell whether it was denial or confusion that reigned on the woman's pretty features.

Gia stepped back and swept her gaze across the others. "And you, funny Chad. And Ranveer and . . ." The next words almost wouldn't come for a moment, yet the possibility of love had been the cruelest part of the deception. "And you, Adi. Are you all in on this?" She knew that they weren't, yet the urge to destroy the house of cards—the *life*—she had been building over the past month by making liars and deceivers of all of them was strong. She wanted to break all of it.

This drama that she didn't understand, which so clearly went beyond Gia dating Sonia's son, was suddenly too much for Dolly. "What is wrong, Gia?" she pressed, her voice almost scathing, like she was telling Gia to stop all this foolishness now.

Gia's eyes fell back on Sonia, whose mouth worked silently a few times before she finally whispered, "No . . . No, don't."

"Don't what?" Gia took a threatening half step toward her. "Don't tell them that you are my mother? That your name is not even Sonia. That you are the world's biggest liar and you left me to rot in a stinking orphanage for my whole childhood while you came here and had . . . had *everything*?" Perhaps, at another time, Gia might have marveled at how she had got so many words out so cleanly, that last repetition not her usual verbal stutter but instead complete incredulity. Rage, apparently, was the key to fluent English.

The color had drained from Sonia's face, and she was now holding a hand out toward Gia, grasping at the air and mouthing the word *no* over and over again. Every time it seemed that Sonia might get close,

Gia shifted slightly, like Sonia's touch would be poison. But then, suddenly, Gia darted forward and brushed the hair away from Sonia's ear, and, like an animal caught in headlights, Sonia let her do it.

Gia glanced across to Dolly. "There is that mole behind my ear you recognized, Dolly . . . Remember that, on my first day?" She pulled back her much longer hair to reveal a mole in almost exactly the same place that Sonia had one behind her own ear. "Just like mine." Gia's heart knocked about like a caught bird. "Yes, I saw Sonia's mole when she bent her head to the water cooler for a drink. At that time I didn't think anything of it." She turned back to Sonia. "But, then I saw the letters at my Uncle Mohammed's house," she went on. "Love letters in your handwriting, Sonia. You cannot deny this." She wasn't.

Ranveer, who had been watching it all unfold with an almost childish bemusement now could not help but join in. "What love letters?"

Her husband's voice brought Sonia back to life, and she turned to Ranveer. "Long ago," she assured him.

"Yes," Gia said, "and long forgotten, just like I was. Until you decided to bring me here and play games with me and lie to me. Have you not already made me suffer enough?"

Each word continued to hit home like a bullet, and Sonia reached out again. "No, Gia. That's not . . ."

Gia turned away, not wanting to hear more lies and unable to stand the sight of the woman any longer. Only then did she realize that half the people under the marquee were watching—her pathetic joke of a life continuing the entertainment in what had already been a most entertaining event for the gossipy clique of the Silicon Valley set.

CHAPTER 22

THEN

Sonia—she had become so used to the name by now, almost as if she had never even had another one—was standing on top of the skyscraper's rooftop terrace. She was enjoying the cool night air outside the vast two-floor penthouse property, where the party was being held. She had never appreciated the value of being outside in fresh air until she had moved to a country that had an almost obsessive relationship with air conditioning. In American public buildings it seemed like an absolute must to walk into a wall of semifrigid air as one entered. At first Sonia had found it to be a pleasant experience, as she had known little air conditioning in her previous life and had arrived in the country at the height of a hot summer, but she soon found her throat always a little too dry, the air she breathed just a little too . . . ventilated. Heading outside at the end of a working day soon became a treat, just so she could savor the outdoors.

She looked down on the city below her, which was expensive looking—shining amber deposits set within a bed of inky blackness—and wondered to herself, not for the first time, how soon it would be okay to leave this work-related soiree without seeming impolite.

"So, what do you do, then?" a deep male voice called out from a little behind her. Even though the impeccable English was smoothly delivered, there was the unmistakable lilt of Indian heritage in there too.

When she had first arrived in the United States, Sonia had fallen instantly in love with the American accent, which seemed so much richer in person than it had on TV and in the movies, yet already she missed the music of her native tongue, perhaps like someone living in the mountains after a life growing up next to the quiet roar of the sea. Reluctantly, Sonia forced herself to turn around, as this was the annual company party at the boss's city residence, and the voice sounded like it belonged to a man old enough to be important within the company that her whole existence in America relied upon. Someone more important than her—which was everyone.

The man she found standing a discreet distance away from her was dressed in an expensive-looking gray suit, the outfit made casual by the collarless white cotton shirt underneath. He had a buzz cut that was a couple of centimeters above military, the dark hair run through with significant streaks of silver, and there was a neatly trimmed mustache that perched proudly on his upper lip. "I've been working on that line all the way across the terrace," the man said. "You would have thought I might have done better than that."

Sonia gave one of her uncertain smiles. She did not recognize him from Clemcon's Mountain View offices, but then she was still a gopher-level worker and had been surprised even to be invited to the annual party. She had blown a whole week's wages on a figure-hugging black dress that she thought did not make her look "too Indian," not knowing why such a concept even mattered to her. It was her first time out of the country, her first time stepping out from under the protection of her family, her first time at a party like this one. Among other shocks, she had been bewildered to find so many Indians so at home in the streets and cafés of San Francisco—and in the hallways and offices of corporate buildings.

She started as the man spoke again. "My name is Shah . . . Ranveer Shah." He paused and looked at her as if the name or the way in which he had said it should have some significance. "Like Bond . . . James Bond?"

Was that like a spy in a movie or something? She had never seen it, so she forced a tight-lipped smile that felt awkward. Finally, she remembered her manners enough to introduce herself. "I'm . . ."

"Sonia," Bindu told Saumya. "Your name is Sonia. You'll need to remember that."

Saumya and Bindu were standing just beyond the entrance to Indira Gandhi Airport, and Saumya frowned at her sister. "I don't understand why I have to change my name. I have not broken any laws, and your friend has gotten me a work visa. This makes me feel like a criminal."

Someone hurrying with too much luggage on a trolley nearly bumped into Bindu, who made a deft sidestep before replying. Saumya looked down at her own small carry-on bag against the mountain of baggage that the man was pushing.

"It's not like that at all. Your work visa is under the name Sonia," Bindu explained patiently—although a little less patiently than the previous five times. "You will understand when you get there, but it is better, if you are not white or obviously do not come from America, to do everything you can to fit in. It will make things easier if everyone is not trying to figure out how to pronounce your name all the time."

"But my name is easy to pro—"

"Plus," Bindu pressed on, "it will help because . . . you know . . ."

Bindu had trailed off, but—perhaps for the last ever time, Saumya realized—she had read her sister's thoughts the way she had been able to for almost all their lives.

"Because I'm starting a new life," Saumya finished for her. "Leaving my old one behind." When she had started speaking, Saumya felt almost in control of her emotions—matter of fact, almost—but suddenly a loud sob escaped her, causing a passing child holding a parent's hand to glance briefly up at her. "And leaving my daughter," Sonia added. "So I can forget that I am doing that."

Bindu's face fell, guilt spreading across it. "Don't," Bindu whispered, barely audible over an airport announcement in Hindi. "You know it was the child's best chance."

Saumya did not want to make her sister feel guilty. It was hard and confusing to at once be so furious with her, to feel so betrayed by the choices Bindu had made on her behalf, and yet to know that her sister was also doing everything she could to help her. "But we don't know what they will do with her, where they will send her," Saumya pressed still. These had been her almost constant waking thoughts for weeks now.

"To a loving, wealthy foster family, perhaps," Bindu tried brightly.

Unlikely, but then, who knew? That was part of the horror of not knowing, that it was equal parts hope and despair, that her feelings were so binary in nature. Saumya's lips continued to tremble, but she had no more words, and time seemed to be slipping away from them. Bindu stepped forward and placed a slender-fingered hand on her shoulder, and Saumya felt her touch like a calming scent.

"You deserve this new chance," Bindu told her. "Go and have an amazing life and do amazing things, *Didi*." Bindu's heartwarming final speech was ruined when her lips began to tremble as well. "No, not *Didi*," Bindu corrected herself. "Not my big sister anymore. Not Saumya. Go now. Go and be . . ."

"Sonia Pandey," she told the silver-haired gentleman who had introduced himself as Ranveer. "And I . . . I do nothing very interesting." Sonia put a hand up to her mouth, suddenly feeling that underselling her job in this way might have been the wrong thing to say. "Administration," she tried, then plowed on, "minor accounting." Her mind raced, but she quickly realized that she didn't really have anything inspiring to say about her job. "A dull-dull person in a company of creatives," she finished with a tight smile.

"Whoa, stop selling yourself there, Sonia," Ranveer said jovially. Sonia smiled despite herself. "But you should see me with a spreadsheet. I am a master of conditional formatting. And formulas. No one writes a formula like I can write a formula."

Ranveer's face lit up and he laughed, a deep, warm sound that went on long enough to seem genuine. He appeared pleased that she was already coming out of her shell. "Girl, your ego is writing checks your paperwork skills can't cash."

Sonia's eager smile dropped. She was utterly confused. "I . . . Sorry?"

"I was, um . . . How do you say . . . ? Paraphrasing a film. *Top Gun* with Tom Cruise; have you seen it?"

"I've heard of Tom Cruise," Sonia answered. Who hadn't? "But I am not watching films much."

Ranveer cocked his head to the side, and a broad smile spread outward from the center of his face. "Well, we shall have to do something about that," he told her. He continued to look at her appraisingly, and, after a few moments, Sonia began to fiddle with her hair.

"What-what?" she asked, worried.

"Your turn of phrase."

Sonia blushed. She wasn't always aware of it, how not being a native English speaker affected the way she spoke. She noticed it more at work sometimes, especially when she had to talk to someone on a bad telephone line. "I am . . . I have not been here very long, just about three months. In America."

"No, no, it's not . . . I love it. Your voice is like music."

Sonia was stunned by the unexpected compliment. If anything, it had seemed like he was picking fault with her. "That would have been a better opening line," she told him after a moment, still blushing, but now at the compliment.

"It might have," Ranveer agreed with a small nod. "So, where did you come from, Sonia?"

"India."

Ranveer chuckled at the one-word answer. Sonia was being obtuse, not stupid, and she could tell that he knew that. "No shit."

Sonia didn't go on, and Ranveer spoke again. "Fine, a woman of mystery. I can get behind that. I am from Mumbai originally."

Sonia smiled and nodded politely. "Never been."

"Ah, it is a most wonderful city," Ranveer said, his eyes going misty and his voice becoming heavy with distant romance. "Busy, exciting, creative. How I miss her."

"Why does every Indian person I meet here say that?" she asked him. Sonia realized too late that she had stopped him in midflow. Perhaps it was a little rude. "I—"

"No," Ranveer put in, "that's a fair point. If India was so perfect, why did we all leave it, eh?" He looked at her searchingly again. "I'm glad I came tonight; I almost did not."

"Why not?"

"Well, I didn't have to, for one thing."

"You do not work . . . ?"

"At Clemcon?" He seemed almost to find that one funny. "No, I contract to hire upper management. A headhunter, if you will. I only usually turn up at these events to see which staff might be worth stealing away. Spot the promising ones early on, as it were."

Sonia was not sure whether he was joking but decided to play along. "That seems like a good reason for being here. Why would you not have come to do that?"

Ranveer shrugged, a weary expression coming into his strong, lively features. "These things are always a little bit the same. I think I might have been to one too many in the last fifteen years or so."

"I almost did not come too," Sonia found herself confessing.

Ranveer scoffed at that. "Why not? You are young enough that you should come to every party. It is a crime otherwise to deny the young men your company. Have fun while you can."

Sonia thought a moment about the best way to reply, especially as he had lavished some serious praise on her. The best way to repay a compliment was with honesty, she supposed, which always seemed to be such a hard thing for her these days. "I was not sure I deserved to have fun."

She pressed two fingers to her forehead as her mind flashed back to three hours before.

Sonia was running late. She had almost decided not to go to the work party—damn the consequences for her career advancement. Then fear had changed her mind, and she was now rushing around her studio apartment, hopping on the worn red carpet as she pulled on tights and redoing makeup that had been put on too quickly. The news was on her very own television set. Her family had owned a TV in India, but her parents had almost never allowed anyone to put it on, and Sonia now found its noise comforting in a life where she was almost always alone outside of work. She found the news the most comforting thing of all. Even though the content wasn't very happy much of the time, she liked the sound of the booming voice, the pictures of places that were not only the beige walls of her tiny apartment. She was idly listening in while reapplying her lipstick as the news anchor began on a new story.

"In international news, a 'Black Day' was observed by the Muslim community in the city of Ayodhya in India today." Hearing the name of her former hometown, Sonia moved so she could peer at the TV screen.

"Muslim shopkeepers did not open their stores and hoisted black flags to commemorate the one-year anniversary of religious riots in the city," the news anchor went on. "Muslim groups observed a "day of sorrow," even as many blame the growing Hindu Nationalist sentiment fostered by the government for the riots that claimed many lives a year ago, riots that originally broke out when a mob attacked and disrupted an interfaith wedding in the city."

Sonia's heart beat wildly as she watched the images from a year before of cars and property being set on fire, the bile steadily rising in her throat. Thirty seconds later, the news moved on, but she was running to the bathroom, retching noisily into the toilet bowl.

When the spinning in her head slowed, she went back into the living area and to a table in the corner, where the colored lights from traffic signals on the street below cast an ever-changing glow through her open curtains. She opened the secondhand laptop that she had saved up for and searched for the riots, part of her appalled that she had not done so before, wondering if a part of her subconscious had kept it from the front of her mind until the news story pushed the issue. Although she had quickly taken to her administrative duties and computer use at work, technology had not been a big part of her life at home.

Soon, she had found videos showing acts of looting and violence, and then, moving a finger along the lines of an article describing the events of 1992, she found the pieces of information that she did not realize, until then, she had been looking for: *At least 36 dead . . . Whole family burned alive . . . Muslim businesses targeted by Hindu mobs . . . Worst religious violence in the region in decades . . .*

Sonia's chest froze over, icicles on the inside. She had known none of this, had thought only of what had happened at her wedding and the sounds she had heard from inside her storage shed as she had hidden from the gangs. It had been easy to imagine that they were only after her, the young Hindu woman who had dared to try and marry a man from the wrong religion.

Bindu had never told her that she had, in fact, been responsible for so much death and destruction.

Perhaps she should not have come to the party and been so honest with this man, after all, because now she was fighting back tears and on the point of breaking into humiliating sobs in front of this virtual stranger. She could see, too, that her words had shocked Ranveer, and he was probably, right about now, thinking that he had made a mistake in coming over and talking to her.

"I do not believe that for a moment," Ranveer finally replied, his voice still kind. "Maybe I'm a silly old romantic approaching middle age too fast, but I believe that beauty shows on the outside, and you're far too beautiful to be all that bad, Sonia."

Although his expression was quizzical, he didn't ask the questions that must have been on his lips. She felt grateful for that.

Instead, Sonia just shrugged. "What is it you said? If India is so perfect, why are we leaving?"

"Well, you know what, Sonia? I think I'll just judge you from the moment I walked over to talk to you tonight, how about that? Who cares about the past, eh?"

"In that case, you must think I am evasive and possibly-possibly unstable," Sonia replied.

Ranveer laughed out loud at that, the sound seeming to be carried away and off into the night air. "I would go for interesting . . . Refreshing, even."

"Even with my spreadsheets?"

Ranveer held out an arm to her. "Would you like me to accompany you inside? There are many eligible young men in there who are currently being denied your company."

"I am not eligible," Sonia replied, "and I am not interested in those young men." She took a breath and said what she wanted to say, and, with it, a year's worth of hurt subsided just a little. "I like your company, Ranveer Shah. You are knowing when not to push."

She screwed up her face, before adding, "And the air conditioning is too strong in there. What is it with air conditioning in this country? I spend all my day freezing to death and choking on dry air."

Ranveer agreed with a chuckle, carefully managing the pleasure in his expression, although she could *feel* that he was pleased with what she had said. "You're right, and the air is balmy out here tonight."

Sonia followed another impulse and put her hand on his arm, which was still outstretched. Suddenly, the ground began to shake, and Ranveer took hold of her, steadying them both.

"What was that?" Sonia squeaked.

"That's okay," Ranveer said, the shaking quickly subsiding. "Just a small one. Your first earthquake?"

"We have earthquakes?" she asked, alarmed.

Ranveer laughed. He had the nicest laugh—full and musical. "You really did not do your research before moving here, eh?"

Sonia shook her head, still freaked out.

"That was just a little baby," he told her, and that thought had Sonia clinging to his arm even more tightly.

"Tell me something about yourself, Ranveer Shah," she said, "to take my mind off the shaking ground." They began to move slowly toward the other side of the roof.

"What would you like to know?"

"I do not know. The usual, I suppose. Who is important in your life?"

"I have two children," he said, although the way in which he said it was hard to pin down. The man was plainly many years her senior, so a marriage was to be no surprise. Yet Sonia had a life here, in the United States. It was perhaps a meager one by local standards, but it was more than she could ever have expected—or maybe even deserved, given what she had seen on the news this evening—and she had no need of becoming involved with a married man, no matter how kind he might seem or how much she ached for solace right now. Perhaps he felt her body stiffen slightly.

"Their mother . . . She was not made for family life. Good at socializing, at playing the wife of a businessman, but, when Roma was born—that is my eldest—she struggled right away. We had a boy, too, but she only lasted a year after that."

"Lasted?" Ranveer's English was better than hers, but it sounded to Sonia like a strange turn of phrase, nonetheless.

"She ran away in the middle of the night with a DJ from Vancouver she met at a party, all very dramatic."

He spoke the words with the air of someone who had not been very surprised at this act of drama. All the same . . . "And left you alone with two children? Young, I am thinking."

"Yes, little Adi was only a year old. Roma nearly four. That was last year." He sighed and smiled. "It has been an adjustment, and we are managing. There is a nanny, of course, but it is important to me not to be an absent father. They already have an absent mother."

Absent mother. Sonia's heart and stomach both clenched viciously. However, unlike Ranveer's wife, Sonia had been given little choice.

They reached the opposite side of the roof, and Sonia reclaimed her arm, now putting her hands on the cool railing for reassurance. "You are a big-shot headhunter and a . . . how do they say, 'single parent' of two young children? This is very impressive, Ranveer Shah."

He took a long moment to reply, and Sonia did not look at him. However, when he finally spoke, his simple words won her heart right then. "It is not anything impressive, Sonia. It just is."

CHAPTER 23

Gia's apartment, although not brand new, had been recently renovated when she moved into it—she could smell the freshness of the paint on the pistachio-green walls—and had the feel and look of a thoroughly modern western apartment. Compared to where Gia had lived before, her residential space was not only vast but was also a thing of stunning beauty that she had cared for with great love and attention in the weeks since she had come to San Francisco. The past couple of days, however, she had let things go a bit—and it was extraordinary how quickly the place started to resemble a rubbish dump.

Gia was sitting in her pj's, watching TV. It was still relatively early in the morning and should have been too early for ice cream, although it didn't take much deciding to get up, head to the freezer, and grab herself a pint of the extra-creamy vanilla. It tended to help, at least temporarily, with the low, twisting feeling like a towel wrung dry that was pulling her apart from the inside.

She returned to the sofa and flicked through the cable channels, already beginning to discover the universal truth about television—that it soon began to feel like you had seen everything before, even the things that were supposedly different each day. Yes, even the news could be like that, although she found herself gravitating toward this constant feed of local, national, and occasional world events, living vicariously through everyday tragedies that—a little like the ice cream—made things temporarily less painful, in this case by appearing to be even more traumatic than her own problems.

The doorbell stopped Gia in the midst of her channel flicking, and she looked longingly at her ice cream, then at the TV, before finally sighing and placing the tub down so she could go and answer the door.

Her Uncle Mohammed stood just outside her apartment—not so long ago a welcome sight but now one that she had been doing her best to avoid. Another sigh escaped her lips, this one even more dramatic than the previous one—and she slouched petulantly in the doorway.

"What do you want?" Gia barked rudely at the man who, until a few days ago, had been the closest living relative she knew of. He was currently vying for the title of "least favorite."

Mohammed frowned. "Hello, Uncle, how nice to see you," he shot back sarcastically.

Gia was determined to look unmoved by his sarcasm, but she reluctantly stepped back and returned to the living room, leaving the door open and the interpretation up to Mohammed about whether or not he should follow her. Reaching the couch, she picked up her spoon and dug back into her ice cream tub.

"You've not been returning my messages or calls," Mohammed said a few moments after joining her in the living area. He had been standing there like a spare part, ignored. "I was beginning to worry. Plus," he added in a lighter, more playful tone, "I wanted the opportunity to come and be nosy, see where you lived."

Gia did not want to play along and doggedly kept eating, peeking out of the corner of her right eye as her uncle gazed around the open living area of her apartment, which, she was realizing, was embarrassingly full of unwashed plates, empty food wrappers, and clothes that needed washing, garments that cost as much as all the clothes she had ever owned before coming to America just dumped on the back of chairs or in piles on the floor. She could not bring herself to care about it. Guilt could piss off.

"Nice apartment," Mohammed said, and Gia thought she might have caught the tiniest bit of envy in his voice. Her apartment *was* much nicer looking than his old—but homely—house over in Oakland, even she could tell that. "This came with the job?"

Gia looked around at the apartment distastefully in the wake of her uncle's question, as if she was realizing for the first time just how tainted the place was. Maybe the truth of it was that she had known that already, but it was taking his comment to force her to face that fact. He was not going to make her feel guilty. *No one* was going to make her feel guilty.

"It came with being Sonia Shah's daughter," she replied, "but then you knew that, didn't you?"

She looked up in time to see Mohammed's expression recoil as if he had been slapped across the cheek, his eyes wide with shock. After a moment, he let out a long, slow breath.

"Only recently."

Gia hadn't expected that reply. If anything, she had expected denial, because lies seemed to be the way of things here on the West Coast of America. "You didn't arrange for the job with her?" she asked doubtfully. He had denied it before, but that was *then*.

"I had no idea, like I said," Mohammed replied. "She had a different name when I knew her, which was a long time ago."

Gia put down her ice cream tub—holding on to the spoon—and sat up a little, looking at him with a mixture of suspicion and interest. "What do you mean, *only recently?*"

"After we had breakfast together, I ran into her close to your work." He drew in a sharp breath, as if caught by surprise by the next thought. "It's strange how the years can dim so many things, yet you can instantly recognize a face more than twenty years later, however different. Then again"—his voice became distant and tinny—"how could I forget?"

The raw honesty of the words, the barely hidden pain, almost stopped Gia. But then, it wasn't *that* recently. "Why didn't you tell me?" she demanded. No guilt, no sympathy. *She* was the wronged party here.

Mohammed's expression—his eyes—seemed to come back to the moment they were in, and he had the decency, at least, to look a little ashamed. "She swore me to secrecy. What was I supposed to do?"

"Show me some loyalty," Gia shot straight back.

Mohammed appeared to weather that shot in the chest for a moment, swaying almost imperceptibly on his feet, before moving to take a seat opposite Gia. "I'm sorry, Gia."

Gia sniffed dismissively, remembering her abrupt departure from Mohammed's house after she had discovered her mother's letter in his box of possessions.

Mohammed had called her twice and texted her multiple times the following day. She had ignored the texts, and she had let the calls go to voice mail, but later she couldn't resist playing back the message he had left her. Haltingly, he had told her about the fate her father had suffered, how he had been dragged away from his own wedding and murdered for attempting to marry a woman of a different faith. Those people in the photograph she had seen at her uncle's house, the grinning boy who had been her father and the woman smiling shyly, her mother—the imperious, stony-faced Sonia Shah, of all people—it still did not compute in her brain. The idea of this couple and their doomed love had held the dreamy quality of folklore, like a traditional tale handed down from generation to generation.

It was tragic and it was horrific, and it had indelibly altered the course of Gia's life. As an orphan's origin story went—and because few at Mercy & Grace had them, many made them up—it was, in its way, romantic and heroic. And deeply ironic, because no one at the orphanage ever gave a damn about anyone's religion. When you hadn't eaten all day and the smell of watery dal found your nostrils, Gia knew by personal experience that you prayed to whichever god would put some of that dal in a bowl for you.

As to her mother, all Mohammed had said in the voice mail was, "She vanished soon after." Really, how annoyingly vague was that?

Slamming the replay button, Gia had fumed as she played the message over and over. She may not have known all the gory details, but this much she knew: that just as he had been sharing such a painful truth with her about her father, he had still lied by omission. He knew she was oblivious to the fact that she was working for her own mother. She was drowning in betrayal as all her feelings swam around her.

The next day she received another text from her uncle, asking if she was okay. Still angry with him at his deceit, she did not respond.

Now, in the apartment she was beginning to hate, Mohammed looked uncomfortable. Gia gritted her teeth, brushing off his apology. "I've thought about the letter I read in your house so many times," she told him. "It's all I know of him. Of where I came from. I want to understand about him now, Uncle Mohammed. I want to know about my father, about what happened. You can't duck this anymore like you always did on our calls. I deserve to know properly about where I am from. What happened. How *she* is my mother."

"It is not a nice story," Mohammed tried. "They were Muslim and Hindu. It sounds romantic to defy conventions for love. But it doesn't always end that well . . . for everyone involved. I wanted to protect you, so I did not share the sordid history with you."

"I'm sure that's what Sonia would say she was trying to do."

"Does she know that you know?" he asked. It was a reasonable, practical question, and somehow it irritated Gia, like maybe he was trying to change the subject again. She did not feel reasonable or practical. In fact, a little madly, a sort of hysteria was pushing itself around her already frayed edges.

"I think that half of San Francisco knows," she replied with a hysterical little giggle.

Mohammed's mouth worked its way upward into an involuntary and inappropriate smile, like her giggle had given him permission to do so. It hadn't. But then his look became the obvious question.

"I had it out with her at a work event," Gia admitted.

"Oh, Gia . . ." Mohammed began to gently chide her, like a responsible uncle might.

"Don't 'Oh-oh, Gia' to me," she snapped back. "It is the so-so-called grown-ups who have been telling all the lies around here!"

Mohammed reflexively threw up his hands in a placating gesture, but then seemed to change his mind and put them down again. "Does Sonia know that you are dating her stepson?" he asked. To Gia's ears, he sounded so disgustingly morally superior in that moment, it made her blood boil.

She leaned forward, riding the crest of her own righteous anger, stabbing her ice cream spoon toward Mohammed. "And that is another thing you could have told me about."

Mohammed started to lift a finger, as if about to disagree with her, perhaps to tell her that dating the boss's stepson is always a bad idea, but the finger floated back down again. "I wanted to," was all he said in the end, quiet and contrite.

"That is what started things off at the event," Gia admitted. "Adi told her about us."

"And Saum . . . Sonia was angry?"

Gia looked distantly at the wall for a moment. "Hypocrite."

Mohammed shrugged. "I guess it's a natural reaction," he tried.

Gia glanced sharply back at him, and his eyes showed that he knew he had erred. No one was taking Sonia Shah's side today, she was making very sure of that. "It's natural to tell your daughter that you are her mother. It's natural not to leave her rotting for her whole childhood in an orphanage while you enjoy living in fucking luxury." She illustrated her point by throwing her hands up toward her own relatively opulent surroundings.

"Do not make excuses for her, Uncle," Gia went on. "She has ignored me and then humiliated me." She could feel the tears coming and felt like her body was betraying her. If she cried now, she would not finish what she needed to say, and she *needed* to finish. "She's lied to me and made me work for her. Made me feel so grateful for this apartment, made-made me scared that she would fire me when I dared to disobey her. I was so scared she would send me back, it's like she owns me, Uncle." Gia stood up, her words suddenly filling her with the purpose that had been missing from her life these last couple of days. She had been in shock, confused and scattered, but now telling Mohammed how she felt was bringing with it such clarity.

"But I do not want to think about her. I hate her, and I'm stuck in this place that she paid for. She is making me dependent on her. If I do not go back to work, then I will be deported." The frustration of that was now bringing her voice to the point of screaming. "She . . . she . . . manipulates me!"

The crescendo reached, the moment of anger spent, Gia collapsed back onto her couch, sobbing, and Mohammed rushed over to comfort her.

"And, and, and . . . the worst thing is that I think I love him," she mumbled, the other half of the deep pain that she had been suffering these last few days bubbling to the surface. "Everything is so complicated now. That is her fault. She has done that too. She has done all of this. I hate her so much!"

Finally, Gia let Mohammed put his arms fully around her, and she sobbed into his shoulder for what seemed like an age.

"There was a time when I hated your mother too," Mohammed told her eventually. Not perhaps the first words she had expected him to break their long silence with. "There was a time when I blamed her for everything that had gone wrong in my life. Understand this is hard for me, too, Gia. These wounds have never healed."

CHAPTER 24

Mohammed had called his brother a fool in their last conversation together as they had traveled to the wedding venue that morning. He had meant it lightheartedly—affectionately, even: "You're a fool, Brother, because you follow your heart and not your head. But maybe I envy you a little bit for that."

Something like that. He would never be able to remember for sure if that really was what he had said. He had a habit of talking down to his younger brother, he knew, and there may also have been dire warnings along the lines of, "It's all smiles and fun and love today, but you've got a whole lifetime of judgment and disapproval ahead of you." He should have been nicer.

Bindu, Saumya's sister, had seen the mob coming before anyone else, and she had found Mohammed first of all. He had followed her pointing finger beyond the edges of the wedding site, which sat next to a dirty road that was still affected by the yearly rains—turning dust and hard earth to sticky, boggy mud. He saw them then, emerging out of the humid haze that hung above the tarmac, coming swiftly on mopeds and on trucks, now resolving from vague shapes in the distance. These were the same vehicles that stood at the side of the highway many evenings, chasing and haranguing those transporting the sacred cow, ever vigilant for Muslims and their evil need to eat beef, or so it went. If he had ever eaten beef, Mohammed could not remember the taste of it.

His heart sank, hope that he hadn't even realized was there sinking down to become the stirrings of fear in the pit of his stomach. He tried to hold on to the flicker of faith that kindled within him—a foolish, wistful thought that they were only coming to stand by and observe, to make sure that their precious ideological rules were not being broken. The two families had planned the wedding as quietly as possible, kept the guest numbers smaller than they might have—although Hassan had complained in that good-natured way of his that it had been impossible to entirely rein in Saumya's desire to make her special day the way she wanted it to be. Hindu-Muslim tension in Ayodhya was like an unpredictable sea, swelling one moment and quickly receding again. What could be tolerated or ignored—or even accepted—one day could be a grave insult the next, and they had tried to catch the religious fervor at its lowest ebb. A reasonable, rational, straightforward man, Mohammed nonetheless hoped against hope that they might.

There was an immediate discomfort among the milling guests, as there was probably not an adult among them who did not know what the arrival of these people could mean. One of the caterer's boys brought out a tray of hot samosas. A tuneless *bhajan* played over the loudspeaker. Mohammed saw Bindu glance back to the scarlet shamiana where Saumya was almost ready to be married and could tell that Saumya's sister—calm, practical Bindu, who Mohammed understood much more than he did the irrationally romantic Saumya or, for that matter, his own brother—only wanted to protect the bride-to-be. She still hoped for her sister's day to be the perfect fairy tale, which, in Mohammed's opinion, all weddings rather impractically aspired to be.

Even as the fear washed over him, he turned back to the approaching group, determined to at least try and help Bindu keep this maybe minor disruption from her sister if he could. Together they stalked quickly past the red-plastic chairs and the makeshift stage that was brightly painted yellow-and-blue boards resting on nothing more than upturned crates. Mohammed felt his own tension rise as he saw Hassan crossing the scrubby field to join them. Overhead, a forlorn crow looked down and gave a hoarse croak that made him start a little.

Hassan was everything Mohammed liked to roll his eyes at—floppy haired, artistic, and without an ambitious bone in his body, while Mohammed was already working on his doctorate in Islamic studies and lecturing part-time at the university. Yet, a wave of love for his brother poured out of him in that moment—how handsome he was, how . . . vulnerable. And how hotheaded too. As the groom, it was not good that he was coming over, anyway—a potential focus for any ire that the mob might be bringing with them—but he was also quick to take offense, and, well, if anyone was to make even the slightest derogatory comment about the Hindu bride-to-be . . .

Their eyes met for a moment as they joined up close to the road, and he felt foolish in his fears as Hassan's expression was a lot more "Here we go" than "Oh shit." For a moment, he had a flash of the teenage Hassan talking to girls, full of confidence and bravado; that particular version of his younger brother had sometimes made him—awkward and unpopular and academic—feel like the junior sibling, and he was right back there for just a brief second, tumbling back down the years in his mind. Maybe everything would be alright after all.

The large, scruffy-looking men with *paan*-stained teeth on the first few mopeds eyed them but stayed on their bikes until the yellow half-rusted truck arrived. A man of about thirty with a scar that ran across his right cheek pushed forward from the dozen or so men who jumped from the back of it. He was dressed all in white, and, despite the journey in such close proximity to so many other grimy, sweaty, unshaven men on a humid day, his outfit was spotless—not even a damp patch under the armpit, nor a bead of sweat on his brow.

"This is the Khan and Pandey wedding, is it not?" he asked with brusque efficiency in his tone.

"It is," Hassan answered cheerfully, "and we would ask you to join us, but there is limited seating, I'm afraid."

Do not be too flippant, Brother.

The man with the scar stopped and eyed Hassan up and down, a look of slight disdain pulling already thin lips even thinner. "We are here to check that everything is in order," the man said. Bindu was staring hard at him, and Mohammed thought then that he looked familiar, as well. Maybe he could even recall a name. The man with the scar seemed to notice Mohammed staring and turned to look directly at him, hard eyes intently fixed, which turned Mohammed's insides to jelly and brought on an instant need to go to the bathroom.

Mohammed looked away, he could not help it, so the man turned his stare on Bindu, instead, which seemed somehow like he was undressing her in his mind as he looked her slowly up and down. Unlike Mohammed, Bindu did not wilt under his gaze, instead lifting her chin in an action that was proud and defiant.

"You will find the menu acceptable," Mohammed put in, as much to pull the man's eyes from Bindu as anything else. "We are soon to begin, but I'm sure we have a moment to show you."

The man with the scar let his gaze slide slowly toward Mohammed, on one side of Bindu, then over to Hassan on the other. Bindu glanced back over her shoulder, perhaps to see where her own brothers—who would, surely, have more sway with these Hindu religious people than Mohammed or Hassan—were, but none were in sight.

"We didn't come to check the food," the man with the scar said coldly. "We came to check you."

Those eyes trained on him were opaque little marbles, and two slivers of ice shot down Mohammed's back as the words sank in, each dropping from one of his shoulder blades. The breeze was picking up, and, even from some way away, he could hear it whistling around the shamiana, causing the thick cloth to flap. Slap-slap . . . slap.

"No man should be getting married to a Hindu woman if he is circumcised," the man with the scar went on. He screwed his face up, a little like a child making a show of being disgusted. "The violation of the human body with the exposed organ, it's not right." He turned to Hassan. "You are the bridegroom, right?"

Mohammed saw his brother gulp, his Adam's apple moving quickly in and out, and knew that he had never felt more fear than he felt for his brother in that moment. His baby brother.

"Grab him."

With those two words, everyone except Mohammed seemed to move at once, Bindu included, and it was the man with the scar who stepped forward to shove her away as she tried to intervene in what they were doing. Bindu stumbled backward, tripping and landing heavily on her backside.

Hassan was being held by two men before Mohammed had even seen it happen. Two men moved toward him, as well, but he stepped backward, and they seemed content to shepherd him away for the moment.

"Let's have a look, then," the man with the scar said, and finally Mohammed realized where he had seen him—standing outside a butcher's shop in the town, wearing a white apron, stained red and brown with new and old blood. That was all he was, a butcher; nobody important at all.

The butcher had signaled toward Mohammed's brother, and now another man came forward to pull Hassan's trousers down, exposing his circumcised penis for all the world to see. The shame and shock on Hassan's face was sickening.

"Bastards!" Hassan raged, through his red-faced shame, but then one of his captors backhanded him to keep him quiet.

Mohammed involuntarily took a step forward.

"Oh dear, someone did him too," the butcher simpered toward Mohammed, faux sympathy draped heavily over his words. Someone behind the butcher handed him a knife. Smaller than the man would usually have wielded at work, it sported a wooden handle and still had a good four inches of blade at least.

"Please, you don—" Mohammed said, with a tremor in his voice.

"Shut up, you," the butcher raged, his sudden outburst shocking in and of itself and sweeping the rest of Mohammed's sentence from his lips. "We could take care of you next."

"Please, no," Mohammed squealed instinctively in reply. "I would never m-marry a Hindu woman." He looked at the floor, feeling both his brother's and Bindu's eyes upon him.

The butcher took two quick steps toward Mohammed, thrusting the knife forward so that it stopped only an inch or two from Mohammed's face, quivering below his eyes that now snapped shut, his head still lowered. "What's the matter," the man sneered, "Hindu women not good enough for you?"

Mohammed opened one eye slightly, fixing it on the blade that trembled there before him. "I wouldn't . . . we shouldn't mix," he said beseechingly.

After several long seconds, the butcher stepped back, his face breaking into a pleasant smile that failed to reach his eyes. "You're right, of course." He turned to Hassan, gesturing with the knife, like it was an extension of him. "This one, on the other hand . . ."

Suddenly, Bindu was on her feet and sprinting back toward the shamiana, her *chappals* falling from her feet. The gathered men ignored her, growing excited in their anticipation of what was about to come. Mohammed wanted to do the same as Bindu had, even if it meant leaving his brother, but found that his feet were concrete blocks. "Lord Ram demands it," the butcher cried. "Come, we'll do it by the river!"

"Lord Ram! Lord Ram!" went up the cries as Mohammed looked after Bindu, now noticing how the rest of the wedding party was already in chaos, the guests running away from the thugs. The invaders had begun tipping over chairs and slashing the floral displays. The loudspeaker was still bleating in the quickly emptying field, the words distorted in the din: "God is one . . ."

Mohammed wanted to stumble after his brother. He could not stop this terrible thing happening—he was a realistic, pragmatic man, after all—but what sort of a brother would not try at least? He was on his feet, so surely he could put one in front of the other, yet he could not bear the thought of seeing it, of seeing the blood or his brother's fear. And, more than that, he was paralyzed by the thought that the mob might yet turn their bloodlust on him. Instead, he fell to his knees and sobbed, the last sight he ever had of his brother seen through tear-blurred eyes as the mob carried him, still struggling, on their shoulders toward the river.

CHAPTER 25

NOW

It wasn't a part of San Francisco that Mohammed tended to stray into very much. He parked at the end of Van Ness Avenue, just before the start of the pier that looped lazily around in front of Aquatic Park. He crossed over to the main pathway, the worn boards creaking underneath his feet. Soon he was looking up at the white art deco structure of the maritime museum, where a lone figure stood leaning against a chrome railing, staring at the watery horizon, waiting for him. When he reached the top of the roof, he found himself stopping about halfway across, as if he needed to keep his distance.

"This is very clandestine," he told her. "I feel like a spy."

She looked disheveled, compared to the last time he had seen her—unexpectedly, after walking his niece back to her first job in the United States, one that this woman had given her. How vulnerable he had been to the woman's unreasonable demand then, still basking as he had been in the overwhelming but complex joy of seeing Gia in person for the first time. He remembered how quickly the shock of seeing Saumya Pandey standing there had been followed by a sense of grim inevitability. *Of course,* he had thought to himself. *Obviously.*

She looked tired now. Not the powerful, confident, almost unrecognizable businesswoman he had run into that first time, just a few weeks ago.

"This is where I first met my stepchildren," she told him. "So many years ago, it seems." She sighed. "I have not been home since the party the other night."

Mohammed rolled his eyes—inwardly, at least, although he could not be sure that his exasperation was not plastered across his face. "So dramatic, Saumya," he chided. "You always had to make such a fuss about things."

"Not Saumya," she corrected him.

"No?" Names were only names. They did not make them who they were. He knew that.

"Not for over twenty years now."

"Everyone calls me Mike," he told her, "even my wife and children. I can't even remember when it started, but, whatever other people call me, I've never forgotten who I am, where I came from."

It felt pompous, perhaps hypocritical, yet he did not owe this woman anything. Not here, not now. They were still half a rooftop away from each other, and Mohammed finally closed the distance, finding himself caught out by the weight of the moment and starting to choke up. For all the anger he might still hold for her, this was a moment of connection. "Can we embrace?" he asked. "Is that something we should do?"

He could see his own emotions reflected in her face. This woman's face was less expressive than the one he remembered from over twenty years ago—perhaps because of age, perhaps because of her traumatic past. Or maybe it was surgery, how would I know? A small sound like a sob eventually escaped her, and she nodded. He was the one to step forward and bridge those years between them, embracing her gently, the feel of this person he had never expected to see or hear from again oddly alien beneath his arms.

"I didn't think you liked me," she said, sounding like she might be trying to inject a little levity into the words.

"I didn't," he replied. "You were that busybody Hindu girl who was leading my brother astray."

Sonia stepped back from the embrace, putting her hand on the railing and viciously wiping away the remnants of tears as if they had offended her. "I can't," she said, shaking her head in denial. "I can't go there."

"Oh, come now, Sonia. You must. Don't you see that?"

Sonia shook her head again, less vigorously this time. "I'm not the same woman, Mohammed. I have a husband, a whole family. I made a business. I made a different life. A different me. I am not . . ."

Mohammed snorted at that; it was as if she could not see herself in the slightest. "You started a wedding business. You spend your life arranging perfect weddings, being fussy and picky and dealing with a flurry of activity, I bet. Sonia Shah is not so different from a girl called Saumya that I used to know."

Sonia's stare turned hard. "Don't judge me, Mohammed. I've worked hard for everything I have now."

Her words, her attitude, all of it was starting to infuriate him. She was acting as if she was the only one in the center of this. "Me, judge you? With my high-powered cab-driving business and my shitty prefab house in Oakland? Where do you live, huh?"

His words seemed to strike home, and Sonia's indignant expression melted, becoming sheepish as she nodded out across the water.

"Where?" Mohammed pushed, genuinely wanting to know where this woman had been for all these years, so close by and yet in another world from the one he had been living in.

Sonia gestured a little more accurately, and he thought he knew the little promontory that she meant, jutting out just a little way beyond the end of the Golden Gate Bridge.

"What? Sausalito? Fuck you, Sonia. You know all about who I was in Ayodhya, the future I could have had for myself until your wedding screwed my whole life up. How is that fair? You were no one when I knew you, just a girl from a middle-class family with a cleverer little sister."

Sonia finally turned away from his last few words, and, his quick anger now spent, a small wave of shame washed over Mohammed. The years of bitterness never fully dealt with had blindsided him.

"I had no idea," Sonia spoke quietly. "I mean, I knew it was horrible—the wedding venue destroyed, what they did to Hassan. I never knew for sure what happened to him, whether he was alive, although Bindu assured me he could not possibly be. She hid me in a shed but never told me what happened in the town after, I had no idea what the mob did to your community, not until I saw about it on the TV a year later, when I was already living here . . ."

They looked out together over the relative serenity of the bay, an idyllic scene with boats idling along on what today was a calm surface. "I ran to save my life that day," Mohammed said, "that was what I did." He had never told this to a soul before, and now he realized that she was just about the only person he could tell. "I saw them carry my brother away toward the river, and I ran. I was so scared. Such a coward. I even lost my parents in all the panic, the confusion. So, I ran home to save my own skin."

He shook his head mournfully, the past like a sparring partner who knew far too well the point where he was weakest.

"What an idiot, eh? They came to where we lived," Mohammed went on, "this mob. My parents were not home yet—I would later find out that your family had given them shelter that day. They were between me and my house, but there was a banyan tree just along the street and set back from the road that I passed without much considering several times each day. With the sun recently set and the light leaching from the sky, I thought it might make a place for me to hide in." He held out his free hand as if touching something invisible in front of him. "I can remember how its trunk was a closely knit, almost entwined collection of individual vines, looking like sinews of muscle in the low light. Except there was one gap, just about big enough for me to climb inside."

He lifted his chin, breathing heavily through his nostrils, a danger-ous glitter in his eyes.

"I got out of sight just in time, and the mob stopped a few yards away from where I was. Some held battery-powered torches, others real torches with flames," he hissed. "The scene was medieval. And I began to realize, as light occasionally illuminated the faces, that I knew some of these people. The mob seemed big. At the wedding, it had seemed like just a large group of angry, evil men, full of hatred, like the bit-part actors in a movie whose names no one will ever remember or care about. Pitchfork Guy Number One. But when they reached my neighborhood, although the mob had increased in size, it was no longer faceless. These were the faces of my everyday life. Even the pockmarked, balding man in his fifties whom I referred to as Uncleji, who ran the hardware store—Jain Electric and Hardware store, it was called—had joined them. I had bought a light bulb from him only two days before, and he had asked me about my studies, about how my thesis was going."

Below them, a toddler walked along holding his mother's hand, and they watched the boy go past together. Even though the mother and son probably weren't within earshot, Mohammed waited before he spoke again. It felt wrong to let the horror of the things that he was speaking of fall on those innocent ears.

"I still do not know how none of them noticed me," he finally went on, "moving from house to house as they were. They came to my next-door neighbor, some of them passing closer to me than the width of this rooftop."

Mohammed shuddered. His limbs were twitchy, his back ached suddenly, and he had a bitter taste in his mouth. He closed his eyes, the images resolving more clearly in his memory as he did so. He did not want to see them any better, yet he also knew that he had kept all this from his mind for far too many years. "I can still picture them with their daggers and their fuel cans. But, this time, they found my neigh-bor hiding inside, the sixty-year-old maulvi from the local mosque. His sister and niece tried to stop the mob from taking him and were kicked and punched to the ground for their trouble. The men kept kicking, even after they were on the floor."

"What happened to him?" Sonia asked, her words causing Mohammed to open his eyes. He realized that he must have been standing silent like that for some time.

"They pulled him right into the middle of the street—this wizened man with wire-rimmed spectacles who liked to set up a table in front of his house and challenge anyone who cared to stop to a game of chess over a cup of Kashmiri tea. 'Kishan?' I heard him say to the man who owned the hardware store, the sound of the other man's name one of disbelief as it slid from my neighbor's lips, of incomprehension. I had seen them playing chess myself only a few weeks before, so my shock was almost as great as his."

Nerves popped along Mohammed's neck, and he bit back a sob.

"I knew then that there was no safe place for a Muslim in India. All my studies, all my hope for educating the world about what it meant to carry my faith. I thought I was empowering myself, my people, yet here I was hiding in the roots of a banyan tree, close to emptying my own bladder with fear.

"When I finally left, now too scared to return to my family home, it was a Hindu family who took me in and kept me safe for the rest of the night. A colleague of mine at the university where I taught. He called on my neighbor's landline to find out how I was doing, and when I began crying, loud, pitiful sobs"—here, Mohammed's voice cracked—"he asked me to stay where I was, and came to collect me in his beaten-up, wasp-colored Maruti car. Maybe another man might have seen that as a sign that it was worth staying, that all Indians were not the same. But all my hope drained with my brother; like yours did, I suppose."

When Mohammed finally turned back to Sonia, he rearranged his face into an attentive smile.

"Sorry," he told her gently. "I had no right to judge you for what happened after the wedding. I didn't mean to. I've had a lot of years to know what you did and didn't do, to know that you did not pick up a bat or a homemade pistol."

"But I know there is fault that is mine," Sonia now protested, blurting the words out like they had corked up within her. "Or Saumya's. It was horrible, what was done to Hassan. We chose to get married. I mean, we didn't know what would happen, but we chose to be together when we knew that some people might not approve, and others paid for what we did. You paid for our decisions. You see why I could not be her anymore? This name came with moving to America, but now I'm glad that it did. I cannot live with owning that past."

"So why bring Gia here? Not just *here* but into your life? Why do that if you are not ready to be the woman who gave birth to her?" Mohammed asked.

"No other choice," Sonia replied.

"No choice?" Mohammed scoffed. That was not—*could not*—be entirely true. Gia had needed saving, but . . .

"I watched Ranveer with his kids all these years, and that's when it began. Slowly, perhaps, but it soon became a terrible yearning to be close to my daughter. I felt her absence every day. I ached to be with her." Sonia swallowed. "I kidded myself into bringing her into the company," she admitted. "I was convinced I could watch in secret, see her become successful, have a life, and not say a thing or be found out." She shook her head. "How foolish of me."

"Do you even realize how incredibly selfish that sounds?" Mohammed asked her. There was no fire in his criticism this time, he was only reciting the plain facts as he saw them. She had seen everything only from her point of view.

Realization blazed in her eyes, and they stood there silently for a long moment.

"I think my marriage may be over," Sonia told him eventually.

It was not an answer to his question, and Mohammed pursed his lips, as if he'd tasted something sour. "I think you'll be okay, Sonia," he told her acidly. "Got the business, after all."

Sonia looked sharply back up at him. "I'm not just thinking about myself, Mohammed. That's the point. There are others I am responsible to, other people who depend upon me—if not financially, then emotionally. My stepchildren for one—I'd always hoped we would grow together and have lasting relationships as a blended family. And there *is* the business, for that matter—the people who work for me. My clients are almost all from the Bay Area Indian community, and you must know how they feel about any impropriety, even here."

"My wife and children do not know all the facts, either," Mohammed admitted. His voice was slow and stretchy, a tape at the wrong speed. "Not really. It's like my past before America is a sealed vault. Poor kids. Poor Farha. So, I get it, I do, but you chose to bring her to your own company, to pull her into your life. The consequences are yours, Sonia. And, you know what . . . ?"

Sonia cocked her head toward him.

"I haven't even heard you say Gia's name once since I got here. Isn't she the most important one in all of this?"

Sonia's expression drooped toward the floor like melting wax. When she spoke, it was almost in a whisper. "I'm scared . . ."

"Of what . . . ?"

"I realized my mistake in bringing her here the first day I saw her—the resemblance to Hassan . . ." Sonia made a small, agitated sound. "Not her face or her fair skin—in that she resembles me, but that posture, that troublesome yearning toward the world, the desire to set things right. I face my past every time I see her. It's like a chisel chipping away at my heart, and it unmoors me every single time." Sonia rubbed her eyes, wiped the wetness from her cheeks. "I'm scared that I can't be the mother she needs."

This stark admission caught Mohammed unprepared; he hadn't expected *that*, not from this "Sonia Shah." However, before he could even try to formulate a response, *boom*. The ground started to shake violently below them. Mohammed was confused, then his brow cleared.

Sonia stumbled toward the railing, lurching forward like a rag doll so that she struck it and had the wind knocked from her. It snapped

Mohammed to attention. He lunged for her, grabbing her hand, and pulling her back lest she topple over and fall to the concrete path below. The ground belched one last time, then, predictably, the long, terrifying moment was over quickly, another movement of the San Andreas Fault line . . . But was there more coming?

"That's . . ." Mohammed began.

"The biggest one in a long time," Sonia finished for him.

Testing a step, unsure whether he was expecting another tremor or suspicious of the roof's current integrity, Mohammed backed away from Sonia. "I should . . ." he began, pulling out his phone. "I should call my family."

"Gia," Sonia said. Only one word, yet the fact that it was the first one to come from Sonia's mouth meant something, and Mohammed hoped that it might be a seismic shift deep within her, and not just the tectonic plates moving.

"Yes," he began, "I should—"

"No!" Sonia interrupted. "You call your family, I will call Gia and make sure she is okay. My stepson, as well. He is in the city too."

Sonia brushed past him and headed to the top of the stairs, clutching her phone to her chest like a talisman that might bring luck. In worrying times like these, perhaps that's what it was. "Sonia, be care—" Mohammed found himself mouthing, unsure about why he felt the need to warn her. Yet, his words were prophetic.

Sonia tripped on a raised bit of the top stair—likely dislodged by the quake—and stumbled. For a terrible moment, Mohammed thought she would pitch forward down the steep, curving stairway, but Sonia's hand shot out and caught the railing. Her mobile phone, however, was not so lucky, and it seemingly leaped from her other hand, making several loud noises as it clattered down the stairs.

Sonia took a deep inhalation and pushed it out in a stream. "Damn, damn, damn," she said as she strained her chin downward, and Mohammed could see the veins banging along her throat.

CHAPTER 26

NOW

Gia sat and waited for him on a small, grassy rise overlooking Potrero Skate Park, just a couple of blocks from where she lived. The undulating concrete surfaces of the skate park were covered in graffiti, and she had been squinting at it, trying to read or make sense of some of the more colorful and expressive pieces, which stood out against the mass of black-and-white tags.

When she had first arrived—ten minutes ahead of the time she had arranged to meet Adi—Gia had considered sitting on one of the picnic benches located along a wall behind where she now sat, until she noticed the piece of graffiti. It was all one piece, beautifully done, with colorful patterns for a background that reminded her a little of some of the paintings by Pablo Picasso. She only knew this because her endless channel hopping yesterday had landed on a program about the artist. She'd stopped to watch because it reminded her of M. F. Husain's paintings, the artist who had been called India's Picasso. On top of the background graffiti was written just one Spanish word, spelled out in bold, slightly 3D-looking letters: FAMILIA.

Nope, she had decided. *Just . . . no.* Not that many years ago, Gia would have given anything for even the littlest thread of "family" in her life. Yet, what she had not realized back then was that, rather than answer all her questions and massage away all her doubts, a little family in the form of finding out about Mohammed had only brought with it more questions, more yearning, more doubt.

Gia glanced up as Adi approached her from the direction of the road. He stopped a few feet away, partially blocking the late-morning sun.

"I was hoping we would have met at your apartment," he said. "I wanted to see where you live."

"The apartment our mother paid for?" Gia snapped. It elicited the response she wanted, and Adi flinched. "You wouldn't want to see my apartment at the moment," Gia went on, guilt immediately softening her tone. "It is a mess."

"I'm sorry I told Sonia about us," Adi said. "It was selfish of me. I thought her being your boss was the only thing stopping us being together."

Gia huffed out a sardonic laugh. "Turns out that it wasn't."

"Either way, I apologize for telling her. I didn't think how badly things might go for you. Sonia got so mad; I had forgotten how forceful she can be. I felt a fool, even before . . . everything else."

Gia regarded him for a moment. He had surprised her. She had no idea what he would say when he got there—or even that he would come when she asked him to—but she had not expected this apology. "Apology accepted," she said. "Now sit down, my neck is beginning to hurt."

He did so, crossing his legs to sit on the grass with her, their shoulders a ruler's length apart, as if carefully measured out. Adi was in his office attire, and as he casually rolled up his trouser legs, Gia was reminded of how delicious he had seemed to her when they first met. He looked at her, fixing her with a stare that still had the potential to melt her insides.

"Does Sonia know you are here?" Gia asked, her brain wanting to switch to another channel.

"Despite how it might have looked the other day, my stepmother is not my keeper."

Gia nodded. "Have you seen her?"

"Um, no. My dad hasn't taken it well, and she's not been back to the house since, you know, the party."

Gia shouldn't care about this, about the marriage of the woman who had left her to rot in an orphanage, who lived a wealthy lifestyle and then deceived her when it mattered the most. And yet, a little pang of sympathy reverberated within her.

Adi laughed bitterly, breaking her train of thought. "Seems selfish to worry about our relationship," he commented, "doesn't it? Ours has only been a few weeks."

Gia's face hardened, though she couldn't find the words to frame her anger.

"I get now why you backed off," Adi said. One side of his mouth crooked upward. "Or maybe I just smell funny."

Gia laughed a little. "I got-got used to the smell."

Looking at his own hands, his fingers entwined together, Adi's voice broke a little when he spoke. "I never got used to the way you repeat words sometimes. I loved it." He turned to her. "Is it terribly wrong, what we did? I don't know how to feel about it."

"We didn't know," Gia murmured. "Our blood is not even the same."

They were silent for a long moment as Gia picked blades of grass and rolled them between her fingers to stop herself from feeling a need to speak. When she did glance up it was because, not far in front of them, a skateboarder dropped from the edge and caught some air over a hump in the middle of the skate park.

Finally, Adi spoke. "I'm sorry. I realize that I should have started with *how are you?* or something. How are you doing, Gia?"

He still had his ability to be charming, of course. "I'm terrible," she replied. "Thank you for asking."

Adi grinned at that, then laughed, as if her quip had given him permission. As it turned out, it was infectious. She laughed, a mild hilarity having taken ahold of her, like a madness might, although it quickly turned into a sob. The sob almost instantly became a flood of tears, and Adi shifted across and put an arm around her shoulder.

"It is not-not fair, Adi." She sniffed. "Why did she do this? Why did she leave me there all this time? Why never tell anyone about me? Was it me? Did she not—" *Love me?*

"No, no, I'm sure it wasn't like that," Adi demurred. "She brought you here, didn't she? Gave you a job in her company, which is a precious thing to her."

Gia pulled away from him slightly. "You aren't defending her, are you?"

"No! I . . . It's a shitty business all around," he finished weakly.

Gia hadn't finished being offended yet, though. "Me? Am I the shitty business?"

Adi shook his head vigorously. "That's not—"

His thought was interrupted when the ground suddenly started to shake, accompanied by an enormous roar that seemed to sound from all around them and was like nothing Gia had heard before in her life. She looked around, her features twisted, and at Adi, before her eyes fell on the skate park just as a boarder in midrun flew off a ramp at the wrong angle and became separated from the skateboard, landing in a skidding heap in the middle of the miniature concrete jungle.

"What is happening?" Gia asked, her heart pounding, but was mostly drowned out by the noise. It was like the cosmos was pushing in on her, vibrating on her lips, her scalp, her eardrums.

"Earthquake!" Adi told her, his voice grave but not cut through with quite the same urgent alarm that she felt. It seemed like the whole world was convulsing, and Gia suddenly felt so tiny and fragile, reaching for Adi, who instantly yanked her close to him. She was glad of his larger, stronger form close to her, even if they were both Lilliputian in a world that was forcefully in motion.

There was a loud crash somewhere nearby, and the sound of a car horn cut through everything else—a long, incessant tone. That was when Gia realized that the shaking had finished and the world was now in another state—a fragile stillness, a few seconds of settling, like all of it was dust from an old disturbed bedspread that needed to find its new resting place. Gia found herself still clutching at Adi's arm and let go of him violently, as if burned by his touch.

"Are you okay?" Adi asked. If he was offended by the way she had pulled back from him, he didn't show it. All Gia could do was nod dumbly back, still lost for words. "Your first earthquake?" he went on, and she nodded again. "No one told you about them, huh?"

"No," Gia finally managed with a small shake of her head.

Adi looked around them as the world started to right itself. Finally, the car horn finished blaring over on the street. "That was bigger than usual," he observed. "There may be aftershocks."

"After . . . ?" Gia asked. Whatever they were, they sounded bad.

"More earthquakes," Adi told her. "Usually smaller than the first, but still . . ."

A cry was now cutting through the other noise, and, looking down into the skate park, Gia could see that it was the skater whose ill-timed run had started just before the earthquake.

"We should help," Adi said, then crossed to the gate and inside the skate park itself. Gia didn't know what else to do other than follow him.

By the time they got there, several skaters stood around their unfortunate friend, who was bleeding in at least a couple of places and, even to Gia's untrained eye, had an obviously broken arm that looked like it could be nasty. She had never been the squeamish type, yet it took a force of will to look at it. Everyone except Adi was panicking—dancing from foot to foot, pacing, reaching out to the injured guy without actually touching him, like doing so might cause something even more catastrophic to happen. Adi, however, strolled up and took control straightaway.

"It's okay," he told them, "I'm first-aid trained. Let me see him." The guy was older than Gia with a patchy goatee, and he wore clothes that looked like they belonged on someone ten years younger. Crouching down, Adi then glanced back up at the man's friends. "Anyone called an ambulance?"

A deeply tanned girl of about Gia's age with blonde highlights held up her phone. "Signal's gone." Gia checked her phone and found the same.

Adi shrugged. "They'll be busy, anyway, I guess. Zuckerberg Hospital is only a couple of blocks from here, isn't it?" He looked down at the fallen skater, whose brow was slicked with sweat, his face contorted with pain, although his cries had transitioned to groans and gasps since they had come. "Let's see if we can move you, huh?" Adi asked, gentle warmth in his voice.

The walk to the trauma center was a slow one, every step painful for the skater, although alleviated somewhat by the banter of his friends, who had joined them on the walk and helped to keep his mind off it. It was a little over thirty minutes later when Adi and Gia watched the skater—Dominic, although already nicknamed Diving Dom by his friends—being taken away by a doctor. The whole experience had left Gia with a warm and fuzzy feeling, as welcoming as a breath of fresh air in a stuffy room—the not entirely metaphorical room that she had shut herself inside for the last few days. She had a newfound respect for Adi, impressed by the way he had taken charge of the situation, the great kindness he had shown Dominic. Gia had felt quite a few different feelings in Adi's company, but the specific aura of safety that he radiated for her now was new. She knew that the shock of the earthquake was a part of it, but it wasn't all of it.

"There is blood on your shirt," she observed, before making an offer that she was still reluctant to make. "You can come and clean up at my apartment if you want. You do not want to have to go all the way-way back to your apartment on the train like that."

"Trains might not be running, anyway," Adi told her. "Not for a while."

"Come on, I might have a T-shirt that will fit you," she told him. Then added with a cheeky smile, "It is pink and says *Absolute Babe* on it."

That made Adi laugh. "Sounds like it will suit me just fine."

They were just passing back through the entrance to the trauma center when Adi's phone rang.

"Phone is working again," Gia observed.

"It's my dad," Adi said, looking at the screen and then glancing nervously up at Gia before answering. "Yeah . . . You okay?"

Gia attempted to wait patiently as he nodded and occasionally replied to Ranveer Shah on the other end of the line, all the while feeling the air charged with tension as fear mushroomed inside her.

"You can't?" Adi asked his father with a sudden increase in pitch of his voice. "Well, the signal went down here at first, so . . . Okay, okay, we will try . . . Yes, 'we.' I'm . . ." Gia saw him pause, then his eye flicked involuntarily for just a fraction of a second toward her. "I'm here with Gia."

There seemed to be a long moment before Adi spoke again, and she could not tell if much had been said on the other end of the phone. "We will try and let you know," Adi finally said before hanging up.

Gia fixed Adi with an expectant gaze, willing herself not to think about the way he had paused before telling his dad who he was with.

"It's Sonia," Adi told her. "My dad can't get ahold of her."

CHAPTER 27

The walk to the office had been fretful for Gia. Adi's words after he hung up with Ranveer rang in her ears. Where was Sonia, and why didn't she answer? Moments after they had set off toward the center of San Francisco and Gia's work, she had tried to call Golden State Weddings & Events, but her call had gone straight through to voice mail.

She and Adi had half run and jogged as much of the journey as they could, cutting what might have been an hour's trip into half that, but they arrived sweaty, panting, and exhausted, only to have to take the stairs rather than risk the lift.

"Why does everything have to shut down in an earthquake?" Gia grumbled as they staggered along the corridor to the office door, her shaking fingertips fumbling with the keypad. She opened the door and found Dolly and Chad sitting in the middle of the office. Dolly peered at her as if Gia was some sort of opportunist burglar taking advantage of the earthquake to break into a wedding business, of all places. After the initial moment of shock passed, Dolly let out a long screech of relief and ran over to embrace Gia.

Over Dolly's shoulder, Gia could see the wall-mounted TV set they sometimes played event videos on, now showing the news. Live updates of the earthquake and its effects took up the screen.

"Thank goodness you're okay," Dolly said, still holding tight to Gia. "I've been so worried and can't get ahold of anybody."

"We called you, and you did not answer," Gia said, failing to keep the accusation from her voice.

Dolly pulled away from her and looked over at the phone, seemingly puzzled, as if the thing might offer its own answer. It didn't. "I tried you, I promise," she insisted. "And I've tried Sonia too. No one's phone seems to be working."

"The signal was down for a while right after the earthquake," Adi told her, "but it seems alright now."

Chad sauntered over to them. Somehow, in the middle of the earthquake and its aftermath, he had managed to get hold of a huge still-steaming calzone and was chomping down on it. It didn't look like one of his usual healthy options, but Gia didn't think it was the best moment to mention it.

"No, this is just what happens in an earthquake," Chad told them around a bite of his stuffed bread. "It's like New Year, when the phones go down because everyone calls or texts at once and nothing comes through for, like, twenty or thirty minutes. Except, instead of wishing their family a happy New Year, they're checking that they're not dead."

Chad grinned over the last part of his statement. Dolly frowned, gently poking him in the ribs. Then she shrugged, as if conceding that he had a point.

"It is frustrating, though," Gia stated as she blinked hard. She didn't like the way her heart was thrashing about, especially on account of someone she had so much right to feel furious with and, perhaps, to not even care about at all. The thing was, for all her life, everyone Gia had ever cared to worry about had shared a building with her at all times. This sort of distress was new and unsettling. The terrible helplessness of it had her insides churning like a washing machine on spin cycle. She would have worried about Mohammed, too, although she expected that he was over in Oakland, which supposedly had not been affected as badly.

"I'm sure Sonia is alright, though," Dolly said, as if reading her thoughts. Her eyes slid over to Adi and then back to Gia again. Gia squirmed with discomfort. In fact, both Dolly and Chad were looking at her far too intensely, and it quickly began to irritate her. For a wild second, Gia considered flouncing off, but she knew that this feeling of concern for the missing Sonia would be far too terrible to deal with on her own.

Chad, being Chad, was much less subtle than Dolly, and he spoke through another large mouthful of calzone. "So, you two . . . ?" he said, his finger wagging back and forth between Adi and Gia, causing the two of them to take half an involuntary step away from each other. "What's that all about?"

This time, Dolly's poke in Chad's ribs was more of an elbow, causing him to spit some of his food out. Gia, taking the only revenge she could currently think of, indicated the pizzalike food and the tomato grease that dripped all over Chad's fingers. "This, it does not look very healthy, does it?"

Dolly answered for Chad. "Comfort eating. You wouldn't think it, but apparently earthquakes make him nervous." She rolled her eyes.

Chad just sniffed and stuffed the rest of the calzone into his mouth at once. Gia had to admit that Chad's lack of tact was, in its own way, comforting. She looked over at the TV again, as they all did, while the reporter continued to drone on about it being "early days" and the imminent possibility of aftershocks.

"You've heard nothing of Sonia at all?" Adi asked Dolly and Chad.

"No, sorry," Dolly answered. She indicated the TV screen "But the news is only reporting injuries so far, so that sounds hopeful."

That didn't sound as reassuring as it was supposed to.

"Early days still, though," Chad put in, as if parroting the doomsayer of a reporter.

Dolly glared at him. "Not helpful. I do feel useless standing here. It's not as if someone is about to think, postearthquake, 'You know, I think I'll just pop into that wedding place and get an idea of prices.'"

"Where do we look if she is not here and she is not at home?" Gia asked.

Before anyone could answer, Gia's phone rang—a loud and stark sound in the otherwise quiet office. It made her jump and brought surprised, nervous looks to the faces of those around her. She glanced at the screen and saw a number rather than a name from her contacts list, although she thought that the number might look vaguely familiar. Then again, numbers were so often slightly similar.

"Who is it?" Dolly asked impatiently.

"I do not recognize . . ." Gia started to reply, but Chad became even more impatient than Dolly.

"Answer it, dammit," he snapped, a previously unheard tension present in his voice.

Gia brought the phone up to her ear. "Yes, please . . . ?"

"Gia?" came a female voice on the other end of the line. The voice was speaking her name, but she didn't recognize who it was.

"Y-es . . . ?" she tried. A thought came to her, a crazy thought that she had somehow been listed as the first contact for someone to call if something had happened to Sonia. It felt like taking an icy plunge as the idea brought with it a wave of nausea and the taste of bile leaped into her throat.

"It's Tasha," said the voice on the other end of the line.

"Ta—" Gia began, still confused.

"From the wedding," insisted the woman on the other end. "You know, Yuba City. Pistachio farms and . . ."

"Yes, yes," Gia said, fishing around for words as the familiarity of the number and the voice finally caught up with her. She breathed deeply and her shoulders eased. What the hell was Tasha doing calling in the middle of an earthquake? *Of course*, the next thought followed on quickly, Tasha had moved straight to New York after the wedding and probably had no idea that there had been an earthquake in San Francisco. Or, if she did, she was calling to check that Gia was okay— and that was, in a weird way, rather touching.

"I left him," Tasha told her.

"What?" Gia asked, still feeling too far behind events and, in particular, this conversation.

In front of Gia, Dolly was already getting impatient and hopping from foot to foot. She mouthed, "Who is it?"

"Jimmy," Tasha said on the other end of the line. "I left Jimmy."

"Tasha," Gia mouthed back a little too loudly to Dolly, which Tasha caught on the other end of the phone.

"Yes, I said that, it's Tasha."

"Tasha who?" Dolly asked.

Unable to take the confusion of the three-way conversation any longer, Gia turned and walked away from the others, hearing Dolly huff impatiently behind her.

On the other end of the line, Tasha finally seemed to realize that she might be interrupting something. "Is this a good time?"

"Um . . ."

Tasha continued anyway. "I just . . . He was pulling the same shit he pulled before, you know? As soon as we got back to New York, he was vanishing at night, and I could never get hold of him during the day.

"So, I've left: screw the lot of them, right? Bloody Singhs."

Gia's heart thundered for this virtual stranger on the other end of the line, realizing that she was projecting some of her own fears as she wondered how Tasha would live and look after herself so far from home in New York. "But where will you live? Will they not annul the wedding if you are leaving him so soon?"

Tasha's voice, previously full of triumph and righteousness, shifted a little to something more serious and measured. "It doesn't matter, Gia, that's the point. I'm here now, and I'm not in dull bloody Yuba City.

"I was tempted to just kick him out of the apartment and see what the family did, but instead I can sell the wedding gifts for a few months of rent on a small apartment and . . ." Tasha seemed to drift for a moment, and, when she came back, her voice was dreamy. "This is New York, right? I can do anything here."

The line between them was silent for a long moment, while Gia tried to figure what, if anything, she had to say to Tasha. "I'm glad for you," she said at last. Then immediately realized—considering how short a time the woman had been married—that might not have been the best thing to say. "I mean—"

"I'm glad for me too," Tasha told her knowingly. "Goodbye, Gia."

"Goodbye," Gia replied, keeping the phone up to her ear for several moments after the line had gone dead, wondering to herself why Tasha had called her, of all people. Maybe she just didn't know anyone else in New York to tell, and, Gia guessed, she might not want this news to get back to her hometown quite yet.

"Gia?" Dolly demanded, finally bringing Gia back to the present. "Was that Bride Tasha?"

Gia nodded her affirmation.

"What the hell is she doing calling now?" Dolly demanded, clearly exasperated.

"She left Jimmy," Gia told her.

Dolly's eyes went suddenly wide, and she leaned forward. "Ooh, really?"

"Yes."

"So, he's . . . available?"

"Maybe we should get back to the missing boss here," Chad interrupted with a stern look at Dolly.

Gia noticed that Adi had fixed her with a strange look.

"What?" she demanded, feeling that maybe she had something on her face.

"She called you?" he asked. "Tasha?"

"Uh-huh."

"Because you stuck your neck out to warn her about Jimmy?"

Gia shifted uncomfortably; Adi's gaze felt charged, yet not in the lusty way she had experienced from him previously. "I guess."

Adi shook his head, as if clearing it, then he looked to Chad.

"Yes," Adi put in. "I can't just stay here doing nothing."

Gia noticed for the first time just how agitated Adi had become—brow furrowed, his strong shoulders hunched. Since the start of the earthquake, Gia had considered him an island of calm, and it was at once unsettling and oddly reassuring to see him beginning to fray at the edges.

"That's right," Dolly said. "You boys head down to the lobby. I . . . er, you know, lady's stuff." She thumbed over her shoulder toward the restroom.

Chad looked suitably disgusted and put out. "Really, now?" he complained.

"Yes, Chad, now," Dolly griped at him. "My period doesn't take days off for earthquakes."

That had the desired effect, and Chad shrank back at the use of the p-word, like Dolly had just thrown a wasp's nest at him. "Look, whatever. Just be quick, okay?"

Adi looked toward Gia as he and Chad started toward the door, but Gia felt Dolly's hand tugging at the sleeve of her pullover to make her stay. "I'll be . . ." she told the two men, and, like Dolly had, Gia thumbed toward the restroom.

Chad rolled his eyes again, and the two men turned toward the door, but they only got a few steps when the building started to shake around them. Dolly grabbed Gia's shoulder and shoved her down below the desk, while Adi darted toward them, his arms outstretched toward Gia. The rattling was brief this time, like a fading echo, and it stopped before he even got back to her.

"Only a little one," Dolly observed, standing up again.

Gia didn't think so. It may have been quick, but those terrible few moments had seemed so much worse for being in a building during the earthquake, rather than outside in the park, and she had momentarily thought that the whole place would come down around them.

"Go," Dolly said, scooting the two men back toward the door, "we'll only be a minute. Make sure you take the stairs, yeah?" She said the last bit as if speaking to children.

With one more uncertain look at Gia, Adi joined Chad, and, once they were gone, Dolly put her hands on Gia's shoulders and gently turned Gia to face her. "How are you?" Dolly asked seriously. "Not just the quake but, you know . . . *everything*."

"It is a lot," Gia admitted, although it felt like a huge understatement. "I am sorry I did not answer your messages these last few days."

"I understand," Dolly replied.

"I have been angry at everyone. Whether they deserved it or not."

With that, Dolly pulled her into a long, tight hug. "I understand that too," Dolly told her. "But you know what, in this life you need to hold on to what you have now, not what you didn't have then. Right now, for instance, you have a wealthy mother who is right here."

Gia pulled back slightly, not wanting to be lectured. "Accepting her as you seem to want me to do is an easy thing to say, Dolly," she told the other woman. "You did not grow up where I grew up."

"No, I know," Dolly answered placatingly. "I can't imagine what your childhood was like, Gia. But I do know a thing or two about going without."

Gia failed to control a doubtful sniff. A normal American citizen obsessed with riches wasn't likely to know what "going without" was in Gia's book. She did, however, feel guilty that Dolly had noticed her derision. When Dolly went on, she seemed to have ignored it, changing the subject.

"He adores you, doesn't he?" Dolly asked.

Gia, of course, knew who Dolly was talking about. However, she wanted to play at least a little dumb. "He does?"

"We are in the middle of an earthquake, and he can barely take his eyes off you!" Dolly exclaimed.

Gia couldn't stop the smile that started to creep onto her face, but silvery tears also welled into her eyes at the same time. "It is ruined, though. It . . ."

Dolly was quick to put an arm around her. "Hush. Come on, now. Let's catch them up. Not that I really think we will find Sonia wandering around the streets of San Francisco. She is probably down sipping cocktails in Santa Barbara or something."

Gia did hope that Sonia was safe, although she also hoped that while she was safe, she was also feeling guilty and miserable and not enjoying a cocktail somewhere.

"Do you not need to . . . ?" she asked, indicating the restroom.

"Lady stuff?" Dolly replied. "No, that was a lie. Don't you lie about your menstrual cycles to get your own way?"

Gia shook her head, having no idea that this could be a thing. Dolly put her arm around Gia and started to guide them toward the door.

"You, young padawan," Dolly told her, "have so much to learn."

"*Star Wars!*" Gia had finally got a film reference.

"Ranveer would be proud," Dolly observed.

"I bet he would not," Gia replied under her breath. "Not now."

Gia and Dolly arrived in the lobby to find Chad standing with her uncle Mohammed, while Adi was in an embrace with his stepmother, Sonia. Dolly magnetically stumbled a few steps forward toward the welcome sight of her boss, but Gia stopped short, conflicting emotions warring within her. It was the first time she had seen Sonia since their argument at the party.

"You were not answering your phone!" Dolly chastised Sonia.

Separating from Adi, Sonia held up her mobile phone to indicate a screen that was a complex spiderweb of cracks. At the same time, Mohammed worked his way past the square bulk of Chad to embrace his niece.

"I'm glad you are okay," he told her. "I was worried about you. I must rush off and get home to my family now, though."

Gia nodded, understanding this, but then looked between Mohammed and Sonia meaningfully. "You were in San Francisco?" Further understanding slotted into place. "You two were together?"

Mohammed smiled sadly. "We were catching up, I guess you could say. It has been a very long time."

Gia could not process this quick enough to know how she felt. She wanted to feel betrayed. Sonia finally walked over toward Gia, hovering as if trying to decide what was the best way to approach her daughter. Gia, however, found that instinct took over, and she deftly skirted around Sonia, avoiding the woman's half-outstretched arms.

"I'm glad you are okay," Gia told her, trying her best not to inject too much kindness into her voice.

"I was so worried," Sonia told her. "I thought I had lost you again. It was just like the time I had . . . had to give you up." Sonia's voice cracked.

Gia glanced over at Adi, so many emotions still warring within her. "Adi looked after me." Gia added a little bite into the words.

Sonia looked uncertainly between the two of them, which only served to irritate Gia further. "Good," Sonia said eventually. Although, in Gia's opinion, Sonia did not make it sound like it was good at all.

With that, Gia started back toward the door, realizing that she still did not want to be in the same room as this woman, glad though she was that Sonia was okay. "I will get home," she told Sonia. "But I shall come into work tomorrow, yes?" That she would have to do. She could not stay away forever, even if she may have considered it for one wishful moment. She needed the money, after all. Her paycheck was the only thing that stood between her and being homeless, between her and paying the bills she had already racked up on a credit card Sonia had assigned to her.

Sonia seemed taken aback, although Gia could not be sure whether it was due to Gia's hurry to leave or the way she had made returning to work seem more like a statement than a question.

"Yes, of course," Sonia answered. "But shouldn't you stay? There may be more aftershocks."

"I will be fine," Gia snapped back at her as she rushed out of the revolving door at the front, feeling everyone's eyes on her back and wondering how she would be able to bear having to continue being around this woman. She hadn't asked for this, any of this, even the raw emotion in Sonia's voice when she'd talked of losing her. Gia didn't know how to respond. Should she be feeling forgiving toward Sonia?

What Gia felt was exhaustion. She was itchy. Her hands were chapped. She fled down the street, the blood pounding in her temples.

CHAPTER 28

Sonia was already awake and working in her office in their gorgeous overlooking-the-water house in Sausalito—the first that she and Ranveer had bought together—when the telephone rang early on Sunday morning. The handset in her office had been left off the hook again, as she so often absentmindedly did—next to a cold, half-finished cup of coffee—so it had run out of battery, and she found herself dashing into their lounge, with its breakfast nook, games, and Ranveer's obscenely big TV to answer it.

She hurried because she knew that Ranveer was still dozing, and she didn't want it to wake him. That good work was undone, however, as Sonia took long seconds to answer it, squinting at the unfamiliar number, which began with a dialing code that was, nonetheless, oddly familiar.

"Shah residence?" she answered in that businesslike manner she had cultivated over the years—sometimes she still kind of listened to herself as she spoke, like some part of her could not believe that she was this slickly professional, almost-American woman who ran her own wedding business, like that must surely be someone else and not the girl who had once hailed from Ayodhya.

On the other end of the line there was a moment of silence, like hesitation. A slight static crackled away, as if the call was coming from some distance. *"Didi?"* a voice asked uncertainly.

Sonia's confusion deepened for a few moments longer, then recognition struck with a mixture of surprise and something else beneath it—something that squeezed her insides, just like fear did. "Bindu?"

"You remember me, then?" her sister said, the tone immediately sharp and accusing.

"I . . . Of course," Sonia replied, caught out by the challenge in that strange yet intimate voice. Good manners, if anything, guided her next words. "How are you?"

"I know why you don't call me," Bindu replied, seeming to ignore the question, "it's the same reason I never called you. Neither of us needs reminding, eh?"

"Bindu . . ." Sonia began in protest, although she had no idea what words she was going to follow up with. Even saying the name, feeling it come from her own lips, felt alien after more than a decade and a half.

"Just remember that I'm the one who got left behind," Bindu put in quickly. "You're a wealthy woman now—a rich husband, even started your own business."

So Bindu had been checking up on her; not too hard, she guessed. But she knew almost nothing about her sister's life. Was that discomfort she was feeling? Trepidation or guilt? On the other end of the line, Bindu had paused, somehow adding more weight to her next words.

"A wedding business, of all things. I almost laughed when I saw that."

Although Bindu's tone no longer had the acid in it, the words nonetheless lit a fire within Sonia. She had a reputation at her workplace of not being a woman to mess with—something else she had consciously worked at—and she was certainly not going to take this from Bindu of all people.

"Laughed?" Sonia growled. "You're right, Bindu, I never wanted to speak to you or see you again. You made me give up my baby. How do I ever move past that? How dare you judge me for what I have made of my life here."

Sonia's outburst was met with several long moments of silence. When Bindu did go on, she seemed more subdued. Tired, even. "I did not call to fight with you, I'm sorry. My life has not been easy, either."

Bindu had never married, according to what Sonia knew, from the internet sleuthing she'd done of her family members from time to time. She taught high school math in a public school to kids who didn't like math—a low-paying, unrewarding job. But Bindu didn't offer this information. Rather, when she spoke again, she talked about something altogether harder. "A few years ago, I started looking for her."

"You did what?" Sonia asked. For a moment, she did not understand.

"I've been looking for her, your daughter. Seeing if I could figure out what those miserable nuns did with her."

The "miserable nuns" statement was an olive branch, Sonia could tell that. Even after all these years, she could imagine her sister's mouth twisting upward at the corner as she said it. Almost as soon as that image had passed, however, she also realized that, after all this time, her sister's face might not give quite the same lopsided grin. It may well have changed and lost some of its soft, youthful lines, as hers had.

The thought filled her with a mixture of horror and regret, causing her to inject more ice into the next words than maybe she meant to, shocking even herself. "You should have left it alone."

"Oh, Saumya," Bindu said eventually, the long silence on the line like the no-man's-land of a battleground between them. She spoke with a sort of judgmental, too-patient pity that instantly refueled Sonia's anger.

"Not Saumya, anymore," she whispered, feeling nerves pop along her neck. "You told me that, *choti behn*." Too many feelings were flooding back in one go, threatening to send her world tumbling down, and Sonia began to feel overwhelmed by them, having to grab hold of the back of the couch to steady herself. Not far behind her, Ranveer stumbled out of the bedroom.

"Who is that so early on a Sunday morning?" he asked irritably.

Sonia instinctively cradled the receiver and half turned away from him in panic, before that insidious part of her made her turn back to her husband and put a finger over her lips as if to shush him.

"Work," she hissed.

Ranveer, still bleary eyed, looked puzzled. "You gave them our home number? Honestly woman, you're worse at separating your business and home life than I am." Although he sounded exasperated, Sonia also caught a hint of pride in there. Everything she had achieved in her own business, Ranveer liked to feel a little responsible for, like merely being married to him had made it rub off on her.

Sonia took the opportunity to shush him again and quickly headed out through the glass sliding doors at the back of the lounge to the patio beyond, which had fabulous views down to the water.

"Is that him?" Bindu asked a little too excitedly as Sonia winced, carefully shutting the door behind her. "Your rich husband?"

Sonia strode toward a leaf-colored chair and remembered to keep her voice down. "Yes, the one who knows nothing of any of this. He . . . he . . . can't." She could feel panic rise within her at just the barest thought of it. "He sees me a different way than that."

Bindu let out a long sigh. The tone with which she then spoke held understanding, even if the words had an edge of harshness. "Has it always had to be like this?" she asked. "Is your life always a lie?"

Sonia did not answer, knowing that her silence was the clearest answer she had. After a moment, Bindu sighed again and went on.

"I'm just going to say it, because I cannot call you and not say it, however inconvenient and terrible it might be for you to hear. Then you can decide on the rest of it and what you want to do.

"I found her, *Didi*. I found your daughter."

CHAPTER 29

NOW

Gia had not expected that walking back into the office building, riding the elevator, and ambling up to the Golden State Weddings & Events office would feel as oddly comforting as it did. Already, the place had a familiarity to it, and an ability to remind her she was doing the job she had so long dreamed of doing. It also had Dolly in it, who already felt like one of the best friends she had known as an adult. For so long, she'd been in a middle ground between the rest of the orphans and the nuns at Mercy & Grace, fitting in with neither.

These inconvenient feelings took her by surprise. She needed to stay strong. The way that Sonia had shown such vulnerability during the earthquake the previous day caught Gia off guard. For just a few moments, Gia had seen unbridled humanity in Sonia's face—the fear and subsequent relief of a mother who thought she had lost her daughter. Gia had reacted instinctively when she fled from the building, only later realizing that she had run from exactly what she needed from Sonia. Honesty, vulnerability. Humility.

Gia glanced over toward Sonia's office as she entered, seeing that the slatted blinds were slightly open and that Sonia had two people in there with her. This, on its own, was a little strange, because Sonia's cramped and untidy office was probably not the best place for entertaining clients. She could see that Sonia was on a call.

"Sorry I am late," Gia said to Dolly, who was by her desk close to the center of the main room. She went on, lying reflexively to cover up what she had *actually* been doing that morning. "I think there are still some delays on the BART after the earthquake, the train took so long."

Dolly hurried over but stopped a few paces from Gia and suddenly looked misty eyed.

"What?" Gia demanded self-consciously, paranoid that her lies had been found out. This was ridiculous, of course, because Gia was a great liar when she needed to be, she knew that if she knew nothing else.

Dolly pressed the palms of her hands together. "Oh, look at you," she said proudly. "Sounding like a San Franciscan already. I was worried you wouldn't be coming in, I admit. You left in a hurry yesterday."

Gia cast a nervous eye over toward the office, where Sonia was still on the phone. "It was all too much," she admitted. "But I have a job to do if I want to stay in America. So," she added with a shrug, "here I am."

She could tell that Dolly was disappointed with her answer but was grateful when the designer did not push the point.

"Well, I'm glad you're here. We're about to go and visit a potential wedding venue."

Gia nodded toward the people in Sonia's little office. She could not see them too well, but they looked to be middle-aged. "For them?" she asked doubtfully.

"That is the mother and father of the groom," Dolly informed her. "They want a waterside wedding, and their last venue has fallen through. Sonia has found a venue that can fit them in soon, and, if they like it, then the wedding is ours. It's good, because we're unusually quiet for the next few weeks, so it will keep us busy."

The door to the office opened, and Sonia—no longer on the phone—walked out after a man in a smart navy pinstriped suit and a woman wearing a parrot-green sari. The man had a thin, black mustache, deep-set eyes, and flecks of dandruff on his shoulders. The woman next to him was dark skinned, with thick black *kajal* on her eyes, and a wrist full of bangles.

Gia could see that Sonia was gripping her trademark coffee cup and looked tired as she neared them. Gia's boss—she found it worked best to call Sonia that in her own head—briefly caught Gia's eye before speaking to Dolly. "Mr. and Mrs. Patel will drive with me. Their son, Vilas, is supposed to meet us there with his fiancée, Zara," she said. "Dolly, can you take the company truck with Gia and Chad? You know where you're going?"

Dolly briskly nodded her reply, seeming to match her movement to Sonia's formal tone. Sonia had only fleetingly nodded toward Gia when saying her name.

"Good," Sonia went on. "We must be quick; they can only fit us in within the next hour to see it. See you there."

With that, Sonia followed the Patels to the door. Gia watched her go and, as soon as the door clicked shut, spoke in a sarcastic voice. "Nice to see you, Gia. How are you?"

"It's her way," Dolly said, "you know this. She's pleased you are here, really."

Gia gave Dolly a doubtful look. "Well, it won't matter soon, anyway."

"Why?"

Gia shook her head, cursing herself for having said more than she wanted to. Dolly pushed on. "Come on, what's that supposed to mean? You can't say something like that and leave me hanging."

Just then, Chad emerged from his office at the back and saved Gia, who stubbornly turned away from Dolly. "Hey, Gia," Chad called out cheerfully. Then he glanced at Dolly. "We good to go?"

Around thirty minutes later, the Golden State Weddings & Events truck pulled up outside of what Gia could see was a grand heritage house. The three-story hundred-year-old Victorian mansion stood proudly on the outskirts of the city. They were, as Dolly had informed her, on the northern tip of the city, close to the water, although Gia could not tell quite how close.

Sonia's little electric car was already there, and the truck pulled up in the space next to it, although there was no sign of Sonia or the Patels. Gia, Dolly, and Chad all got out, and Chad immediately started to take pictures of the grounds and moved to get a head-on shot of the front of the building. As they neared the main door, the front of which was covered by a porte cochere, Sonia suddenly appeared in the entrance, her tone as brisk as ever. "Come on," she chided, "we are already inside." She turned, not waiting for them to follow.

"She is in a good mood still," Gia complained quietly but sourly to Dolly.

"This is a big thing," Dolly told her. "It's not just the wedding. The venue has a preferred-vendor list, and this is just one venue within a whole campus in this area. If we impress them, it could lead to a lot more business. Maybe much bigger events, not just weddings and parties—if Sonia wants to go that way."

The entrance led through an arched doorway to a reception area of white marble the size of a tennis court. A bulbous crystal chandelier hung suspended above the center of the lobby from the middle of the domed ceiling. They followed through after Sonia, straight on into an elevated, semicircular lounge, where much of the space was taken up by a long, curving window with a golden curtain thrown open to view the panorama of the water. Little signs above the doorways told them that the dining room was to the left—as did the long rows of dining tables—and the ballroom was to the right.

The Patels were standing next to the window, looking down onto the garden, gesticulating and talking in an excited manner. Moving farther into the room, Gia could see that the well-manicured garden looked straight down onto the water and across the bay, with Alcatraz Island visible slightly to the left.

Mr. and Mrs. Patel turned and walked back toward them, and Sonia spoke to Dolly. "We're going into the garden; the Patels might want to hold the actual ceremony outside. You join us for a chat in a minute, yes?" Sonia waited until the potential clients had walked past and around into the ballroom until she leaned in and added, "Something to wow them, okay? We need this." She glanced at Gia, almost imperceptibly quickly. "After . . ."

Sonia didn't finish the thought and stalked off after the Patels.

"After the Khosla fiasco," Gia finished for Sonia once she was sure that the boss was out of earshot.

"News gets around," Dolly told her, "and our client base can be . . . *superstitious*. A few bad events, and it's like you're cursed. I wonder if the news of the Singh separation is starting to get around yet. Even though the families are from New York and Yuba City, you can bet it will sooner or later."

"Neither of those things were our fault," Gia tried to point out, only half believing her own words.

Predictably, Dolly screwed up her face. "W-e-ll . . ."

"The Singhs wasn't my fault," Gia persisted. "Tasha still married him."

"Perhaps only as a means to an end," Dolly said. "I mean, I guess the penny would have dropped eventually, but maybe it might have taken a year or so otherwise."

Gia blushed. "Thanks," she complained acerbically.

"I'm just saying. If it's a year after, it doesn't look like it's our fault. Or, like I said, a wedding-planner curse or something."

"But the Khoslas ruined their own party before we did."

Dolly raised her thick but impressive eyebrows. "That doesn't really count as a positive."

Gia was quiet for a moment as they wandered up to properly take in the impressive view. Sonia and the Patels were below them in the middle of the lawn, Sonia periodically gesturing, as if trying to get the couple to imagine the wedding event that might happen in that space.

"Why did she look at me when she said about the Khoslas?" Gia muttered, still feeling aggrieved about the whole thing. "That definitely wasn't my fault. *She* started that one."

When Dolly replied, she did it in the way of someone who knew she was about to provoke a bad reaction but could not stop herself. "Well, the shock of you with her stepson was a difficult one for her to swallow."

Gia rounded on Dolly. "Whose side are you on?" she hissed.

Again, Dolly held up a placating hand. "And she was keeping secret the fact that she was your mother. Yes, yes, I know. No spotless souls in this one."

Gia sighed, feeling a certain inevitability about her day so far, about where everything was heading, the way she felt it *had* to go. She wanted to believe that there was a way forward with Sonia. She'd had that moment the previous day . . . but would it be enough? More likely Gia would be waiting for breadcrumbs of emotion from Sonia and pretending that each one was a feast. And working with her would only make it more difficult.

Gia had been trying hard to put aside her anger, although doing so was in itself a colossal task. There were a lot of years to be angry for—a whole childhood in poverty to be bitter about. So, she was trying to ask two simple questions and answer them without the cloud of that anger coloring her feelings: *Can I ever have a relationship with Sonia Shah? Can I do it with her as my boss?* "Ugh, maybe it's for the best," she said, mashing her hands against her eye sockets where a headache roared underneath.

"What?" Dolly asked, appearing instantly to pick up on their interrupted conversation from earlier. "Come on, you were going to say something at the office."

Chad, who had been taking pictures in the dining room, had impeccable timing again as he sauntered into the lounge. This time, however, Dolly was not putting up with it.

"Chad, piss off and take pictures somewhere else," she snapped at him.

For a moment, Chad looked as if he was about to protest; instead, he shrugged and just puttered through to the ballroom.

Although in some ways Gia felt reluctant, she'd also been aching to unburden herself. Ever since speaking to her uncle earlier in the morning, she'd needed to get this off her chest. Dolly might be the best person to tell. Maybe the *only* person she could tell.

"You cannot say, but I have spoken to my uncle Mohammed," she told her. "I may be able to live with him temporarily, and he thinks he can find me a job, something that might allow me to stay in the US and keep my visa for now, or at least until I can reapply. I do not think I can stay here and in the apartment she rented for me any longer."

Dolly looked heartbroken, and it made Gia's own heart drop, despite her best efforts. "Gia . . ."

Gia waved her hands back and forth to stop Dolly carrying on, feeling like she might cry if the other woman continued. She signaled to Sonia and the Patels in the garden below. "Don't," she said. "Not here, not now. Let me be professional for once, eh?"

She started to walk away but stopped when Dolly spoke again. "Don't do anything too hasty, please."

"I just . . . I struggle to be around her. Not with what she has done, not with the way she is. I do not think she will change enough for me to want to know her. Yesterday, for the first time, I saw-saw something promising in the way she behaved. But it-it is not enough, and I do not think I can, how do you say . . . *cultivate* a relationship with her while I work for her as well. While I am in her debt."

"Stay for this wedding," Dolly insisted. "Do that at least. We will need you if we get it. *I* will need you."

Gia sighed resignedly. "Maybe," she answered, not feeling much conviction, "if we get it."

CHAPTER 30

THEN

Sonia sat in her home office. In the last few years since she started her business, she had found the space increasingly useful. It was a comfort to be surrounded by work at home, as well as in the Golden State Weddings & Events office. The room was almost dark, the only glow the harsh white of her computer screen, which had an email on it—the sender showing as "Bindu." In the main body of the text, a name stood out to her, almost every other part of the email seeming to melt away around it.

Sonia reached out a finger and touched the name on the screen. "Gia . . ." she said, rolling her tongue around the name, seeing how it tasted, worried that it would be sour or bitter. It turned out that the second part of the name was the bitter part, where she let out a small harsh laugh, starting to crumble a little inside. "Kumari."

It was a name that meant the girl had no one. A true orphan's name.

There was also an address on the email, the first line of which read: "Mercy & Grace Orphanage." Sonia pulled up a browser and the Google search engine, quickly narrowing and specifying her search until she found pictures of a crumbling building that looked like it had been built at least 150 years ago. It also looked like it hadn't had much care and attention in most of that time.

Sonia stood up, starting to hyperventilate, turning and gripping the back of her chair so hard that she could feel the numbness as the blood left her fingers.

This wasn't supposed to be happening. There was not a single aspect of this that was supposed to appear again in the new life she'd worked so hard to build; not a single particle of a road not traveled was ever supposed to find its way back to Sonia. Though of course she thought of her, sometimes. Mostly when she saw Ranveer interact with his own children. (His ex-wife had returned from Vancouver a couple of years after running away, her fling with the DJ done and over, and set up residence in the next city. Ranveer and she shared joint custody.)

Sonia's eyebrows squeezed. Her daughter would be sixteen years old now. As an image of a bright-eyed girl in a long, thick ponytail flashed through her mind, something rushed up through her, a shriek or a sob or bile. With a shudder, she scooped up all her remaining energy and started to get her breathing under control, nodding to herself as she came to a decision, however unsteadily.

Turning and walking out of her office, Sonia crossed the spacious lounge with the glass doors all along one side and the distant lights in the darkness. She came to the kitchen, where Ranveer was retrieving a milk pan from the cupboard. He did not notice her, happily whistling the theme tune from the *Pirates of the Caribbean* film—a track from a CD of Hans Zimmer movie scores that she had bought him on his last birthday. The cheapest gift she'd ever gotten him, yet he listened to it almost every day.

He looked so cheerful as he continued to get things from the cabinets, blissfully unaware of her silent, hovering presence. Goose bumps swept up her neck and shoulders as she pondered the bombshell she was about to drop and the upheaval it could bring to their wonderful life. He was a picture of contentedness, but she had to tell him this, whatever the consequence.

"Ranveer . . ." she finally managed to say croakily.

He turned at the sound her voice, a jar of spice in one of his hands. Sonia opened her mouth to speak further but hesitated as she tried to find the best way to form the words; Ranveer beat her to it.

"Spicy hot chocolate?" he asked. "I found a recipe with cinnamon and cardamom and cloves."

Sonia, not being much of cook, knew what those things were but was not sure if she had ever bought them, let alone could confidently use them. Perhaps a little too easily, she let herself be distracted from what she was about to say. "We have those things?"

"I bought them earlier," he told her. "I think I might learn to cook more things, now that I'm practically retired. Or else, it is going to be only sweatpants and movie marathons from here on."

Despite herself, Sonia chuckled lightly and fondly, walking a few more steps into the room, treasuring this moment, holding tightly on to it. Warm bubbles in her chest rose as she batted her eyelashes at this uncomplicated man who had treated her with nothing but kindness ever since she had met him.

"I never expected you to slow down too much," she told him. "You are going to show me up and become a Cordon Bleu chef before we know it. You do not do anything by half measures, Ranveer Shah."

"I think my first project is going to be a three-course meal for the children the next time they visit. I know that with all my years of work, they have been kind of neglected. It's time that I make them feel that they are put first, no? I only hope it is not too late."

Sonia watched him as he fetched some milk and poured it into the pan on the stove. She swallowed, now feeling profoundly unsettled.

"I'm sorry," she whispered.

Ranveer looked up at her from by the stove. "Sorry for what?"

Sonia had not expected him to hear her and, now that he had, found herself reaching for at least a version of the truth that she had wanted to tell him. "I have not been much of a wife to you."

Predictably, her kind husband scoffed. "What is that supposed to mean?"

Tears started to come to Sonia's eyes, but, as had long been her way, she forced them back with a steely reserve. "I've not given you everything that a wife should give a husband. For one thing, most of the things I've cooked were heated at two hundred degrees in the oven, and that is about it."

Ranveer crossed over to her, a look of concern now slightly darkening his naturally carefree expression. "Hey, what's this all about? I never wanted you to be *that* sort of a wife, you know this. You always wanted to work, and I respected that you did.

"Now you are building a wedding business from nothing, and I could not be prouder. People who take the time to grow businesses don't always have the time to cook."

The sides of Sonia's mouth felt like they had boulders pulling them down, but she lifted them, wishing in some ways that his words were not the balm on her fragile ego and conscience that they were.

"I do not want to let you down," she told him. "I would have nothing without you." And she knew that she meant those words wholeheartedly. In that moment perhaps more than any other she came to understand that this man was a top priority for her, *the* most important thing. Maybe that was wrong, maybe that wasn't, but she had not made all the choices that had led her to where she was now. She had made the best of it and somehow found a wonderful man to whom she owed any happiness she had.

Ranveer continued to look at her uncertainly for another moment, but eventually he whistled and headed back toward the stove again. "I'm not sure about that," he said. "Anyway, was there something else? You looked like you wanted to say something before I began to talk about hot chocolate and retirement."

He was not always as unobservant as he came across. Sonia momentarily imagined forcing the words out of her mouth. *I have a daughter you never knew about.* It did not work, these were not words that could come into this place—into their house, into the warm, fuzzy ambience right here and right now. "No."

"Oh, it's trying to boil already." Ranveer grabbed a wooden spoon to stir the milk with. "Do not work too much longer, eh? I thought we might put a movie on."

Sonia took a step backward. "I have a call to make, then that's it."

Ranveer huffed out his mild displeasure, although she knew him well enough, of course, to know that his sounds of displeasure were sometimes almost exactly the opposite. "This late?" he nearly crooned. "Business never stops these days."

Sonia played along with the familiar, comfortable game. "I will be straight out after," she promised him. "Keep my chocolate warm for me and choose a movie."

She walked back to her office, carefully closing the door behind her. She did not want to think about this anymore, did not want to be suffering the guilt that came with her decision, so she quickly picked up the phone and dialed Bindu's number.

"Didi?" Bindu answered eagerly.

The word almost stopped Sonia for a moment, it almost undid her resolve. "Yes," she answered stiffly.

"You got my email with the details about your daughter?"

"Gia—"

"Kumari," Bindu finished for her, "I know. Could not those nuns have been more inventive? I will bet that was Sister Mary's idea. Remember that sour-faced crone who seemed old before her time? She might as well have branded the poor child with the big *O* on her forehead."

She remembered Sister Mary, of course she did. For too many years that grim woman had stood sentinel in her thoughts. Sonia had wanted to do well for herself, for Ranveer. Perhaps Saumya would have wanted to do well for Hassan, for his memory. But it had always been Sister

Mary who she had held those internal conversations with, always fantasizing about seeing reluctant respect find its way onto the woman's age-lined face when she told her of the things she had done, the woman she had become.

"I can't meet her," Sonia told her harshly, before other words that she did not want to escape her found their way out.

"What?"

"She can't know of me, you understand? There is no space here for her. I wish there was, but there is not."

"Space?" Bindu was clearly shocked and not expecting her words. She sounded almost heartbroken. "But . . . she's your daughter. And you have seen where she is."

"I am not a mother, Bindu. I am not. She's not had my emotional guidance all these years, and she has not missed very much, trust me. But what I can do is help her in other ways." It should have been a seminal moment, finding that the child she had left behind was alive and well, but all she felt was nausea, a need for the moment to be done with.

"I have money. I want to ensure that she gets an education, that she always has a roof over her head, that she gets opportunities. Will you help me to make sure that this happens? Can you be the one to contact the orphanage for me?"

Bindu still seemed to be finding her way around the first part of the conversation. "You could—"

Sonia was having none of it and quickly cut her off. "She cannot know it is me. She may not even want the help if she knows who it is from, you understand?"

Bindu was silent for a long moment. "Okay," she finally answered with clear reluctance in her voice. "I will approach the nuns at the orphanage. But I think you underestimate the value of giving this girl something to call 'family' in her life. A sense of belonging. Some support."

"I owe her, Bindu, I know this. But I'm not someone who can give her that kind of support."

Bindu let out a sigh, and, when she spoke, her voice was tinged with deep sadness. "Who did you become, sister? Do you ever wonder how things would be if the mob had stayed away that day?"

Of course she fucking did. Stupid fucking question. "No, what is the point? Saumya Pandey died that day, along with Hassan, the man who was to be her husband." She slung nervous eyes at the door to her office and lowered her voice for her next words. "Saumya Pandey would never do the things I have done."

CHAPTER 31

THEN

They were just beginning to settle into their Sunday evening when the telephone started to ring. Farha got up and stood over the telephone. She peered at the instrument, which rested atop a shaky three-legged table against the family room wall.

"Hmm, looks like an international number," she told her husband.

"Just ignore it," Mohammed told her, irritated by the interruption of the Bollywood movie they were watching, wondering just where he had put the remote control so he could pause the TV before they missed anything.

"It is annoying, though," Farha observed, staying to glare silently down at the telephone, as if she could somehow send her bad vibes through it to whoever was interrupting their weekend viewing.

Finally, the call went through to the answering machine, and a woman with a thick Indian accent began to speak. "Hello? I'm looking for Mohammed Khan. My name is Bindu; you will remember me as Bindu Pandey."

Mohammed was on his feet in a flash, and he pushed past Farha to grab the handset, ignoring the confused and annoyed look his wife gave him. "Hello?" he said, instantly thinking that he should have stayed on the couch rather than leaping up to answer the phone. He moved back past Farha, shooing her interested look away from him and heading toward their bedroom.

"Yes, this is Mohammed," he added as soon as the door closed behind him.

"Hello," said the voice on the other end, "I do not know if you remember me?"

"Bindu, of course I do," Mohammed answered, his mind a confused swirl of thoughts, but his good manners still very much in place. "How are you?"

"Well enough, thank you," Bindu replied in a formal tone of voice. "How did you . . . ?"

"Track you down? Not easily. It's taken me close to two years. I found a cousin of yours. They say that you all but disappeared from your family shortly after the . . . riots." She paused for a moment. "America appears to be the place to disappear to."

"Is it?" Mohammed asked, as much to find words to fill the conversation with as a genuine question. His mind raced with thoughts of the past. More than anything, he wanted to know why this woman who he had so nearly been related to was calling him after all these years. "You have a family?"

"No, I never married, but I am happy. A job with steady income, a home of my own . . . And you? Was that your wife?"

Mohammed felt a chill inside at the sudden personal line of questioning, like two worlds that were never supposed to meet were coming into contact. If two parallel universes met, would they both be destroyed? "It was."

"Good," she said, and he recognized a genuine note of pleasure in her voice. "What do you do for work now? I remember how clever you were."

Mohammed could not keep the veneer of politeness up anymore, however. "I'm sorry, I do not mean to be rude—"

"But what am I doing calling you like this?"

Mohammed let out a sigh, feeling impolite for pushing her. "Yes."

There was a long beat on the other end of the line, although he had not remembered Bindu as someone who needed to create dramatic effect. "I've been sitting here for thirty minutes trying to find a good way to say this," she said, "but there is no way to soften it, to prepare you. So, I shall just have to tell you. You have a niece, Mohammed. Hassan's daughter."

Mohammed, still standing up in the bedroom, stumbled backward and landed with a slight oomph on the bed. "Hassan? He . . . How?"

"Saumya was pregnant at the time of the . . . wedding. She, um . . . She gave the child up, and the child then ended up in an orphanage. That is the short story."

Mohammed felt his temper rising, a mix of indignation and sudden retrospective helplessness. "You knew this? Why did you not contact me? I could have helped."

Bindu's reply was flat, unamused by his sudden show of bravado. "You were gone, Mohammed. Your whole family had vanished from Ayodhya. And, to be honest, I was more concerned with my sister at the time."

"Saumya?" Mohammed said, suddenly realizing that he had not thought of Hassan's old bride-to-be once during the whole conversation. "Does she know?"

"Saumya is . . . I cannot reach her."

Mohammed did not quite know how to put that sentence and a half together. "Is she . . . ? She's alive?" He had no reason to believe otherwise—at least, he had not heard of her death in those terrible days that followed the wrecked wedding, but then if there was a child, of course she had lived.

Bindu took a moment to answer, and, when she did, she had changed the subject. "I am more concerned with the child now than I am with her."

"The girl is in an orphanage, you say?"

"Yes, in Noida, not far from New Delhi. I have not been there but it looks . . . It is not good, Mohammed, but she is well, and she is fed. Her name is Gia."

Mohammed took a deep breath, trying to take in her name, to fully *feel* the idea of her, although Bindu's words—*it is not good, Mohammed*—had set off a slight feeling of panic within him.

"Can we get her out? I'm . . ." Despite everything, he found himself forcefully swallowing his pride to say the next words, as if he were in some way answering to a past world, to a past him and even to a past her. "I am only a cab driver. I came here illegally at first, so I've never been able to . . . I do not know if I could afford to bring her here. I have a family—"

Mohammed glanced at the door, and, when he went on, he did so in a whisper. "They know little of the past. But I want to help. It is Hassan's daughter, after all."

"All of us are hiding from what happened that day, Mohammed, I understand. Even though we were not the ones who did anything wrong. You are a good man, however. I knew that you were the right one to call."

He was a good man, wasn't he? He tried to be. "We will figure it out. I can find money somehow."

"It's okay," she said. "Money is not the problem. She will stay where she is for now, but she will be looked after, given every opportunity, although she will not know exactly where the money is coming from."

"Maybe she needs more than money, Bindu. Maybe she needs a family."

"Oh, Mohammed," Bindu said, sounding at once pleased and sad. "I always liked you. That's why I tried so hard to find you, and it's taken me a long time to do that. Family is exactly where you come in."

A few minutes later, Mohammed opened the door back into the family room and found Farha standing right on the other side of it, so that he almost walked smack into her.

"Who was that?" his wife demanded.

"No one," he clearly lied, pushing past her and hoping that his evident disinterest in holding the conversation would convince her to leave it be. Fat chance. He sensed his wife follow him across the family room.

"Don't lie to me, Mike."

Mohammed rounded on her, not in the mood to—not feeling *at all able* to—have this conversation. "Okay, it's none of your business. Is that better?"

Farha's face only hardened. "She called you *Mohammed*. No one calls you that. Who was she, Mike? Where was she calling from? India? Is she from your past?"

Mohammed shot her an impatient look, trying to warn her off as he felt close to the edge of losing his temper. Farha, however, took the initiative on that one.

"You never tell me anything!" she screamed, only inches away from his face. "You're my husband, the father of my children, and I don't even know who you are."

Mohammed felt the storm beginning to erupt within and took a long, slow breath trying to find the words that the situation needed. "I'm Mike. What does anything else matter?"

"You tell me, Mike," Farha spat. *"You tell me."*

Farha turned to where a young boy had appeared at the end of the hallway that led toward the two children's bedrooms and the backyard beyond. Their eldest son, Hassan, was standing there, looking worried.

Mohammed held out a placating hand. "It's okay, Hassan. Adult stuff."

Farha, however, continued to address her husband. "We are your family, Mike," she told him, indicating the boy. "You should put us first."

"I do."

Farha's head suddenly snapped up, like something had just occurred to her. "You said his name. You said Hassan."

Geez, she must have had her ear pressed right up to the door, and Mohammed couldn't help but be a little appalled. "You listened?"

"Was it about your brother? I thought he was . . ."

She stopped herself, acknowledging that their eldest child was still in the room, his expression uncertain, scared.

"He is," Mohammed said quietly through gritted teeth.

Finally, Farha's face softened a little, and she stepped forward, putting a sympathetic hand on his chest. "He is the only thing I know of your past, and you never even said what happened to him. If you can't tell me"—she indicated his son—"tell *us*, then who can you tell? The strange woman on the telephone, this Bindu? Who is she?"

Mohammed pulled away from her and took several steps toward the door, thinking that he might need to leave, that he needed to get away and just drive—get far from everyone and everything. However, it occurred to him at the last moment that his front door really did represent a threshold right now, and he turned back to his wife.

"I . . . I have a niece that I did not know about."

CHAPTER 32

NOW

Gia had once been better at getting up in the morning. An uncomfortable bed and a thin blanket, which, for a little while, had even been a cloth sack, had made getting out of bed when she lived at Mercy & Grace Orphanage much easier. Now she had a thick duvet and a spring mattress, which were like insistent fingers that tried to stop her getting up when her rude, attention-seeking alarm beeped out its unrelenting, brain-grating tune.

These comforts, however much she did appreciate them, nonetheless still felt tainted, and she found herself keeping up an inner guard—determined not to let herself enjoy any of them too much.

Her alarm had sounded at four thirty that morning, and she'd been ready for Dolly to come and pick her up at five. The sun was just beginning to crack the eastern horizon as the Golden State Weddings & Events truck pulled onto the grounds of the General's Residence where the Farooq-Patel wedding was to take place on this day, and Gia's brain still felt like it was back in her bed.

Dolly—who looked far too bright eyed and ready for the day for Gia's liking—drove the truck down a ramp and straight into a service entrance where Sonia and Chad were already waiting. Along with someone else Gia had not been expecting to see.

"Morning," Sonia said to both of them in her usual brusque way, placing a to-go coffee cup—where on earth had she managed to get a barista coffee made at this hour?—down and immediately heading around toward the back of the truck. Chad shuffled past, his unruly but now-immaculate shock of recently-dyed-to-black hair looking like he had been up since two thirty to get the appearance right, but Adi—the unexpected member of the team—lingered, his hands in his pockets, his eyes half downcast. They hadn't seen each other since the day of the earthquake, and Gia could feel her heart beating like a drumroll.

"Sonia said you would need an extra pair of hands today," he offered in explanation, without being asked for it. Perhaps, Gia thought, her eyes had betrayed her.

"Yes, it was not possible to access the location last night," Gia answered in a light tone, thinking that this might be the most mundane thing she had ever said to him. She wondered if they would ever say anything more interesting to each other again.

"I . . ." His eyes flicked up at her for a brief moment. "She needs help," he finally said, seeming to repeat himself. "She's alone. Her marriage is on the rocks."

There was no accusation in his voice, only sympathy, and it began to stir something within Gia, not unlike milk curdling in her stomach.

"Adi! Gia!" Sonia called out from the back of the truck. "Come and start carrying things, will you? We have a long morning ahead of us."

Both of them jumped a little, like kids caught with their hands in the cookie jar, and they scurried to help. Dolly and Gia had spent so much of their week making hanging decorations for the *mandap* and designing a "set" for the *nikah* ceremony, which was to be held in the garden, overlooking the water. There were endless table centerpieces, while the flowers were due to arrive before nine, and the caterers would begin setting up at ten. They had pulled all the linens together, but they still had to have everything in place before the families began arriving for the ceremony.

"Once everything is outside," Sonia told Gia and Adi, "then I want the two of you to start on the assigned-seating lists. But Gia"—she pointed at her—"make sure you are taking pictures of everything as it goes up. I want you to capture how we are changing the venue."

Gia nodded, always glad to be asked to use her phone and to take photos—to create. And this might be her last chance to capture anything like this.

"Maybe a post or two this morning but no photos yet, in case the families are checking out our social media," Sonia added.

Sonia was beginning to get her head around the whole social media thing, which Gia was feeling both good and bad about. Every time Sonia spoke about the company's social media presence, Gia felt validated, felt like she had been carving out a niche for herself within the company, even if she automatically begrudged any idea of needing validation from Sonia. Yet, at the same time, she had wanted the Instagram account, Twitter, and the Facebook business page to be *her* thing, and her thing alone. She did not want Sonia's strong will, her forcefulness, coming into it.

But then, of course, she remembered that she was leaving, that she was not supposed to care. She should let these worries go.

Gia had spent most of the last week with Dolly, buried in a world of gold and silver adornments, floral wedding arbors, shamianas, and endless, endless decorative options for the Big Fat Indian wedding, as she had come to think of it. Almost every time she had spoken to Sonia, Dolly had been present, and Sonia had essentially been speaking to the designer, not her. Having seen Sonia open up the way she had, it had first been frustrating and, ultimately, annoying that Sonia had not found the time to speak to her alone. Yet, throughout the week after the earthquake had occurred, this farcical, formal way in which they had related to each other had become a comfort, because Gia had realized something else. Sonia was protecting herself, just the same way that Gia did. The desperate outburst in the foyer of their office building was all that Sonia had to express herself and, it having not yet yielded some gushing response from Gia, Sonia had no more to give on that front. And so, instead, she had reverted to type . . . the Ice Queen demeanor she did so well.

"You want to take a picture before we start putting the chairs up?" Adi asked her when the waitstaff arrived with the first of the chairs and tables brought up from the service area. They would drape them with pristine white tablecloths. In the middle they would place the centerpieces of red roses and baby's breath that had delicate silk butterflies dancing among the fresh blooms. Sonia wanted each table to be adorned with china, crystal, and silverware for every guest who had RSVPed yes. They had thirty-six to cover. It was going to take a while.

"I guess," Gia replied. The empty grounds had an incredible backdrop toward the shimmering water of the bay and Aquatic Park Pier, yet the garden itself was still a blank canvas and was not going to make the best picture.

"I miss you," Adi said behind her as she framed the photo for a panoramic view, trying to decide how much of the breathtaking background to keep in and how much to save to make the "after" photo seem all the more impressive—like Golden State Weddings had somehow brought San Francisco Bay along with them as well. *Man*, she was good. The job that Mohammed *might* be able to secure for her was one answering telephones for the cab company. It would not, she understood, be as rewarding creatively, but then maybe it would not have to be forever.

Adi's quiet declaration caused Gia to fumble the shot, and she silently cursed Adi as she kept her back to him. She could not do this. She had been glad to see him, but now she realized that she could not deal with him *and* her and a whole wedding to be put on.

"Did you hear me?" he asked, his voice quivering a little. Gia had taken off a hooded jacket that she had been wearing against the chill early air, and she now shivered a little as the westerly breeze found her, making its way in from the sea, even though the wind's touch was warm.

"I can't," she said, still not turning around. Then, a moment later, against her better judgment, she asked, "Are you okay?" She quickly snapped the picture a second time and began to set out the tables, not seeming to wait for the answer.

"You've not met my sister, Roma," Adi said, expertly clutching champagne glasses in a four-leaf-clover pattern as he deftly changed the subject. Gia knew that he had a sister but little else about her. "She is one of those people that you only love because you are related to her."

That made Gia look up, trying to suppress the grin she felt pulling at the corners of her mouth.

"I don't mean that really," Adi said, catching her reaction. "I love her, of course I love her. Although we are very different. She is three years older than me and always believed she was the boss of me. She likes shiny things a lot more than I do. She's mad about clothes and wants every part of her life to be aesthetically pleasing." He laughed. "Princess Bling is what I call her, and I think she secretly likes the nickname.

"But she is also hard nosed in a way that I could never be. She can be cold when she wants to, and she has always monopolized our father's attention. She cannot help this, you understand, doing so is like breathing for her. And, I have never resented it."

Adi finished with the table service on his end and turned to Gia. "She never really accepted Sonia. All these years, and she still treats her like she is the woman who invaded our lives. Over time, she has become less . . . *overt* about it. I'm not sure she even means to hurt Sonia anymore. Yet, as far as Roma is concerned, Sonia is still a second-class citizen in our lives. She always comes last, always sits a little on the outside."

"Not-not for you?" Gia asked.

"I've known Sonia for longer than I knew my mom. And now my dad won't even talk to her. Neither will Roma." Gia saw his face break a little, for a moment, like Jell-O losing its shape. "So, you ask me how I am? I feel like I'm losing my family, and now I can't even talk to you."

Adi didn't wait for any response, instead walking past Gia and around the building—the quickest way back to the storeroom and the huge stack of tables they still had to get through. Gia lingered, trying to take in what she had just heard. Sonia had been putting up a shamiana toward the other end of the rear garden, and, just as Gia was about to turn and head back down to get more chairs, a gust of wind, stronger than anything the day had offered so far, caught the uncompleted cloth tent and caused it to sway violently, half collapsing the structure, the scarlet, gold-lined exterior crumpling inward in places.

A shriek sounded inside of the tent, and Gia and Adi instinctively ran to help. As she got closer, Sonia began to yell. "Help!" she cried. "Help me!" It was Sonia's voice—and yet, not at all like Sonia's voice. Gia grabbed and pulled at the fabric, which seemed so much more voluminous when much of it had fallen to floor level.

She fought through it, lifting the heavy tent with great effort to continue making progress, and suddenly a part of it lifted to reveal Sonia, who had fallen to the floor, now curled up almost into a ball, her arms over her head as if protecting herself from some unseen assailant's blows.

Gia did not know what to make of what lay before her. She had lifted the tent enough for Sonia to make her escape, but even now the woman continued to lie on the ground, curled up in a ball, whimpering, seemingly unaware that she could easily get out from under it.

"No," Sonia cried quietly, "don't let them come."

"Sonia," Gia said, first softly, then again more firmly to grab her attention. Finally, Sonia looked up at her, disoriented, glancing about herself as if she was surprised at where she was.

"Where is Chad?" Gia asked. Last she had seen, he had been helping Sonia set up the tent.

Sonia finally came back to the present, the change rippling across her face and dramatically transforming what Gia could see there. "He went to find my phone," she said, getting to her feet and brushing herself off. "I left it inside."

Sonia pursed her lips and avoided Gia's eyes, as if still embarrassed. "Are you okay?" Gia found herself asking, mostly because the whole thing had unsettled her so much. "That was . . ."

Gia struggled to find the words but could see in Sonia's eyes that her boss knew exactly how odd it had looked. "This needs to be perfect today," Sonia told her, regarding Gia with something twitchy and uncertain in her eyes. "Not only because of the opportunity it provides us for future business, for getting away a little bit from only the weddings of the fussy Indian community. But because it is a hard wedding. Vilas is Hindu; Zara is Muslim. It needs to be the best wedding, so then *that* is all people will want to talk about."

These were, perhaps, the most words that Sonia Shah had said to her in one go since she had come to San Francisco. Certainly, it was the most since she had discovered that the woman was her mother. Gia looked for something to say, feeling the gravity of the moment between them, but her mind was stuck on a burgeoning revelation, like a rock tumbling down a hill.

You are damaged, Sonia Shah, Gia thought as she looked at her. *You are irrevocably broken.* Or maybe Saumya was the broken one, the shattered pieces of her left behind somewhere in India, with the attack having poisoned her psyche. Cornered and battered, the horror and guilt and sadness had taken physical form, and this new person had been created from what was left. Gia had known this, after a fashion, yet she had not understood what any of that meant until she had seen the terror-stricken Sonia screaming for help beneath the cloth of a collapsed shamiana, until she had understood the importance of this Hindu and Muslim wedding to her. Sonia Shah may have transformed herself into a different woman than Saumya Pandey was—a guarded, secretive, bruised shell of a woman—but she was still human.

Gia felt an internal release, like a tourniquet loosening. She tried again to open her mouth, to say something, anything that could convey even a little of this to Sonia, but Chad—with typical timing—came huffing and puffing across the lawn toward them, Sonia's phone in his hands.

"You should do cardio as well as weights," Gia grumbled irritably at him.

Chad ignored her, his eyes meeting Sonia's. "I took a call, from Vilas," he said, a hint of guilt in his eyes, "I was worried it might be urgent."

"Yes?" Sonia nodded impatiently, dismissing his guilt over answering the boss's phone.

"We have a very big problem."

CHAPTER 33

"What is it with people?" Sonia complained as she drove Gia across the San Francisco–Oakland Bay Bridge toward Oakland in her little electric vehicle. "I swear, lately there has not been an event that has just been easy, straightforward. Why do people book events with us and *then* decide to sort out their family dramas?"

The call that Chad had answered on Sonia's phone was from Vilas Patel, the bridegroom-to-be, having an anxiety attack because his future in-laws—reluctant in-laws, apparently—had decided that they were not going to attend the wedding. Vilas's parents had taken a "screw 'em" attitude—"just go get your bride, we'll take care of everything else," they had assured their son, and they had taken charge of organizing the wedding. But Vilas wanted Sonia to intercede, to try and persuade his in-laws-to-be for Zara's sake.

"I mean," Sonia went on, slapping a hand to the top of her chest, "do I *look* like a family counselor or something?"

No, Gia thought, *you definitely do not.* What Gia could not work out, however, was why Sonia had instructed Gia of all people to come with her. Surely—as apparently the wedding was going ahead with or without the bride's parents—her time would have been better spent back at the venue, as they had been on a tight schedule as it was.

"I do not see why it is our problem, either," Gia said, earning a raised eyebrow from Sonia. "It is their own stupid problem if they miss out on their daughter's wedding."

"And it is *our* problem if the couple looks miserable in all the pictures and the talk is of the lack of a mother and father of the bride, rather than what an incredible job Golden State Weddings & Events did." Sonia shook her head. "Ugh, I cannot believe all the problems we have had lately. And this one looked so promising. Why us?"

Although Gia had the sense that Sonia's question was rhetorical, that she did not *need* an answer, a rather obvious one came to mind, and—right now, for the first time properly alone with Sonia since Gia had discovered that the woman was her mother—it seemed like an opportunity to air her thoughts. "Maybe it is my presence. I might be bad luck."

For a brief moment—perhaps only half a second—Sonia glanced at her unguardedly, shock and concern showing. Then it was gone, and Gia found it hard to be sure that the look had ever been there at all. "That's ridiculous," Sonia muttered. "There is no such thing as bad luck, only bad choices. Like when you told Tasha about her fiancé's mistress in Yuba City. And that turned out okay, anyway."

"Kind of."

"Well, okay for us, which is what matters. And none of the rest of our recent problems have been your fault."

"There was the time where you screamed at me in Palo Alto for-for dating your stepson behind your back," Gia put in rebelliously. Was she trying to start an argument?

Sonia opened her mouth as if to disagree again but instead started to laugh. Despite herself, Gia joined in. It was ridiculous, not at all funny, yet here they were, almost in tears about it. As their laughter subsided, the seemingly incessant awkwardness between them—which had been there right from her first moment working at Golden State Weddings & Events, well before things became more complicated—started to return. Gia swallowed loudly, wondering whether to say what was in her head. When else, though, if not now?

"I am serious, though. If you think how things have been since I came into your life . . . Has anything worked out all that well for us, and for you especially? Now I hear your husband will not even speak to you after finding out about me. Maybe I am bad luck for you. I came from such a terrible time in your life, and maybe that is where I should stay."

Gia was shocked by what she found herself saying. If she had, in any way, imagined reconciliation between them in these last few weeks, those fantasized moments had involved a groveling Sonia Shah who had so very deeply seen the error of her ways. Yet here Gia was, calling herself "bad luck." Still, maybe this was the easiest way to say goodbye. Easier for both of them. It felt like she was taking charge of the situation, being the adult abou—

"Watch out!" Gia cried as Sonia veered across into her neighbor's lane and earned a long blast of the horn from the semitruck that was overtaking her. Sonia swerved back, the short, proportionally high-sided vehicle rocking disconcertingly on its suspension for a moment until she got the car pointing straight again.

Gia's eyes went to Sonia's hands on the steering wheel, which seemed to be gripping it hard enough to crush it. "Sorry," Sonia muttered, her eyes focused on the road ahead. Moments slid slowly away as Gia waited to see if Sonia was going to say anything. To disagree with Gia, to tell her that she was not bad luck. Or even to agree with her, because then that would make things so much easier. Yet Sonia's eyes stayed on the road ahead, and Gia, out of the corner of her eye, occasionally caught her mouth working silently, unknowable words or phrases slipping from the woman's lips.

They had passed over the bridge now, were dropping in toward an industrial-looking landscape.

"I recognize this," Gia said. "Uncle Mohammed lives this way."

"Yes, the Farooqs live in Oakland, like your uncle," Sonia replied. Then, after a moment she added, half to herself, "All these years, and I had no idea he was here. So close by."

"Would you have visited him if you knew?" Gia asked, unable to resist putting a little acid into her voice—poking, probing for a reaction. "Been friends?"

Sonia glanced strangely at her for a moment, then returned her eyes to the road with a simultaneous shake of the head. "No, I suppose not. I'm not sure he ever really liked me back then. I'm not sure I cared for him too much, either. Hassan was our common link, the reason we put up with each other." They pulled up at a traffic signal. Sonia glanced sharply over at Gia for a brief moment. "He adores you, you know, your uncle."

"I know. He's . . ." *Say it, Gia. Say it and have it done.* "I might go and live with him for a while." Sonia's expression was unreadable, but she nodded slowly—in understanding, it seemed, if not in agreement.

"Longer to get to work," Sonia pointed out, like a bit character in a movie foreshadowing what was coming.

Say it, Gia. Tell her. She did not, of course, know if she had any other job yet, but she wanted so much right now to have this done, to tell Sonia right here, to her face, that she was going to remove herself from the woman's life. If she owed her mother anything, perhaps she owed her that. Not an email or a letter, but words spoken to her face.

That was when a call came in, and Sonia tapped on the dashboard screen to answer it hands-free. "Vilas?"

Gia could hear the clear distress on the other end of the line. "I am going to their house," the young bridegroom-to-be said, sounding as if he was walking and slightly out of breath. "I'm just around the corner. I'm going to have it out with them."

"I'm five minutes away," Sonia told him. "Why don't you slow down, just wait until we're there? There are things that . . . are better if they come from me."

There was a long pause on the other end of the line. Only the sound of Vilas's labored breathing could be heard, and the brief roar of a vehicle driving past. "Okay."

Vilas hung up and Sonia winced. "We do not need this."

"I do not know why you brought me along," Gia told her. "What am I going to do, post the Farooqs' refusal to come to the wedding on Instagram?"

"You are kidding, right?" Sonia said, sounding shocked. "You are my secret weapon here, Gia. You are my heart."

CHAPTER 34

A neatly trimmed hedge that grew about three feet tall bordered the Farooqs' driveway. The house was in a nicer residential neighborhood of Oakland than where her Uncle Mohammed lived, Gia noted. The bridegroom-to-be, Vilas, was standing on the sidewalk just outside of the house. Gia noticed the face of a middle-aged South Asian man with a scraggly beard briefly appear at one of the windows, looking out momentarily before disappearing again.

She felt like a policewoman turning up at some sort of domestic call, or perhaps a small siege.

"You have not been up to the door?" Sonia asked Vilas as she crossed over to the driveway. Vilas was dressed in jeans, a white T-shirt, and white sneakers, his forehead creased with worry, and his eyes looked ringed and haunted. His fingers kneaded his mobile phone like it was a stress ball. Vilas did not look like someone who was due to be married that afternoon, although Gia could tell that the man's symmetrical features and tanned skin in the traditional red turban would be a delight to photograph later on. He was going to be a dashing groom, Gia knew, with or without the presence of those idiots inside the house.

"No, but they know I am here," Vilas answered. "Abdul Farooq, that . . ." He resisted reaching for whatever probable expletive he had been planning to use. "He shouted from the door that he was going to call the cops if I came any closer."

Sonia made an exasperated sound. "Let's see if he calls the police on me, eh?" She marched down the drive like a woman who was not about to take any prisoners. Gia loitered for a moment, smiling awkwardly at Vilas and wondering if Sonia had expected her to follow. Finally, feeling almost like a bungee cord was in place between Sonia and her, she stumbled down the angled drive and toward the front door, which opened slightly.

The grim face of Abdul Farooq—the father of the bride—a thin, pigeon-chested man, appeared in the opening, and Gia noted that he had pulled the chain across, as if he expected Sonia to try and shoulder-barge her way in. Gia might have understood the sentiment if it had been muscle-bound Chad rather than Gia following the Golden State Weddings & Events boss down the driveway. Then again, Sonia's face probably looked like it could break down a door right now.

"Go away," Abdul Farooq said to Sonia. "We're not coming, and we've nothing to say about it."

"Is it the flowers?" Sonia said, an acid hiss in her tone belying the flippancy of the words. "We could change the arrangements; it may not be too late."

Abdul glared at her, clearly unamused and looking almost as exasperated as Sonia had a moment before. Gia stood just behind Sonia's shoulder.

"The catering, then. We emailed you the menu for your approval. You didn't respond, but it should suit all tastes and beliefs."

The man's face became dark with rage. "Don't be ridiculous," he spat. "You know why we are not coming."

When Sonia spoke again, her voice was a little softer, inviting Abdul Farooq to unburden himself. "Why don't you explain to me why, so I understand?"

Abdul's eyes flicked to Gia, up to Vilas at the end of the drive, then the other way, as if checking whether any of the neighbors were watching. He sighed, removed the chain, and opened the door farther, stepping back. "Why don't the two of you come in?" He shot daggers up at Vilas, however, a warning that he was not invited.

Walking into the hallway, Abdul was already striding toward the sitting room that Gia could see lay beyond it. Above the entrance to the sitting room was a framed painting of what she thought was the Kaaba in Mecca (she had done some googling when she had found out she was half Muslim) and a tapestry depicting a mosque in Medina. Sonia stopped suddenly, looking up at the Mecca painting for a moment, so that Gia almost walked into her, brushing her arm lightly as she half stumbled in avoiding her.

Sonia glanced at her and, for the second time that day, wore an expression that Gia had not seen before. She was glassy eyed, almost fearful. Sonia's hand grabbed Gia's arm for a moment, as if she were steadying herself.

"Are you okay?" Gia asked reflexively.

"Yes," Sonia answered, clearing her throat and managing a half smile, which actually reached her eyes for once. "Déjà vu, that is all." She leaned in, half whispering. "Now, I need you to try and work on the mother, Maryam, if you get a chance, while I handle him."

The sitting room was awash with religious iconography—the wall was embellished with endless calligraphic motifs and verses from the Quran and Arabic proverbs. And their daughter was marrying a Hindu boy. What a slap in the face, eh? Brought up by nuns in an orphanage with kids from all religions, no one's differences had ever seemed more important to Gia than the bond they shared by having no one beyond the walls of Mercy & Grace. Only a few years ago she had discovered she was half Muslim by birth herself—and who ever would have told her or known that to be the case?—so Gia was struggling to have sympathy with these people, who were just bigots as far as she was concerned.

"Oh, Abdul," Maryam Farooq said as Sonia and Gia entered behind her husband, the disappointment in her voice evident. She was a small, round woman, with a cream-colored lace scarf wrapped around her head from her jaw to her crown, and multiple rings on her fingers.

"Do you want a scene on our front porch?" Abdul grumbled back at his wife.

"We've already got that boy hanging out by the road," Maryam retorted.

"That boy is your future son-in-law," Gia chided the older woman, before even thinking what she was saying. It earned a sharp glance from Sonia and slightly shocked looks from Abdul and Maryam. Gia should, of course, have kept quiet and looked abashed about her outburst. But she was Gia Kumari of Mercy & Grace Orphanage, and she did not pull punches, because no one else ever did.

"It is the morning of his wedding, and he is so stressed, his asthma is acting up," Gia added.

Maryam, recovering from the initial shock of the way Gia spoke to her, now snorted unsympathetically. "Every man gets stressed on the morning of their wedding, this is as old as time."

Abdul Farooq, however, was more direct. "We are not going to accept that, that . . . *Hindu* as a member of our family. Perhaps we cannot stop Zara, she has always been a willful girl, but we do not have to be a party to it. We do not have to condone it. If we go it is like we will be showing our approval, and everyone will see us doing so." His voice had reached a small crescendo as he spoke, passion gathering within it, and he finished with a vehement shake of his head.

"May we have tea?" Sonia asked, looking over at Maryam. "It is a warm day already, and I have not drunk a thing yet."

Maryam looked over at her husband, as if for permission. Abdul Farooq wore a troubled frown and was staring at a point on the crimson *kanni*-patterned carpet, but he gave a small nod. *Clever,* Gia thought. Once they were inside the house, these clearly traditional and devout Muslims would not refuse asked-for hospitality, whatever the circumstances.

As Maryam headed toward the kitchen, which was over to the left, Sonia caught Gia's eye and gave a nod of the head that indicated she should follow the groom's mother. Gia did so, but Maryam looked at her resentfully.

"I thought you might like some help," Gia quickly offered.

"I am capable of making some tea," Maryam sniffed, then she cast an eye back at Gia while gathering cups. "You are not grown up in America, no?"

"I have been here not much longer than a month," Gia told her.

"Your English is good, even if your manners are not. Are you educated? What made you come over here?"

Gia felt her jaw set but inwardly took a long, full breath. The woman was trying to anger her and put her off from talking about the thing that they both knew she had come out to the kitchen to talk about. "The nuns in the orphanage taught me English," she answered, then added, unable to entirely quell that little bit of defiance, "the other orphans taught me my manners."

Maryam Farooq smiled a little at that. "You're a tough cookie, eh? Pass me the pot." She pointed to a finely painted teapot in delicately blended enamel colors. It looked like a family heirloom, and Gia was careful about how she passed it over. Maryam placed a traditional-looking kettle onto the gas stove. *Geez*, even Gia had discovered the joys of an electric kettle. How old-fashioned could you get?

"So, what are you," Maryam went on, "a charity case? That or you are very good at your job." The other woman searched Gia's eyes, perhaps looking for a sign that she was getting riled up by her rudeness.

Gia, for her part, was trying not to show how close to the bone the woman was striking. "Can I not be both?" Gia finally answered, beginning to wish that she had been a bit more careless with that expensive-looking teapot.

"I would rather Zara was with a girl like you than a Hindu," Maryam said as she spooned loose-leaf tea into the pot.

"Thank you, I think, although I doubt Zara swings that way," Gia replied, keeping the irony of her half-Hindu heritage to herself.

But her quip was lost on Maryam, who continued to vent her frustration.

"Maybe you came from nothing, maybe you are just a street rat, but at least you are a defiant, clever street rat. Trying to make something of yourself. That is better than a—"

"Hindu," Gia finished for her. "Yes, you said. But why are you making this all about Vilas?"

Maryam frowned as she searched about for the strainer. "What do you mean by that?"

"You are upset that he is a Hindu, I get that. I don't agree with it, but I get it. But what has that got to do with turning up to your daughter's wedding?"

"Because she is marrying *him*!" Maryam snapped, seeming incensed.

"You have a whole lifetime to despise your son-in-law if that is what you want to do," Gia said. "But the wedding is going ahead either way. How much will you regret going, really? Will you be sitting on your couch in twenty years' time saying, 'Oh, I really wish I had never gone to my daughter's wedding'? I do not think so. But you may well be sitting there wishing that you had. Missing out is always harder than not missing out, trust me."

Maryam Farooq's eyes had slowly narrowed as Gia spoke. "Is that your pitch, young . . ."

"Gia"—she thrust her chin upward—"Kumari."

"Young Gia. You will try to bully me with a fear of missing out?" The kettle began the low, throaty rumble of the boiling process.

"Is Zara your only daughter?" Gia pressed, not wanting to let up, not wanting to let this wily, difficult woman get the upper hand in their conversation.

The slight smugness melted, and Maryam's features went rigid. "She is our only child. I could not again, after . . ."

"And what is a typical day in the Farooq household like?" Gia forged on, feeling a little cruel in the way she rolled over the woman's pain, but she had one last part of her pitch, and she was going to say it. *Yes*, because she wanted to win, she had always wanted to win, to get things right, to be in life's plus column. Needing to stand out above the crowd had been the story of her whole childhood. But this was also because it suddenly mattered to her—a feeling that niggled away inside her like the need for coffee in the morning had recently started to. This family did not *have* to be broken, it was not necessary, so she would do her best to ensure that it stayed as whole as it could. What happened today, she realized, may well echo down the decades.

"Wha . . . ?" Maryam began as the pitch of the kettle began to rise. "Well," she went on, clearly unsure. "Zara's father, Abdul, is still almost fifteen years from retirement. He works in the pension department at Cisco. I have a cooking club." Finally, she lost her patience. "What are you getting at?"

"And life is fulfilling?"

Maryam began to bristle now, just as the first wisps of steam began to escape the spout of the kettle. "Are you judging me?"

"Yes-yes, I am," Gia replied, "but not in the way that you think. I have only recently started to understand family."

Maryam nodded slowly at that. Sometimes, when people knew that you were an orphan, they would treat you like you had a disability or a disease. At best they saw you as "unfortunate"; at worst they could not even bear to touch you, as if the bad luck of losing both parents might rub off on them or something. It had not occurred to Gia until this moment that she had recently gained a parent, that many of her peers at the orphanage would have seen this as a "fortunate" event. Either way, the one and only thing that Gia liked about Maryam Farooq so far was that the woman appeared to respect her for being an orphan. Or, at the very least, for being an orphan who had risen above her station.

An old, familiar ache bloomed in Gia's chest, but she swallowed it down. Her breath caught, part of the betrayal she had felt with the boss who had turned out to be her mother, what she was struggling to get over. It was not only being abandoned all those years ago and left to grow up in an orphanage. It wasn't that Sonia Shah had never felt what it was to scarf down a moldy roti with burnt dal and feel relief there was something lining your belly. It wasn't even the fact that Sonia had lied to her these past weeks. No, the worst thing was that Sonia being her mother had threatened to take away her life's greatest achievement— being hired into her dream job. Because *feeling worthy* was just about every orphan's dream, and, when she realized that Mohammed had not arranged the job, she had—foolish girl—let herself believe that she had somehow landed the position on merit.

"Nothing is more important than family," Gia said, now fighting with the first stirring of the kettle's whistle. "And no part of family is greater than the importance of a child to their parents. I never got to see that, all my life, yet now I see it everywhere. I guess it is, what-what is the word . . . biological? Yes. The greatest drive every animal has is to make new life, but humans raise their children for years, dedicate half a life to making them the best people they can before sending them into the world.

"I never knew this, but parents live through their children, and their grandchildren. Do you want to risk all of that for a principle? Half of the marriage that is happening today is of a Muslim woman called Zara. Your daughter."

Gia's last words were against the incessant whistle of the kettle, yet Maryam Farooq seemed briefly oblivious to its shrieking. "Kettle is boiling!" noted Abdul Farooq's voice from the sitting room, which jolted Maryam enough for her to turn off the gas and snatch it from the stove. Carefully, she poured the steaming water into the teapot and set it to brew while Gia slowly stepped back a couple of paces, listening to see if she could hear what was happening in the sitting room.

"Why am I here, Mr. Farooq," she heard Sonia ask, "when I should be preparing the wedding venue? I get paid if I deliver a wedding, not if I deliver the parents of the bride."

Gia found herself grinning inwardly, remembering Sonia's *actual* reasoning for their need to intervene and make everyone happy, as she had put it in the car on the way over. Sonia was wily, clever, manipulative. She would have made a good orphan.

"Yet here I am, because I have lately come to understand the cost of missed opportunities, the true weight of regret." *Then again.* "If you do not go today, Mr. Farooq, this will be the biggest mistake of your life, I promise you. Take it from someone who knows."

CHAPTER 35

It is strange how silence can have different qualities to it. Sitting next to Sonia in her electric car on the way out to Oakland had been different to how it was on the way back, even though the two of them were saying nothing, as they had for much of the first journey. The first half of the journey out of San Francisco and across the bay had been tense, the silence between them strained. When Sonia was not speaking, the space—whether the cramped confines of her vehicle or the more open space of the company's main office—always felt charged. Her silences never seemed to invite anyone else to break them, either.

It did not feel like that right now. Gia's heart boomed so hard she pressed her hand over it. It seemed that both of them wanted to break the silence, to speak and let sweet words fill the space. Yet still neither had as they ascended a serpentine road flanked with streetlights and the occasional barking dog on their way back to San Francisco. Gia could suddenly bear it no longer. She wanted to say something meaningful, something about them, something that would build on the words she had heard Sonia speak to Abdul Farooq, words that seemed to resonate with their own situation. In the end, frustratingly, all she could find was the most mundane, obvious thing.

"Do you think they will come?" Gia asked. As relevant as it was, the question sounded facile to her the moment it left her lips. Why was it so hard to speak to this woman? Gia was the most verbose person she knew. Well, except for Dolly. And maybe Chad.

"We gave it our best shot," Sonia answered, keeping her eyes on the road. "I'm not sure what you said to Maryam Farooq, but she looked like she wanted to adopt you right there and then."

Sonia's face paled suddenly, like she realized that she had said the wrong thing. From the outside, perhaps it would have been funny, yet it only amplified the awkwardness between them, the feeling that they were two people for whom it was impossible to connect, even if they wanted to. The silence swelled around them, Gia's warm feelings having popped like a blister.

Passing between the glass-fronted high-rises, Gia's mind floated back to their half-finished conversation from the journey over. Who knew when she would find herself alone with Sonia again? At work, they were never properly alone, and Gia knew that she would never be able to bring herself to call up this woman and say, "Hey, let's talk about our mother-daughter relationship." The whole thing felt surreal; she did not even feel related to her. And, if a connection was even to be possible, then she could not be her employee, her subordinate. In that moment she made up her mind, knowing that what she had to say could not wait.

"I'm going to leave," she said. Her words tumbled out, one light-ning breath.

"Leave?" Sonia said, her voice almost a whisper. She looked straight ahead, her eyes on the road as they took a left. The traffic was quiet for the time of day, and they were getting the run of the lights, so they would probably soon be back at the General's Residence and carrying on with the preparations for the wedding.

"Golden State Weddings."

Another beat. "And do what? You are on a work visa." The voice was too calm, too sure. Annoyingly so.

"Uncle Mohammed, he thinks he can find me something where he works. Sponsor me to stay."

They turned right. It was a straight run of not more than a mile to the wedding venue. Sonia snorted derisively. "And do what, drive a cab?"

"Answer the telephone, do administration, I do not know." She did not like the scathing note in Sonia's voice. It had been good enough for her uncle all this time; who was Sonia to sneer at him and look down at him? Then again, Gia did not yearn to do it, not as she had yearned to work in event planning.

"Why would you do that?" Sonia asked, her tone gravelly. She seemed genuinely puzzled, like she could not possibly know where this was coming from. It was infuriating.

"Because I can-cannot work with you!" Gia fired back. She had not shouted at Sonia, yet it felt like she had, and her heart was racing. Sonia's lips tightened, but she did not immediately reply, so Gia went on. "I cannot be your daughter and your employee. I cannot work through my feelings for the life I have never had with you and call you 'boss.' We have barely even talked about this."

The entrance to Fort Mason was looming in the distance, and Sonia remained silent, which only drove Gia's anger even further. Her brain clicked and clattered, a wooden roller coaster ascending its hill. *She* was the one who had grown up without parents, who had been lied to and brought here under false pretenses. All her life she had felt adrift, rudderless, and untethered. *She* was the one who should be emotionally closed off.

She tipped her head back and squeezed her eyes closed.

The car now swung right, passing the low shrubberies that were reminiscent of the surrounding Californian landscape. Making their final turn toward the General's Residence, Gia realized that Sonia was crying, her sobs quiet like she was doing so under the watchful gaze of a strict librarian. It struck her hard, her stomach tightened like a fist.

"Hey," said Gia, although she did not know what words were supposed to follow that up.

Sonia took a shuddering breath. "I have lost everyone," she said, pressing her fingertips to her forehead. She stopped the car and unlocked the door. Gia opened her mouth to reply, trying to find the right words. The right words were *No, that is not what I meant*, but, by the time she had realized that, Sonia was already a dozen strides away from the car.

You never had me in the first place, Gia thought, *and that is the problem.*

⚜

"What did you say to her?" Dolly demanded as Gia walked into the kitchen, which was a modern update crammed into the Victorian-mansion-turned-wedding-venue. Dolly sat at the crisp white island counter, sipping hot tea from a Styrofoam cup. On the stove top behind her sat a silver kettle.

Dolly's expression was furious. Her voice was angry and compressed, carbon pressed into a diamond. Before Gia had a chance to answer, understanding lit up Dolly's face for a moment before it darkened again. "You told her about leaving! How could you? And now of all times!"

"I . . . I didn't know she would start crying!" Gia shook her head. Why hadn't she waited until after the wedding? It had seemed so "now or never" in the car with just the two of them, Fort Mason growing closer and closer.

It wasn't fair that Gia suddenly felt like the bad guy. Had everyone forgotten that *she* was the child who had been discarded, left to rot in an orphanage? Why should *she* be feeling as if she had done something wrong, as if *she* had something to hide? In her mind's eye, she pictured the cracked, whitewashed plaster that covered the orphanage's stone walls that, over the years, had become even more cracked, so that scorpions living, loving, and procreating in its insides would creep out, sending the girls into a screaming frenzy. She cringed at the memory of

253

the press of people on the dreadful commute via public transportation for her polytechnic class, young men hanging out of the doorways as though on the prow of a sailboat. Walking the streets of Delhi after class, gazing at lights in every window, seeing the families inside, none of them hers.

Dolly got up, scowling, as the kettle began to squeal, and she turned around to turn off the burner. Facing Gia, it was as if anger wafted off her like heat. "Is your mother not allowed to have feelings?"

It felt like a vein popping in Gia's head, with the oxygen churning in and out of her body, her chest heaving as if she'd run a marathon. She had been remarkably calm these past weeks following the initial blowout at the Khosla party, yet having Dolly of all people shouting at her was just too much.

"She is not my mother!" Gia screamed back. "She is Sonia Shah!"

Dolly blinked for a moment. "She is a woman who has had to leave her marital home, who is trying to build a relationship with her daughter." Dolly stepped forward suddenly, grabbing Gia's wrists and shaking them. "You don't get it, do you? Everyone's life is a mess, it isn't just yours."

"It's not right!" Gia cried back, trying to pull her arms free of Dolly's grip and failing. "As a little girl, I used to dream of having a sweet, kind mother who would be my friend. Who would be loving and honest with me. Instead, I get the Ice Queen, who lies to me, who tempts me with all things shiny, who manipulates me. Was I asking too much?"

Dolly shook her arms again, but gently this time. "Yes. You wanted perfect, and perfect is always too much, even if you deserved it and life has dealt you a terrible hand. Perfect is for the movies. That's why we watch movies, Gia, because we know that life will never be like that. It is a fantasy. There is no 'You had me at hello.'"

"What?"

"The end of the movie *Jerry Maguire* . . . You know, 'Show me the money'?" She waved her hands by way of illustration. "Never mind, you've never seen it, have you?"

"That is shitty. What is the point of life if it cannot be good?"

"No, it isn't shitty," Dolly said, drawing herself up like an actress in a movie musical about to burst into song. Her hands came to Gia's cheeks, some of her fingertips brushing lightly against her skin. "It's beautiful. Imagine how boring life would be if it was like a movie and we always knew how it would work out. Movies end for a reason—so we don't have to watch Renée Zellweger put up with Tom Cruise's snoring or see the time they had a furious fight about whether or not she put the top back on the milk."

Gia raised her eyebrows. "I do not want to see that, either," she admitted.

"And at the same time the film doesn't show them on a Saturday night cuddling on the sofa and watching *Top Gun* and *Mission: Impossible*, because that would not be interesting to watch."

Gia let out a long sigh. Her anger was spent, but it was being replaced by much more somber feelings. "I get what you are saying. What is the expression . . . ? 'You must take the rough with the smooth.' But all I wanted was a little normal. Normal would have been perfect for me. Like your life."

Gia suddenly noticed that they had an audience. Chad—and one of the site staff who had been present when they arrived earlier—were watching them from the doorway. Chad was holding a giant slice of watermelon, while the staff member—a middle-aged man with thickset shoulders, slicked-down black hair, and the mannerisms of a British butler—looked deeply concerned. "Don't mind us," Chad said to Gia and Dolly, then turned to the man beside him. "This is our methodology; we like to work in a tense, creative atmosphere."

Dolly shot a furious look at Chad and grabbed Gia's arm again, pulling her out of the room and out of the building, toward the service entrance where the company truck was still parked. "Come, I've still got table decorations to bring in. You can help me."

"You want to know about my childhood?" Dolly went on once they were alone. "My dad fell off an extension ladder while painting the front entrance of our house. I was seven years old at the time."

"Oh." Gia had not known. She stared at Dolly for a moment.

"He was unconscious for just a few seconds, and he was taken to a local hospital where he was checked out. The doctor told him everything was fine. He insisted that he felt fine, and he quickly returned to his normal activities. Life went on as if nothing had happened. No big deal. He returned to his work as a biochemist. You know what happened six months later?"

Gia shook her head and lifted her shoulders. Although Dolly's voice remained conversational, her eyes had hardened.

"He mixed a much higher concentration than what is legally allowed of a chemical in a mortar that then exploded in his hands. He lost two fingers, and the damage to the lab cost millions. He had been having some strange symptoms for a couple of months, but nothing he could put his finger on exactly. Just episodes where things seemed 'off.' When they took him to the hospital, they said it was symptoms associated with the traumatic brain injury over six months earlier that had never been treated. Daddy was never hired as a biochemist again, even though he has a doctorate from a top American university. He's worked as a hotel porter, a cab driver, a groundsman, and I don't even know how many other things."

Gia swiped her hand under her nose. *How heartbreaking.* They turned and headed down the sloped backyard toward the service entrance.

"We had no money when I was growing up, always a missed paycheck away from eviction. My mom worked until cancer stopped her, and my brothers and I got after-school jobs as soon as we could." They reached the truck, and Dolly continued talking as she stepped inside and rummaged around. "But I never minded any of that, and I get that I still had more food in my belly than I bet you did most of the time."

Dolly turned and carefully handed a dozen boxes of sweets sealed in red-and-yellow-cellophane paper to Gia. "Here, take this. I get how hard this must be for you, Gia, I do. To discover you had a mother who was living a much more comfortable life, that she kept herself secret from you, like you yourself are a dirty secret."

Yes, Gia thought, looking up from the brightly wrapped favors that she was holding as Dolly went back for more, *that's just how she has made me feel.*

Dolly came back over, and, though it may have been a trick of the light, Dolly's eyes seemed glassy to her. "But you're not dirty, Gia. You're someone to be proud of. Look who you became against all the odds." A tear fell down Gia's face, even though she was trying hard to blink it back in. "Give her time," Dolly urged. "Calmly tell her how she's made you feel. It will not magically all be okay in an afternoon, but you will get there if you give it a chance, I know it. Nothing about what Sonia did is okay, and I think she knows that, but it doesn't mean that she still doesn't have a lot to lose. A husband, a business, and a standing within the community that is built on having a positive, wholesome reputation, not being a social pariah. In an ideal world those things do not matter, but I have just told you about the world we are living in, Gia."

Gia wanted to argue at that. She fished around for the words, but her brain was blank. How could she be a source of shame or disgrace just by being alive?

"Doing shitty jobs all his life destroyed my dad," Dolly said, stepping down from the back of the truck. "It made him bitter, resentful, earning crumbs while he had the skills to . . . I don't know. I just think he felt like a failure, like he was wasted potential." She faced Gia again, arms crossed on her chest, the heat of the day making the strawberry birthmark on her neck stand out brightly. "Did you think this was my life, Gia?"

"No, I did not."

"And yet here I am," Dolly said, "a happy and successful American-born girl, living my own dream. Well, the first part of my dream. Until I find myself that rich man to marry, that is."

Gia laughed, although the action pushed out another tear.

"If Sonia has given you nothing else in your life, Gia, she's given you the chance to do something you love. Don't give that up just because you're upset right now, or one day maybe you'll be as regretful as my dad."

CHAPTER 36

"They're not here yet," Dolly hissed in Gia's ear. From the corner of her eye, Gia could see that the wedding procession had assembled and was making its way on foot along the curving drive toward the porte cochere at the front of the General's Residence. The sun was struggling to break through the fog, with a breeze blowing in off the water, catching saris and silk scarves and making the dancing seem livelier—as if to warm up cold limbs—the riot of color more vibrant as bhangra drums beat out the inevitable march of the bridegroom's last journey as an unmarried man. Closing the chapter on a single life gone before, anticipating a new life as a husband and father to come.

Vilas Patel was a different man to the pale, distraught man that had lurked at the edges of the Farooq property in Oakland that morning. He was mounted on a white stallion and wearing a silver-and-gold-trimmed red turban from which hung marigold garlands like a flowery curtain around his beaming face. His yellow-slippered feet resting on the wide stirrups glowed in the fiery light of the setting sun. They had done it, *all of them* had done it. There was an odd bond between the family and the wedding planners, Gia was coming to understand, one that only really presented itself on the actual day of the wedding. One a client, the other a vendor, yet a shared nervous energy took over and there was mutual relief—amazement, almost—when things came together and everything was in place.

Except one thing.

"Shush," Gia mouthed, turning to show Dolly that she was shooting a video on her phone.

"Sorry," Dolly mouthed back, stepping away to ensure that Gia would have the best view of the wedding party as it approached.

Vilas Patel met his bride at the front door to the property, his olive-toned face gleaming, his coffee-colored eyes dancing with hope and delight as they fixed on her, none of the complexities of this moment evident in his expression. *These are beautiful lies that we tell ourselves,* Gia thought, not quite knowing where those words had come from. She was not a poet or even that sentimental, yet this thought seemed to perfectly fit the moment—this part of a wedding that was the "happily ever after" of familiar fairy tales. It was like a band at a rock concert making their entrance onto the stage and playing the first song.

On impulse, Gia moved to be among the wedding party as it began to crowd under the porte cochere, trying to keep the phone camera steady as she joined in and swayed with the rhythm, jostling in between shoulders as everyone followed the bride into the grand entrance area under an ombre light cast by the chandelier and overpolished, cherry-colored flooring. Gia wondered, as the procession turned into the ballroom and on through to the garden, how many of the weddings held there had such lively beginnings.

The sky was starting to bleed coral and tangerine, sunshine leaning between the distant peaks. Gia put up a hand to cover her face from the bright yellow, gasping at the site of the ceremony, where a *mandap* combining a sleek gold structure and swaths of pale-pink drapery dominated. Clusters of soft-toned pink and blue blooms hung on the side, mirroring both the sheer fabric and the luminous waters of the bay.

While Chad filmed from one side, Sonia stood discreetly to the other side, dressed in dark sapphire, clipboard in hand, as she watched everything like a silent conductor. Dolly was in shimmering green and gold, and she crossed to stand beside her boss. A moment later, Adi hurried up from the direction of the service area, wearing a simple blue-gray *kurti*.

Zara peeled off toward a small shamiana that had been set up to one side, the material a deep scarlet with gold lining. It was the same tent that had collapsed onto Sonia early in the day. The shamiana had been Sonia's idea, Gia remembered, a private, enclosed spot within which the bride could freshen up, including a small dressing table with a mirror. Adi had checked and rechecked the shamiana. It should not be collapsing on Zara.

Vilas continued on and stepped up onto the elevated stage of the *mandap* to await his bride, as the guests hurried to find seats among the white, satin-covered chairs. In the center of the stage, a small fire burned in a stone brazier, while four ornate gold-gilded chairs sat on either side. A pandit with a heavily etched face and a red mark across his forehead sat beside the fire, chanting mantras and adding oil to the flames so that they burned a brilliant orange. Soon he would be issuing instructions to the bride and groom on what to do and say. Vilas's parents arrived to join Vilas, hugged him warmly, and took the two seats to the left of the stage, behind where Zara would sit. The other two seats were still empty, and Gia, hurriedly uploading her video to the Instagram page, because the wedding was happening "now," glanced around for any sign of the Farooqs.

It had felt like she and Sonia had gotten through to them but, even on a wedding day, not all fairy tales came true, she guessed. Dolly's story, her picture of "real life," was still with her.

Gia went and joined the others, and a few moments later, Zara appeared from between the tent flaps of the shamiana, attended by two bridesmaids of her bridal party. She looked first to the *mandap*, then her gaze quickly swept across the whole gathering and back again. A determined smile was on her face as she approached the *mandap*, but Gia's heart nearly broke for her, and anger boiled up at the Farooqs, only to be turned on its head again a few moments later as two sweaty, exhausted-looking late arrivals came shuffling from the direction of the ballroom.

Everyone gathered turned to look as Abdul, wearing a black achkan and cream *churidaar* pajama, and Maryam Farooq, wearing a black hijab and Gucci sunglasses, walked outside. They hurried along the central aisle between the two halves of the seating and onto the stage, finding their seats under the bemused but grateful gaze of their daughter. *And they were worried about everyone seeing them*, Gia thought with a grin.

Sonia, however, was not even watching, and Gia followed her look to where Ranveer Shah stood, dressed in a finely embroidered white-and-red *kurta* in an older, more flamboyant style than the one his son was wearing. He crossed to them, and Sonia turned to meet him, while Gia strained to hear the first words that would come out of his mouth, although it was Sonia who spoke first.

"I'm sorry," she said, her voice low as the wedding guests were beginning to settle.

"Love," Ranveer replied in the tone Gia was now beginning to recognize as his movie voice, "means never having to say you're sorry."

Hmm, Gia thought, *not sure I know that movie.*

TWO HOURS EARLIER

"Yes?" came the voice on the other end of the phone, the question an immediate challenge, although the voice sounded fatigued and disinterested.

"Ranveer?"

"Yes?" This time he was more interested, because he didn't recognize her voice, Gia realized. Then again, why would he? They had spoken about three times in total since she had arrived in San Francisco.

"This is Gia."

"Oh." One syllable, a sound like a boulder falling to cover a cave entrance. *None shall pass.*

"Do you blame me for existing, sir?"

"Of course not," Ranveer blustered at her bluntness. "Existing is not a crime, but you might understand why your presence is . . . difficult for me."

"I do not think my existence has been easy for anyone. Not for you, not for the nuns at the orphanage who had another mouth to feed, not even for my uncle, who wanted to put having to flee his old life behind him. It was not easy for a young woman called Saumya, either, whose husband-to-be was murdered on her wedding day, then she had to make a horrible decision to give her baby up. To give me up."

"I did not know that."

"Because Sonia would never have told you, sir. Because she is a cold, hard, difficult woman who does not easily share her feelings."

Ranveer laughed unhappily. "I do know that."

"Then why marry her?"

That question seemed to stop him for a moment. It was rude, it was direct, she knew this, but it was also a question that Gia needed to know the answer to. The tension grew for a few moments, and Gia thought he might be angry, or maybe even hang up on her, but there was surprisingly deep, heart-wrenching emotion in his voice when he spoke . . . wistfulness, perhaps even yearning.

"Because she is clever and also sarcastic and funny when you get to know her."

"No, she is not," Gia said without thinking. This was not Sonia Shah he was describing.

"She is hilarious, but it takes a long time for her to be that way with anyone. She is like the largest clam with the biggest pearl inside; there is a lot of prying open needed."

"And this is why you loved her?" Gia had not meant to use the past tense, although perhaps the point she had to make went back years—to the woman who had fled India, who had found Ranveer Shah.

"Yes, I suppose."

"Then you fell in love with the woman who had already given birth to and left me, who omitted to tell you the full truth all these years. I have come to realize that she could not be anyone else, Mr. Shah. If I want a mother, I must accept this. Do you want a wife?"

"I do." He did not hesitate.

"Then come to the General's Residence in Fort Mason as soon as you can. Wear something for a wedding, and think of something good from a movie to say to her, yes? Something cool."

He paused for too many moments.

"Yes?" Gia demanded.

"Yes," he replied hurriedly. Then, "You are a little like your mother, you know."

"Good . . . I think. And by the way, I'm going to keep dating your son."

"Wha—"

The couple had circled the sacred fire seven times, and the lavish wedding meal had been consumed inside, although there was still plenty left to pick at, and Chad, for some reason, kept handing out acai bowls that had not been any part of the catering plan. There was dancing in the ballroom, and the fire in the *mandap*, although extinguished, still gave off a familiar smell—an acrid, smoky scent arising from twigs and oil against a slowly darkening sky where the first, brightest stars were starting to show.

Gia and Adi had just finished putting the chairs back in the storage area. Every time they were alone they found brief seconds to lock fingers, brush hair away from eyes . . . let lips touch and trace. For longer. And longer. She was getting good at this, especially seeing as her improvised statement to Ranveer about continuing to date his son had not been shared with Adi at that point. Gia had realized that it was within her power. The anger had been let out; a sense of control had seeped in. She only had to reach for it, not letting fear or loss direct her actions toward Adi. After the last trip with the few remaining chairs and the long, lingering kiss they had shared afterward, Gia felt that she had probably made it clear enough.

"So, you and Adi are still a thing?" Sonia asked, interrupting Gia's thoughts as she stood beyond the end of the *mandap*, right at the back of the garden where it ran along the water's edge.

Gia touched a guilty finger to her lips in memory of those caresses just minutes before, momentarily forgetting that she was supposed to be unrepentant. "You saw?"

"Children are never as sneaky as they think they are."

"We are not—" *Children*, she meant to say, yet her own mouth seemed to have disagreed with her.

"You are my child," Sonia said. "Can I call you that?"

"Of course," Gia answered. It was true, after all. Whatever else, *that* was true.

"Is Ranveer's presence here your doing?" Sonia asked.

Gia allowed herself a small smile, one that Sonia probably wouldn't see in the darkness. "It could have been Adi's."

"But it was yours." There was a slight pause before the next two words, like Sonia had to do a little working out on how to say them, like they might—*shock, horror!*—be unfamiliar to her lips. "Thank you."

Sonia inhaled deeply, a long, slow breath, and they stood in silence as music carried distantly to them from inside and giggling children ran across the lawn somewhere behind.

"Please stay." Two words from Sonia Shah's lips; so naked, both the words and the voice that had spoken them. "I need you."

EPILOGUE

Gia stood at the top of Ranveer and Sonia's sloping garden, just outside their house in Sausalito. Above her, the sky was a cold, steel gray, and the breeze blew through her hair and rustled the trees around her—those that still had leaves, as most of the deciduous ones were now laid bare.

Perhaps she would have been cold but for the pastel-pink jaunty peacoat that Dolly had helped her pick out on their shopping trip the previous weekend, and but for Adi's arms around her. The two of them were quietly looking out across the water together, enjoying the majestic view that swept down the hills into the main part of the town and over to distant silhouetted landscapes. Adi pulled back from her, the charcoal-colored oven mitts he wore on his hands lingering as long as possible. "I'd better go and check the oven," he told her.

Gia grinned and glanced over her shoulder. "I like you in those mitts, by the way."

Adi gave her one of his smoldering looks, which dissolved into a silly face as he waved both hands at her and grinned stupidly.

"I take it back," she added.

Once Adi had gone inside, Gia picked up a telephone handset that she had earlier taken from its cradle in the house and placed it on the table of the nearby outdoor dining set. She stared at it for a few moments, a little nervous about the call she was about to make. The number was a long international one.

"Aunty?" Gia asked, her voice cracking slightly so that she had to clear it. "I am not calling too early?"

There was a long, rich laugh on the other end of the line. "Some might say it is very, very late. And don't call me *aunty*, it makes me sound like any other generic aunty in your life. Call me Bindu Maasi." *Mother's sister.*

"Okay, Bindu Maasi. I have a lot to thank you for."

Nearly ten minutes later, just after she had ended the call, Gia heard the chugging engine sound that she had been waiting for, gravel grumbling under tires. A moment later, a battered yellow Volkswagen pulled into the drive below, a familiar door slammed, and she let out an excited breath. "Uncle Mike!"

Gia turned and hurried back inside through the sliding glass doors, closing them behind her against the late November chill. There, on a cream-colored leather sectional, Dolly sat next to a young Caucasian man with jet-black hair that was parted in the middle, falling in two straight curtains to below his elfin jawline and secretive dark eyes. His black suit was crinkled and frayed at the hems, like he wore it a lot. Dolly wore a red sweater with a turkey plastered across the front in vivid brown and white sequins. Both Dolly and the man were looking intently at the coffee table, where Chad—kneeling on the other side of the table—was placing the last of three acai bowls in front of them. He wore a white T-shirt that was two sizes too small for him, and that declared him "The Acai King."

"This one has chocolate-covered pomegranate seeds in it," Chad told them, "and I call it Coco-Yes-You-Do."

Dolly looked up and caught Gia's eye, her expression that of someone who needed saving. "Gia! What ya doing, Gia?" she asked eagerly.

"My uncle and his family are here."

"Oh, great, I'll co—" Dolly had started to stand up but stopped midway when Chad thrust one of the acai bowls almost into her face.

267

"No, you don't," Chad told her firmly. "You've both got Acai Surprise to try as well."

Dolly gestured toward the kitchen, which was just out of sight, close to where Gia had come in. "Thanksgiving dinner is nearly ready; I won't want to eat any of it if I fill myself up."

"I've got an event next week," Chad complained, "and getting this right is going to make or break the fourth-quarter profits for the Acai King. You said you'd help!"

"Are you the Acai King, or is that the business?" the man sitting beside Dolly asked. "I'm confused."

Gia patted Chad on the head as she passed. "Look at you, a proper entrepreneur."

Dolly took the aggressively proffered bowl and began to mumble. "Hmm, Acai Surprise. I'm not sure that anything in an acai bowl should be a surprise, you know."

Gia left the lounge and turned right down the stairs to the front door. She opened the door to find her Uncle Mohammed; Mohammed's wife, Farha; and their two children. Farha was carrying a large ceramic bowl covered with foil.

Unable to contain her excitement, Gia put her hands together enthusiastically. "So glad you all came."

The usually confident Farha, who Gia was used to meeting in her own home where she was definitely queen bee, held up the bowl meekly. "I brought a *saag*-and-corn side dish, is that okay?"

Mohammed frowned at her. "Of course that's okay. They weren't expecting caviar."

"Very thoughtful," Gia said helpfully and then leaned around to look at the two boys, who were both glued to their mobile devices. "Hey, you two," she said. Both nodded in greeting without looking up from their phones.

Mohammed leaned in, as if speaking confidentially. "Is Dolly still with that poet fellow?"

"Troy," Gia replied.

"Yes, him. Is he here?"

"Yes, in the lounge," Gia answered. She added, a little vindictively, "They're engaged now, you know."

Mohammed looked mortified. "Engaged? I thought she wanted someone wealthy. Poets are never wealthy. They are hardly ever even famous until at least fifty years after they're dead."

"Dolly doesn't need to be kept by any man, Uncle Mike, she's a career woman, you know. She's going to head the wedding and family events part of Golden State, now that Sonia is concentrating on building the corporate parties side of things."

Mohammed squeezed her arm. "And you're busy? Glad you stayed and joined the wonderful world of publicity and videography? Does Sonia miss the weddings?"

"She told me that she was done. That the Patel-Farooq wedding was the culmination of the dream Hindu-Muslim wedding she'd always imagined."

Mohammed crinkled his brow, gathering his thoughts, then nodded. "Yes, that was also Hassan's brave, idealistic dream for modern Indians."

They both retreated into their thoughts until Gia continued, "As for me, with Chad leaving, I had to get nifty pretty quickly with a camera, but now, I'm loving it. In fact, I may be looking into movie direction next." From his furrowed brow, Gia could tell she was going to get a volley of questions from her uncle.

Hurriedly she held out her arms. "Coats?"

She ushered all of Mohammed's family inside and put their coats on a big rack by the bottom of the stairs. "Anyway," she said, carrying on the earlier conversation, "Dolly fell in love and realized that it's more important than money, apparently."

Farha scoffed at that. "This is true, until you have children."

"Well, as long as the boy doesn't try lecturing me about Khalil Gibran again," Mohammed said. "I mean, the nerve. I ran a module on his works at the university in India. The boy reads a copy of *The Prophet* and thinks he knows all there is to know."

Smiling about how much freer—bit by bit, at least—Mohammed was becoming with speaking about the details of his old life in front of his wife and boys, Gia led them up the stairs and into the lounge, where Ranveer, Sonia, and Adi had all come in from the kitchen. Adi still had his oven mitts on, while Ranveer wore an apron with a picture of Remy, the rat from the film *Ratatouille*, on it. Just after Mohammed's family walked into the lounge, Ranveer popped the cork on a bottle of champagne, making Farha and Mohammed jump, although the two boys continued to play a Candy Crush game on their phones. Sonia placed some glasses on the table, shooing away Chad's acai bowls.

"I hope we are not late," Farha said a little nervously. "Teenage boys move slower than sloths."

"You're just in time," Sonia said. "Thanksgiving dinner will be in ten minutes. And Adi's sister isn't even here yet, anyway, but that's not unusual."

"Enough time for a drink," Ranveer said, looking at Mohammed. "I know you drove, but may I interest you in half a glass for a toast?"

"Sorry, Muslim," Mohammed told him. "And a poor one at that. Abstinence from alcohol and pork are the only things I manage to keep to."

Sonia theatrically produced an apple-cider bottle and held it up toward Mohammed. "I remembered that, even if my husband didn't. We have nonalcoholic too."

"What shall we toast to?" Adi wondered.

"No earthquakes in the last six months," Gia put in with a chuckle. "Or ever again, thank you very much."

"Family, of course," Ranveer put in with a smile at Gia. "This weird, imperfect family. To have us . . . almost all together."

"Weird and imperfect?" Sonia asked her husband. Her lips curled, and her voice was sweetly sarcastic.

"Yes," Ranveer pushed on. "And I have had to learn, even later in life, that this is the best kind of family, and how it makes your life richer and more meaningful."

"Like dogs," Chad said, garnering a confused look from almost everyone else in the room. Chad looked around, as if everyone else was in the wrong for not instantly agreeing. "I mean, have you ever met a pompous purebred dog? Whereas the mongrel that could be a mix of a dozen different breeds of dogs, that's the one who will steal your wallet and run off with the prized bichon frise from next door."

The silence continued for several seconds.

"Weird is good," Chad added, as if this fully explained his previous statement.

Ranveer cocked an eyebrow at Chad. "Where was I?"

"Family," Gia put in, raising her own glass of bubbly and thinking that this particular mongrel was doing pretty well for herself, "I'll drink to that."

ACKNOWLEDGMENTS

Every book is a journey. And I know I never could have traveled so far and so well without the love, support, and efforts of many people.

First, I want to thank my amazing agent, Jessica Faust. You believed in this book from the time I pitched it to you, and your astute ideas for additional plot points only made the story richer and deeper. I feel so grateful to be on #TeamBookEnds.

My acquisitions editor, Erin Adair-Hodges, thank you for coming aboard and hitting the ground running with a strength and grace that is truly unmatched. Your supportive reaction to and your sincere belief in me and my story touched my heart more than you know. With you at the helm as an amazing editor who always manages to elevate my work, I believe I can reach unparalleled heights.

I can't fully express my gratitude to my editor Jenna Free, who pushed me to make every scene and beat stronger until the story lived up to its potential. You are the most incredible collaborator and literary guide, yes, but I am in awe of how your masterful notes and thoughtful insights helped me find better ways to tell this story.

To my incomparable publicity team—Kathleen Carter and Brittany Russell—who worked tirelessly to promote my previous novel and will no doubt champion this one. My copyeditors—Hannah B. and Ashley Little—who made sure the novel was in tip-top shape before it entered the world, I am deeply grateful to both of you.

To my fiction cohort at Saint Mary's College: Katie Z., Katie D., Hannah Onstad, Jennifer Pollock, Dani Herrera, Anna Torres, Carly Blackwell, Bobbi Solano, and the incredibly gifted novelist and professor Ruchika Tomar, thank you for workshopping this story and for your valuable feedback. I am a better writer for having worked with you, and I can't wait for our books to live on the same shelf.

While I might have written the words you just read, there was a special group of people who held my hand through it all.

My Dad, Joginder Singh Ahuja, who is the rock in my life and my gentle cheerleader.

My niece Harnoor Walia, who is always the first one to read my books and respond with positivity and enthusiasm.

My husband, Tony Judge, without whom I simply would not be here. I am so lucky to have a partner who fiercely advocates for my writing and champions the stories I want to share with the world.

My kids, Amaraj and Ghena Judge, who give meaning to my life.

Amaraj, I begin each book by brainstorming with you. Thank you for the hours of discussion about my writing and for being my Mother's Day gift forever.

Ghena, every time I say "I can't," you shrug your shoulders and tell me, "Of course you can." Your confidence in me is contagious and keeps me going when the words seem to dry up.

And with that, a major thank you to my readers. Without you none of this would be possible, and I am truly grateful to have an audience that wants to learn more about the rich culture of their neighbors.

ABOUT THE AUTHOR

Photo © Anantha Anvaji

Anoop Judge is the author of *No Ordinary Thursday*, *The Awakening of Meena Rawat*, and *The Rummy Club*, which won the Beverly Hills Book Award. Her essays and short stories have appeared in the *Green Hills Literary Lantern*, *Rigorous*, the *Lumiere Review*, and *Doubleback Review*, among others. She earned an MFA from Saint Mary's College, California, and was a recipient of the 2021–2023 Advisory Board Award and Alumni Scholarship. Born and raised in New Delhi, Anoop now resides in California. She is married with two nearly grown and fully admirable children. For more information, visit https://anoopjudge.com.